W9-CAB-885

VIDEO KILL

JOANNE FLUKE

KENNEBEC LARGE PRINT
A part of Gale, Cengage Learning

GALE
CENGAGE Learning·

Farmington Hills, Mich • San Francisco • New York • Waterville, Maine
Meriden, Conn • Mason, Ohio • Chicago

LIBRARY OF CONGRESS CATALOGING-IN-PUBLICATION DATA

Fluke, Joanne, 1943–
    Video kill / by Joanne Fluke. — Large print edition.
        pages ; cm. — (Kennebec Large Print superior collection)
    ISBN 978-1-4104-7063-8 (softcover) — ISBN 1-4104-7063-6 (softcover)
        1. Serial murderers—Fiction. 2. Murder—Investigation—Fiction. 3. Large
type books. I. Title.
    PS3556.L685V53 2014
    813'.54—dc23   2014010523

Published in 2014 by arrangement with Kensington Books, an imprint
of Kensington Publishing Corp.

VIDEO KILL

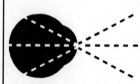

This Large Print Book carries the
Seal of Approval of N.A.V.H.

A LETTER FROM
JOANNE FLUKE

Long before Hannah Swensen baked her way into my life, I found myself in the throes of a love affair with Stephen King, John Saul, and Dean Koontz. I didn't know any of them personally, but I was head over heels in love with their novels. Whenever I opened one of their books I escaped from mounds of dirty clothes, grocery lists, and den mother duties. I was transported to a life of excitement and jeopardy where anything could and did happen. Not content to simply gobble up other people's stories, I decided to try my hand at writing suspense.

I wrote *Video Kill* for two compelling reasons. The first was that my local museum was showing Alfred Hitchcock films on Saturday afternoons and members had to do was show their card to attend the screening. Free movies would have been enough to lure me, but there was also a free children's activities class at the same time! Free movies and free babysitting? How could I resist. The second reason was also compelling. When I went to see *Psycho,* I happened to be seated right next to the woman who'd acted as Janet Leigh's eye double. My new-found friend told me all about the long minutes she'd spent on the shower floor, trying not to blink while "Hitch" got just the right shot of her eye.

After watching some of my favorite films again, I started to ask myself "what ifs." What if someone out there liked Hitchcock films even more than I did? What if that person was so obsessed with Hitchcock films that he or she decided to reenact the murder scenes with real people, really and truly for real?!

It was the germ of a novel and right after the museum's Hitchcock festival closed with *Strangers on a Train,* I went home and started to write. This book is fun, and it's scary. I love this book. I hope you'll love it, too.

This book is for Jay Jacobson,
good friend and movie buff.

PROLOGUE

Los Angeles, California

She was perfect. Her gleaming black hair ran in a rippling cascade down her back, passing the curve of her tiny waist, just brushing the swell of her hips. Her dress was made of a soft rose-colored material, designed to caress her perfect figure. With dazzling white teeth, generous lips, a dainty nose with a hint of a tilt at the tip, and violet eyes fringed by dark sweeping lashes, she could have been Hollywood's most beautiful movie star. Instead, she had opted for a position with more power. She was a studio secretary.

The vision of loveliness turned at the end of the corridor to usher them into a small waiting room in the penthouse suite on the top floor of the Cinescope Towers. The lower floors were for producers and minor executives, but the twenty-second floor was reserved for the power that ran Cinescope

Studios. Alan Goldberg.

When they were seated, she buzzed the inner office to announce their arrival and then turned to them with a smile. It would be just a few moments. Mr. Goldberg was taking a call. Would they care for coffee? Or perhaps something stronger?

Both Erik Nielsen and Tony Rocca opted for coffee, even though they'd gone through gallons the night before. They'd been up all night, revising their movie concept for today's meeting. They'd already been turned down by every other major studio in town, and both men knew that this interview was their last chance.

As Tony and Erik waited in the reception area, sipping freshly ground coffee from expensive china cups, Alan Goldberg sat at his desk, talking to his uncle in Hawaii. Despite the fact that Alan physically resembled Wally Cox, the actor who had played mild-mannered Mr. Peepers, it was a mistake to underestimate him. As acting head of Cinescope Studios, Alan wielded plenty of power. Employees at Cinescope quipped that Alan Goldberg was one floor below God and twenty-two stories above the unemployment office, which was where you headed after an unsuccessful interview with him. But there was one person who was even more important than Alan in the Cinescope hierarchy. His uncle, Meyer Goldberg.

"But, Uncle Meyer, Rocca and Nielsen are seasoned writers. It's not right to dismiss them without even hearing their concept."

The voice on the other end of the line went off into another tirade, and Alan reached for his bottle of aspirin. He chugged three down with the last of his coffee and glanced around his office idly, trying to remember when his Uncle Meyer had last been sane and competent.

Alan's private office was a haven of masculinity, an expert blending of gleaming wood, leather, and muted tweeds. Two walls were entirely covered with built-in mahogany bookshelves that were served by a sliding library ladder. They contained the original leather-bound shooting script of every movie that Cinescope had ever made.

Alan had inherited the library, the office, and his position three years ago. By that time Cinescope Studios was an established institution. Meyer Goldberg had founded his empire in the forties, an era when careful Jews were changing their names. The actor Leo Jacoby was billed as Lee J. Cobb, and Sam Spiegel took his screen credits as

S. P. Eagle. It might have been easier to operate under a gentile pseudonym, but Uncle Meyer had never taken the easy way out. The ornate wrought-iron gate in front of his studio still read MEYER GOLDBERG'S CINESCOPE. Because Alan's uncle had possessed the knack for producing the movies America wanted to see, Cinescope had thrived from day one.

There was a pause in the conversation, and Alan chimed in with his usual "Yes, Uncle Meyer." He wasn't listening, but that didn't matter. Uncle Meyer never paid attention to what he said, anyway. The monologue from Hawaii resumed again, and Alan reached out to pour himself another cup of coffee. As he drank it, he held the receiver loosely to his ear and thought about the history of Cinescope Studios.

Madcap comedies had been the rage in the forties, and Meyer Goldberg had produced the right number of reels to keep America laughing right into the next decade. Then he had abruptly switched to another genre, inexpensive "B" movies for the drive-in market. Cinescope had churned out hundreds of teenage beach-blanket movies and horror thrillers with monsters that were just real enough to convince a high school girl to cuddle up next to her boyfriend in

12

the safe island of his souped-up car. When the television market had blossomed in the midsixties, Cinescope was ready. The "tube" had eaten up Cinescope productions even more voraciously than Meyer's badly acted monsters had gobbled up their pretty victims. By the end of the seventies it was one of the major studios producing at least four hit series a season and a larger proportion of network Movies of the Week than any other studio in town. Meyer Goldberg had been riding on the crest of a greenbacked wave when Alan had left for Harvard Business School.

Alan's friends had kept him abreast of the progress at Cinescope. The studio was expanding, and construction was almost complete on a mammoth twenty-two-story, glass-walled tower. That was good. Other news was not so good. Meyer Goldberg had made some big changes in studio policy. Smoking was now forbidden within the studio gates, meat was no longer served in the commissary, and sparkling grape juice had taken the place of champagne at studio premieres. Even coffee had been banned. It seemed Alan's cigar-smoking, poker-playing uncle had been reborn as a Southern California fitness nut.

At the end of his junior year Alan had

received a frantic phone call from his uncle. He had to return immediately. It had been a sweltering summer day, three years ago, when Alan had jumped the first plane to Los Angeles and rushed to his uncle's side.

Alan had found his uncle pacing the floor of his brand-new office. The outside walls were huge panes of tinted glass, affording a view of the entire Los Angeles basin on a clear day. This particular day had been far from clear. Meyer had explained that Alan would have to take over, his health was of paramount importance, and he simply had to leave Los Angeles. The sight of the smoggy air lurking outside had been too much. He'd installed Alan in the penthouse domain, signed the legal papers that were necessary, and promptly defected to the cleaner air of Hawaii.

The day after his uncle had left, Alan had celebrated his independence by removing every NO SMOKING sign in the studio. His second act had been to order a coffee machine for every office. After a tasteless vegetarian lunch at the studio commissary, Alan had written a memo restoring meat to the menu. Then he'd hired the most beautiful girl in the secretarial pool as his personal assistant and spent the remainder of the day behind closed doors with her.

There was a moment of silence on the line and then a sharp question. Alan roused himself to give the appropriate response. "Yes, Uncle Meyer. I went over the figures on Rocca and Nielsen's last film. But the fact that *Free Fire* didn't show a profit has nothing to do with their work. Our accountants played games with the numbers. You authorized those transactions yourself."

There was another sharp comment, and Alan had all he could do not to groan. His uncle was being unfair, but there wasn't much he could do about it.

"Yes, Uncle Meyer. I'll follow your orders and tell Rocca and Nielsen that we're not interested. Just for the record, I think you're making a mistake."

Alan hung up the phone quickly, before his uncle could think of a reply. Then he buzzed his assistant and told her to give him five minutes before she brought in Tony and Erik. He needed time to compose himself. His uncle's call had been disturbing. It had been the first time in three years that Uncle Meyer had shown an interest in the studio. Was he thinking of returning?

To take his mind off that dire possibility, Alan swiveled his desk chair and looked out at the view. Since this was August, a month with frequent smog alerts, a dirty brown cloud was slowly spreading across the Los Angeles Basin. Alan began to smile as he watched it roll in. Uncle Meyer would never come back if he knew the smog was this bad. Alan would be sure to tell him. From now on, as far as Meyer Goldberg was concerned, the area directly surrounding Cinescope Studios would be in a perpetual three-stage smog alert.

Alan was still watching the progress of the smog with great pleasure when his secretary tapped on the door to usher in Tony and Erik. He smiled and rose to greet them. Uncle Meyer's instructions had been clear. He had to turn them down, but he'd listen to their presentation first. If their concept was good, he might be able to put in a good word for them somewhere else.

Tony Rocca crossed the room in rapid strides and stopped in front of Alan's desk. Tony's quick, decisive movements always left Alan feeling old and tired even though he was ten years younger than Tony's thirty-five. Tony was a ball of pure energy, and he was never at a loss for words. He'd told Alan that he'd inherited his gift of blarney from his Irish mother but his Italian father was responsible for his physical appearance.

Today Tony was wearing a satin camouflage jacket with the *Free Fire* logo on the back, calculated to remind Alan of the last movie they'd written. His brown hair remained unruly despite the expensive hairstylist he visited regularly, and he reminded Alan of a member of a street gang. Perhaps it was the perpetual dark circles under Tony's dark brown eyes or the fact that his wiry, compact body seemed constantly ready to spring into action. But there was an element of the tough streetwise punk in Tony Rocca that no amount of money seemed able to erase.

As Tony reached out to shake hands, his jacket parted slightly and Alan caught a glimpse of the Rocca trademark, a brightly colored billboard T-shirt. Tony had a different T-shirt for every occasion, and Alan's curiosity got the best of him.

"Take off the jacket, Tony. I want to read your shirt."

Tony grinned and shrugged out of his jacket. Today his shirt was fire-engine red with large orange letters that proclaimed POLISH ASTRONAUT. Tony snapped a smart salute and clicked his heels together.

"I have good news from the old country, Mr. Goldbergski. You will be pleased to know that Poland is launching a manned space flight to the sun."

Alan knew Tony wanted him to play

straight man, and he couldn't resist. "That's ridiculous, Tony. The spacecraft would burn up long before it got there."

"Our country's finest scientists have solved that problem. We will go at night."

Alan groaned and waved Tony to the side. "Thank God you don't write comedy." Then he turned to Tony's partner. "Greetings, Erik."

"Alan, good to see you again."

Erik gripped Alan's hand firmly and smiled. He had Viking blond hair, eyes that were the color of a calm lake on a sunny summer day, and the kind of honest, guileless face that used car salesmen envied. Not much rattled Erik, outwardly at least. Alan knew he came from a long line of poker-faced Minnesota farmers who were masters at hiding their emotions. He was wearing what he called his "banker's clothes," a three-piece suit, long-sleeved white shirt, and conservative tie.

Alan gestured toward the two wing chairs in front of his desk.

"Sit down, guys. I'm afraid we'll have to get right to it. Forty-five minutes and I'm due in a board meeting."

Five minutes passed and Tony realized that he was still sitting on the edge of his chair. He forced himself to sit back and look relaxed. The signs weren't good. Oh, Alan had laughed at his joke about the Polish astronaut, but when Erik had handed him a bound copy of their treatment, he'd barely glanced at it. Tony suspected that Alan had already decided to turn them down.

Erik was describing the second murder, and Tony tried to concentrate on the story. They'd gone over it so many times last night that Tony knew Erik's exact words before he spoke them. They'd really worked on this one, and Tony knew they made a good team. Erik made the verbal pitches and wrote the dialogue. Tony came up with the initial concept and blocked out the scenes. Of course they overlapped some, but generally the work was well divided.

Erik was well into the setup when Alan yawned. Another bad sign. All traces of the enthusiasm he'd shown when they'd pitched *Free Fire* were gone.

Tony could feel the sweat start to gather under his armpits as Erik outlined their idea with no wasted words. *Video Kill* was the story of a psychopath who recorded his victims as he murdered them. Naturally the police triumphed in the end, but not before the populace panicked and the audience was treated to six grisly killings. Tony held his breath as Erik finished. They really needed this sale.

Alan sat perfectly still, making a little steeple with his fingers. It was so quiet and tense, even Erik's poker-face began to show signs of strain. Finally Alan looked up and frowned.

"Cinescope's never been big on blood porn."

Tony jumped in with both feet. Erik pitched, and he handled the hard sell.

"That may be a mistake, Alan. Look at what *Friday the 13th* did for Paramount."

Alan nodded. "True. But don't you think the killings are a little too bizarre?"

"Bizarre is the new normal, Alan."

"Good point, Tony." Alan smiled slightly. "The real problem here, as I see it, is with logistics. The worst police department in the country would spot a killer who lugged around all that bulky video equipment."

"Your studio security guard didn't spot me." Tony reached under his chair and brought out the slim briefcase he'd carried past the main desk. "Take a look, Alan. Everything's digital now and I've got a full video rig inside. And by the time this movie is ready for release, they'll be manufacturing something that's even smaller."

"That's true." Alan nodded. "You've fielded all my objections, and if it were up to me, I'd buy."

"Wait a second." Tony looked confused. "I thought you did all the buying."

"I do. Unless a higher authority overrides my decision."

"Meyer?"

Alan nodded. "I got a call from Hawaii this morning. Uncle Meyer reviewed the numbers on *Free Fire,* and he wouldn't buy from Rocca and Nielsen if you stormed his little hideaway on Waikiki with the original *Gone with the Wind.* Off the record, I like your concept, but my hands are tied."

Tony sighed and began to gather up his papers. He knew when he was beaten. "Okay, Alan."

"Wait just a minute!" Erik rose to his feet, and Tony was shocked at the anger on his partner's face. "I went over those numbers myself. Twenty-nine standing sets, Alan? We only used three. And two and a half million for animation that we didn't use? Cinescope managed to write off an entire year's overhead against *Free Fire.* No wonder it didn't show a profit!"

"Look, Erik." Alan looked embarrassed. "Uncle Meyer authorized the budget transactions before he left, and I admit that what you say may be partially true but . . ."

Erik cut him off. "I know we can't prove

anything, Alan. By the time we found a team of auditors who were willing to tackle Cinescope's books, your boys would have everything covered. All I want is the truth. Look me straight in the eye and tell me that Cinescope honestly lost money on *Free Fire* and I'll pack my bags and hightail it back to the farm."

Alan winced. "I can't do that, Erik. I admit Cinescope screwed you, but there's nothing I can do about it at this late date. Uncle Meyer was perfectly clear over the phone. He refuses to buy from Rocca and Nielsen."

Erik gave a brief nod and sat down. He'd made his point. Now it was up to Tony to use Alan's concession to their advantage.

Tony began to grin. "Okay, Alan. Don't buy outright. Take an option instead. We're hurting for cash right now and we'll let this baby go cheap. You don't have to check with your uncle to give us an option, do you?"

"No. I have the authority to option. How cheap are we talking, Tony?"

"Only twenty thousand for a year's option, provided you throw some television work our way. Just a couple of assignments to keep us afloat, Alan. That's all we need."

Alan looked thoughtful. A twenty-thousand-dollar option was the sort of thing he could take out of petty cash. And he had a struggling detective show that could use some fresh writers.

"Let me make you a promise, Alan." Tony leaned forward, closing in on the deal. "If you option *Video Kill* today, I personally guarantee that by this time next year, Meyer'll be chomping at the bit to film it. It's a hot concept and it's going to get hotter."

Alan took a long time to consider, but finally he nodded.

"All right, Tony. I'll get you guys a couple of television assignments, no problem. As far as *Video Kill* goes, I'll take a year's option, but don't hold your breath. There's no way it can go into production without Meyer's approval."

Tony stood up, a huge smile on his face. "We understand that, Alan, but you just bought us some time. Thanks to you we've got twelve months to come up with something that'll make him change his mind."

Alan stood up to shake hands. The interview was over. After they left, he picked up the bound copy of their treatment and paged through it. *Video Kill* would make a dynamite film, but Uncle Meyer never changed his mind. Even if Tony and Erik came up with a fucking miracle, the old man would drop it like a smelly sock the second their option ran out.

1

Eleven Months Later
Sunday, July 4

"Hi, Mr. Brother. It's good to see you again."

Christie Jensen, the pretty brunette at the ticket counter, smiled as she greeted the man at the front of the line. Working the Fourth of July matinee was a drag, but now she was glad she'd agreed to come in. Mr. Brother was her favorite regular. The other guys in line often asked her for dates, and she politely explained that it was against company policy. But Christie knew that she'd say yes to Mr. Brother without a second's hesitation.

Mr. Brother was far from what her younger sister termed "to die for" or "terminally handsome." He was of medium height with light brown hair which was thinning a bit on the top. His body was lean and well muscled even though he didn't seem the type to play tennis or jog, and this afternoon he was wearing tan slacks and a matching sports shirt, open at the neck, no tie, topped by a well-cut, brown tweed jacket with leather patches on the elbows. Christie could tell that Mr. Brother's clothes were expensive.

Christie had spent hours trying to identify exactly what it was she found so attractive about Mr. Brother. She admitted that his apparent wealth might have something to do with it. After all, he drove a beautiful tan Mercedes, and she'd never ridden in a car that expensive. Or perhaps it was his courteous, almost old-fashioned manner. He had the slightest trace of an accent, something European, Christie thought. He reminded her of the cultured aristocracy she read about in her favorite romance novels. Mr. Brother was friendly enough, he never failed to greet her by name, but he kept an aloof distance. And there was an air of subdued mystery about him that Christie found intriguing.

"Good afternoon, Christie. One ticket please, for the matinee."

Christie looked into Mr. Brother's darkly intense eyes and wished she could think of some bright, witty thing to say, but her mind had gone perfectly blank and the rest of the

26

line was growing restless. She knew there'd be complaints if she delayed too long with one customer, so she settled for giving him her best smile as she handed him the computerized receipt that read BIJOU MATINEE ADULT. The whole encounter had taken less than a minute and then he was walking away. Christie knew she'd blown her chance again, and she turned to the next person in line with obvious reluctance.

Brother strode through the archway that led to the center aisle. This was his place of refuge, a private hideaway where he could be alone to think. It was a great relief to slip out, like a snake shedding its confining skin, and become Little Brother again.

He moved past the empty seats to the very center of the back row, where he could stretch out his legs and no one would be likely to bother him. The smell of popcorn was overpowering, and Brother suspected it was deliberately funneled in through the air conditioner vents to attract customers to the concession stand in the lobby. Theater owners were using every marketing trick they could devise to make money in an industry that was slowly dying, bled dry by DVDs and television. If the number of matinee tickets sold this afternoon was any indication, the battle was lost.

As the lights dimmed and the movie began, Brother gazed around him and smiled. The Bijou, in the heart of downtown Los Angeles, was a crazy quilt of architectural styles. The cognoscenti called it a monument to bad taste, but Brother had always felt comfortable here. Soft pink lights twinkled from the top of stark Corinthian columns, Romanesque arches were decorated with Moroccan tiles, and a Chinese lacquered balustrade ran the length of the balcony. It had been a center for entertainment in its day, but now the huge interior was practically empty.

Three elderly ladies, dressed in a style that had been fashionable years ago, were the sole occupants of the middle section. They had probably come inside to escape the heat, lured by the theater's senior citizen discount. The left section housed two middle-aged couples and a man slumped in his seat near the back, gently snoring his way through the feature. Predictably, the current crop of teenagers had taken over the balcony, huddled so closely together in pairs they reminded him of the two-headed freaks on county fair posters.

The front four rows of the theater were filled with the one group that had turned out in full force. At age twelve and under, half price, the prepubescent children were more interested in throwing popcorn and poking each other than in the movie being shown. Brother couldn't blame them. *Triumph of the Jubees* was a thinly plotted tale of extraterrestrials with bright pink fur and sickeningly sweet mannerisms. The only reason Brother had chosen to see it was to admire Lon Michaels's brilliant cinematography. Through some miracle, Lon had managed to turn this perfectly idiotic concept into a quality film. It was a pity that Cinescope didn't give him something more deserving of his talents.

Brother sighed and imagined his own film completed, projected on the giant screen at the Bijou. No one would snore, or throw popcorn, or giggle through his film. There would be public acclaim and glowing reviews. Critics would applaud him for having the courage to make a statement so radical, so daring, that not even the greatest filmmakers in history had attempted it.

When the film was over and the credits rolled on the screen, Brother got to his feet and left the theater. It was almost four o'clock, and his standing dinner reservation was at five. Since his mother had died last year, Brother took all of his meals out. Preparing meals for himself seemed a waste of his time, and he could well afford restaurant prices. Dinner would be at Le Fleur, as usual. A private table in the rear dining room was reserved for him.

Brother redeemed his Mercedes from the lot and pressed down on the automatic door lock button. There were plenty of junkies and street gangs in the downtown area, and an expensive car like his sometimes attracted trouble. As he rounded the corner, he saw a bag lady pushing a Vons shopping cart containing all of her belongings.

The downtown area was a schizophrenic mixture of conflicting styles and cultures. Urban renewal had left high-rise buildings and sparkling new mini-malls in its wake. Shiny, modern architecture was interspersed with the original downtown, now an impoverished skid row. In the daylight hours businessmen in three-piece suits and fashionably dressed women claimed the area, but as the sun went down, they picked up their calfskin attaché cases and Gucci purses and headed for home. That was when the night shift came out. Drug dealers sold their wares in plain sight on street corners, ethnic gangs roamed the area searching for confrontations, and the homeless huddled in doorways and slept miserably on bus stop benches. People who drove through the downtown area after dark did so with great dispatch, their car doors locked and their windows rolled up tightly.

As Brother turned west on Sunset Boulevard, he saw the copper dome of the Griffith Observatory gleaming over his right shoulder. The traffic was light, and Brother drove a bit faster. Most people had vacated the city for picnics at the beach or barbecues in suburban backyards. They'd be clogging the freeways to return to their homes later tonight, but right now the streets were virtually deserted.

In no time at all Brother was entering the Sunset Strip, an area flanked by offices, designer boutiques, and expensive restaurants. The Hollywood Hills rose steeply to the right. Homes clung tenaciously to the side of the hill, reinforced by pylons driven deep into the bedrock. The hills had once been a prime real estate area for the stars of the silver screen. Brother knew that if he drove a bit farther down Sunset and purchased a tourist map of "Famous Movie Stars' Homes," a significant number of them would be in the Hollywood Hills.

Le Fleur's bright green canopy beckoned at the end of the block, and Brother negotiated the narrow driveway. A valet parker, sitting on a stool in front of his kiosk,

31

rushed to assist him. Brother got out of his car and relinquished his keys, and another uniformed man hurried to open the restaurant's front door for him.

"Good evening, sir. Your table is ready. Happy Fourth of July."

The maître d' smiled, a flash of white in the dimly lighted interior, and Brother was seated immediately. While he was waiting for his cocktail, he again considered his project. He had begun his preparations over a year ago by making a detailed study of Lon Michaels's work, copying the expert lighting techniques and camera angles until he felt he was reasonably competent. Of course, Lon had no idea that he had taught Brother all he knew about cinematography.

The waiter delivered his Manhattan, straight up, no twist. Brother removed the miniature American flag that had been used to decorate it and took a generous swallow. He would direct and produce his masterpiece himself, in the tradition of the true auteur. His film would be presented as a fait accompli, and the credit would be his, alone. He had already written the shooting script and purchased the equipment he needed. He had even gone through the Players Directory and cast the actress he needed for the first segment. He was ready to shoot immediately, but he would have to rush to complete his cinema verité in time for a Christmas release. Would it be wiser to delay shooting for a few months and plan on a definite summer debut?

Brother pondered the question as he finished his appetizer. The waiter had just served his entrée, the aroma was exquisite, when he reached a decision. Summer release, winter release, it made no real difference. The strength of his concept would guarantee its success.

An hour later Brother was at home, in his mother's five-bedroom, two-story, Queen Anne–style home, which sat on a choice lot in Beverly Hills. He still lived and worked in the "children's wing" upstairs, a bedroom, a bath, and a huge playroom-turned-office, which his mother had designed for him thirty years ago. The downstairs had been his mother's domain, and the housekeeper still cleaned it regularly, dusting the delicate china figurines and polishing the expensive antique furniture. Nothing had been altered since the day of his mother's death, and Brother kept entirely to his own section of the house. The children's wing had a separate entrance, and it was perfectly adequate for his needs.

Brother sat at his desk and sipped a small

cognac. He had checked his equipment and everything was ready. A video camera was tucked into his carrying bag, along with a shooting script for the first scene. The Academy Players Directory lay open on his desk, and brother felt a surge of excitement as he examined the picture of his actress again. She was an unknown, but she was perfect for this first, starring role. Sharee Lyons might not realize it, but she would earn her place with the immortals tonight.

It was past eleven at night when the cross-town bus dropped Sharee Lyons at the stop on Sunset Boulevard. Sharee, who had "startling sea-green eyes" and "shining hair the color of pale moonlight" according to her, sat down on the slatted bench and switched to old tennis shoes for the eight-block walk to her apartment. Then she tucked the gold, spike-heeled sandals she'd borrowed from a girl in her acting class into her tote bag and dashed across the busy intersection.

As Sharee turned down a side street, she clutched her beaded evening bag tightly to her chest. There was a crisp hundred dollar bill inside, her tip for serving canapés and displaying her perfectly capped smile at a producer's party in Beverly Hills. It had been a lucrative evening, and the producer had given her an ounce of caviar, a bottle of domestic champagne, and an invitation to come to an audition tomorrow for a small part in the series he was currently taping.

Firecrackers rattled in the distance as Sharee hurried past the once-stately apartments south of the boulevard. The Fourth of July was going out with a bang. There had been a huge display of fireworks at the party, but Sharee had been too busy serving hors d'oeuvres to see much of it. If she did well at the audition tomorrow, she might be attending the same party next year as a bona fide guest.

The Regency Palms was at the end of the block. Sharee cut through the deserted courtyard and took the crushed gravel walkway that led to the middle building. Plastic potted palms lined the narrow path at four-foot intervals, and she was careful not to brush up against the thick layer of grime that covered their fronds. Her gold lamé blouse was also borrowed, and she'd have to pay a dry cleaning bill if she got it dirty.

There was a sack of garbage on the bottom step, which Sharee dropped in the Dumpster before she climbed the concrete stairs to her second-floor apartment. She could hardly wait to get into some comfortable clothes and practice the scene the producer had given her. For once she didn't have to worry about being quiet while she rehearsed. Her neighbor in 19B was traveling for a week with his band, and the young actress on the other side was spending the three-day holiday with her boyfriend in Malibu.

Sharee unlocked the door to her apartment and pushed it open. Darkness greeted her, and she fought down her childish fear. While she no longer believed in monsters or ghosts, she still had to gather her courage to step into the dark apartment and lock the door behind her.

Heart pounding, Sharee ran across the living room to snap on the light. Then she heard the shower running in the bathroom. She'd been in a hurry when she left for the party, and she must have forgotten to turn it off.

Sharee tossed her tote bag on the couch and hurried down the hall. Clouds of steam rolled out to meet her as she opened the bathroom door. She was just reaching for the knob to turn off the shower when she saw a man in a black executioner's hood standing at the far corner of the room. Steam swirled around him, and he looked as if he'd just materialized from a horror movie.

At first Sharee was too startled to scream. Then she spotted a video camera on a tripod next to the shower. Sharee's mind clicked into action again, and she laughed as her earlier fears evaporated. She knew who owned that brand of camera. The man in the executioner's costume was Bob Beauchamp, a colleague from her acting class, and he was filming another of his surprise projects.

"Bob! You rat!" Sharee faced him squarely with her hands on her hips. "How did you get in here? And where did you rent that ridiculous costume?"

There was no reply, and Sharee's smile faltered. Her green eyes showed a tiny flicker of fear as the executioner stood silent and unmoving, watching her through the eyeholes of his mask. Sharee felt her throat go dry, and she swallowed with difficulty. It wasn't like Bob to carry a joke this far. Surely he could tell she was frightened.

"Come on, Bob. That's enough! I brought home a bottle of champagne from the party. If you stop recording, I'll share it with you."

Silence filled the room, and suddenly Sharee realized that the executioner was at least four inches taller than Bob. Terror swept across her face, making a parody of her beauty. She willed her frozen body to move, and with what seemed like agonizing slowness, she turned to run. The executioner's arms were like steel cables, reeling her back, and Sharee clawed at him in a frenzy, kicking and twisting and biting to get away.

Sharee's long, polished nails raked deeply, and for one brief moment she had the advantage. But before she could recover her balance, he had her again, his grip even tighter this time. Sharee thrashed wildly as she felt herself lifted. She struggled blindly against the inevitable, like the butterflies her older brother used to pin in his collection box, but the executioner shoved her roughly forward, under the stream of scalding water.

A thin, high, inhuman scream punctured the haze of her panic. The sound grew louder, bouncing off the white tiles, and Sharee dimly realized that it was coming from her own throat. As the knife slashed downward, her scream reached a crescendo, tapering off into deafening silence.

A puzzled expression crossed Sharee's face as she crumpled, her hands sliding against the wet, slick tiles. There was no pain, only bone-chilling cold as the knife rose and fell. And through the steam and the gathering cold, she saw the gleaming eye of the camera as her blood colored the water pink and then red until it disappeared down the gurgling drain.

Brother left his star in the shower, lifeless green eyes staring up into the spray. One last shot of her crumpled body with a slow pan to her beautiful untouched face, and it was finished. He picked up his equipment and stepped out into the warm summer night, secure that he had captured the first segment, exactly as he had intended.

A string of firecrackers rattled in the distance as Brother walked across the silent courtyard. At first he was startled, but then he remembered the date and smiled at its significance. Today was the Fourth of July, a perfect time to start his production. The birth of the nation and the birth of his masterpiece. People would remember them together for years to come.

2

Monday, July 5

It was shortly past seven in the morning when Tony Rocca stopped at the Mister Donut on Hollywood Boulevard and bought two cinnamon twists for his partner, two maple bars for himself, and a cup of coffee to go. The frizzy-haired matron at the cash register, who had obviously taken full advantage of her Mister Donut employee discount, peered over the tops of her glasses to read his T-shirt. Her bright red lipsticked mouth moved painfully as she sounded out the words. This morning Tony was wearing a navy blue short-sleeved Hanes that proclaimed GENIASES CAN'T SPEL in bright red letters.

Balancing the coffee precariously on the passenger seat of his dark green Volvo, Tony eased his way back out into traffic. Three blocks later he turned down a side street and pulled into the lot of the Schwartzvold

40

Building.

Tony parked in his space and locked his car. This morning Tony opted for using the front entrance. He needed a little fresh air after the party yesterday. Tony and his wife, Allison, had hosted a Fourth of July barbecue at their home in Studio City, and Tony had sampled one too many of the margaritas he'd mixed. He cut through the alley and dashed up to Hollywood Boulevard.

Tony liked this area with its old substantial look, but it was definitely rundown. People were still waiting for what they called the "Hollywood Renaissance." The land barons were playing a slow game of chess with their Hollywood holdings. There hadn't been any strong moves thus far, but they'd created enough interest to raise the rents. The owner of the Schwartzvold had announced an increase last month. Tony had accepted the rent hike even though he was really strapped for money right now. It was worth it to work in Hollywood, where there was a feeling of film history.

Frederick's of Hollywood was a bright purple erection at the end of the block, and as Tony walked past, he noticed that they'd changed their window display. Perhaps he'd drag Erik inside one of these days, just to see him blush and stammer. For someone who could write the best raunchy dialogue Tony had ever read, Erik was strangely provincial when it came to the real world. Even though they'd been friends for years, there were times when he didn't understand Erik at all.

Tony had been a tough punk from L.A. when he'd enlisted and been sent to the Middle East. Once there, the giant melting pot of the army had teamed him with an unlikely buddy. Erik had been a straight-laced Minnesota farm boy on his first trip away from home, but his innate common sense coupled with Tony's streetwise cunning had helped both of them survive the horrors of combat. When their tour of duty was over, they'd lost touch except for the annual Christmas card. At least, Erik had thought they'd lost touch. Since Tony had a buddy in Minnesota, he'd kept tabs on Erik. He'd found out about the family farm that had gone bankrupt, the college degree that Erik had financed through the GI Bill, and the move he'd made to L.A. after his parents had died. Tony even knew about Erik's disastrous marriage to a young starlet who'd screwed him six ways to the center. And fifteen years later, when they'd gotten together again at a veteran reunion, Erik had filled in the missing years. He'd told

Tony about the farm, the college degree, and his job teaching English in L.A., but he hadn't mentioned his marriage. Since Tony was well acquainted with Erik's touchy sense of privacy, he hadn't brought it up, either.

As Tony walked rapidly down the street, he nodded at the white-haired man who was kneeling on a folded rug in front of Greta Garbo's star in the sidewalk. It was one of hundreds of such tributes that lined the sidewalks at the intersection of Hollywood Boulevard and Vine Street for a mile in either direction. The stars were set in a three-foot square and were inlaid in brass with the celebrities' names in the center. Tony had spent many happy Sunday afternoons as a child, taking what the guidebooks called "The Walk of the Stars" and attempting to identify all the names. One thing he'd learned from these excursions was how to read upside down. Every other star was set in backward for people who were walking in the opposite direction.

The man looked up and nodded. He was what the sociologists had termed a "familiar stranger," a man Tony saw every morning in the same place at the same time. He was in his seventies, Tony guessed, and he was wearing the bright green windbreaker and visored cap he'd worn for the past three years. As Tony approached, the man rubbed vigorously at the star with Brasso cleaner, making the metal sparkle in the sun. Last Friday Tony had found him scraping the gum off the sidewalk with a putty knife and muttering angrily to himself.

Since Tony had to pass this spot every morning to get to his office, he had worked up several scenarios about the old man. He could be a relative of the famous Garbo or her loyal, retired chauffeur. In Tony's best scenario the old man was a former lover paying homage to his lost lady. Even though he was rabidly curious, Tony wasn't about to ask questions. The real story might not live up to his fantasies.

Tony walked carefully around the star and earned a fleeting smile of approval from the old man. On his way down the sidewalk, he sidestepped Merle Oberon, walked over Elvis Presley, there was no way he could be serious about a man whose face had been painted on black velvet, and tromped directly in the center of Harry Cohn, the ruthless Columbia Pictures mogul.

"Serves you right, White Fang," Tony said aloud. "You stomped on plenty of real stars in your day!"

Fred Astaire, upside down, was the sentinel in front of the Schwartzvold Building, and Tony used his key on the front door, then made sure it locked tightly behind him. He'd come in one morning last week to find an old wino sleeping in the lobby.

On his way to the elevator Tony checked the row of metal mailboxes in the lobby, even though there'd been no mail delivery yesterday. There was nothing in the box marked ROCCA & NIELSEN except an outdated circular for a Radio Shack sale. Tony dropped it in the battered wastebasket that was chained to the wall and headed for the elevator. He hoped it was working today. The thirteen-floor climb to the tower office would just about kill him.

There was a metallic squeal as the old-fashioned elevator doors slid open, revealing the dark, wood-paneled interior. Tony felt like Daniel entering the lion's den as he stepped inside and the heavy doors screeched closed behind him. If the elevator got stuck, not an uncommon occurrence, he could press the alarm button until he was blue in the face, but no one would be in the building to hear it. Writers were the only people crazy enough to come in this early.

Tony sighed with relief as the elevator ground to a halt and opened its doors. The cage had stopped three inches above the floor, but Tony wasn't about to quibble with the ancient Otis about minor inconveniences. He unlocked his office door, switched on the lights, and immediately took three aspirins with a swig of lukewarm Mister Donut coffee.

The first sight of his office in the morning always made Tony groan. Allison had hired a high-priced decorator while he was away on location for *Free Fire.* She'd given him free reign to throw out Tony's old army-surplus office furniture and replace it with new things that were cheerful and bright. Unfortunately, she hadn't stipulated how cheerful or how bright.

Brilliant orange, blinding yellow, and eye-popping turquoise fought for dominance on Tony's expensive tubular furniture, but dazzling fuchsia was the hands-down winner when it came to his desk. The framework was dull black covered by a sheet of fuchsia Plexiglas. It was the same color Revlon had christened "hot pink" in the fifties. Marilyn Monroe had worn it on her lips and Pepto-Bismol had bottled it. Now it had found a home on the four-by-eight-foot glass rectangle of Tony's desktop. Tony managed to hide it with papers most of the time, but he had cleared his desk before he'd gone home on Friday.

Tony went to the bookshelf and got down the unabridged dictionary and the world atlas. They were the biggest books in the office. When he opened them on top of his desk they almost covered the glaring pink surface. That meant he'd have to hand-hold the script he was proofing this morning because there was no longer room to work at his desk, but it was well worth it.

The script was a rewrite for a television detective series that Tony and Erik had gotten from Alan Goldberg. It was not the first incident of Alan's generosity over the past eleven months. Cinescope occasionally gave script assignments to writers who couldn't write, as did every other studio in town.

Selling to episodic television consisted of three hurdles. Pitch, story, and script. The writer's first hurdle was to "pitch" story ideas. If the producers liked an idea, and if network approved, the writer had jumped the first hurdle. Then he had to jump the second hurdle by working his idea into a story. This story, an embellished action outline with indications of appropriate dialogue, was often rewritten by the studio story editor to make sure it conformed to the guidelines of the show and the personalities of the leading characters. A completed story earned the writer over fourteen thousand dollars and a crack at the third hurdle, script. If the producers had faith in the writer's ability, he was given a script assignment. For completion of this script, the writer was paid twenty-four thousand dollars in round numbers. That made a grand total of approximately thirty-eight thousand dollars up front, plus a generous residual fee for every rerun. A writer who had leaped all three hurdles and written a script for a popular television series could expect to earn as much as eighty thousand dollars for his work.

Tony sighed as he remembered Alan Goldberg's account of the original writer. The guy had been a master storyteller and he'd been given a story assignment on the strength of his brilliant verbal pitch. The story that had followed was less than acceptable. It had been revised and strengthened by the in-house story editor, and the end result had been promising. The original writer had been given the go-ahead on script because of his excellent credentials.

The first attempt at script had been abysmal and the second no better. It was too late to cut off the original writer. He'd fulfilled his contractual obligations and the studio was required to pay him in full for his inferior product. To add insult to injury, the studio was stuck with an unusable script.

Alan had called in Tony and Erik to fix up the script with the implicit understanding that they wouldn't arbitrate for any screen credit. The original writer would get full credit, and since his name alone would be on the script, he could show Rocca and Nielsen's rewrite to other producers to get future assignments. Such inequity bothered Tony, and he sat down to proof their work with a scowl on his face.

Tony finished the first act and the second maple bar simultaneously. He wiped off his hands and went to make coffee. Erik always arrived at the office at precisely eight-thirty, and the first thing he needed was "Swedish Plasma."

As he poured water into the machine, Tony looked out the tower window that dominated the small kitchenette. The room was Gothic-Deco. The design was Gothic, but it had been repeated all over the little cubicle. Tony liked the mixture of styles, and he was grateful that Allison hadn't set her decorator loose on anything but his private office.

The view out the kitchenette window was worth the price of the whole office suite. Tony could see the Capitol Records building, and he loved its design. It was built to resemble a stack of records on a turntable, and it was a Hollywood landmark.

The smell of fresh coffee brewing was irresistible, and Tony poured a cup before the pot was fully ready. He was about to go back to tackle the second act of the script when the telephone rang. Tony raced for his office, reached over the desk from the front, and picked it up on the second ring. It was Alan Goldberg.

"Hi, Alan." Tony leaned over the atlas, his left elbow resting on Borneo. "We should have your script for you by tomorrow morning."

"Good, but that's not why I'm calling. Did you catch the news this morning?"

"News? No, Alan. I've been working on your script. What's up?"

"A miracle, that's what's up! It looks like you guys were right on the money with *Video Kill*."

"That's great, Alan." Tony's mind whirled, trying to make some sense out of Alan's words. "How so?"

"Apparently some sickie stabbed a woman last night in Hollywood. He left a video of the whole thing for the police."

Tony was so astonished, he almost dropped the phone, but Alan went on

50

without waiting for his response.

"They're running an exclusive on channel five. Watch it and call me back."

Tony didn't even bother to hang up the phone. He just dropped the receiver and rushed to turn on the office television. His hands were trembling as he sat down and watched the segment. Alan was right. A killer had recorded himself murdering a woman and left the video behind for the police.

An interview with Chief Detective Oliver "Sam" Ladera of the Los Angeles Police Department was next, and he substantiated the facts the reporter had just given. That meant their crazy idea for a movie, the one everyone had said was too far-fetched to be believed, had just turned into reality.

Erik Nielsen jumped out of bed at the instant his alarm rang. He'd learned to wake up fast when he was in combat. For one brief moment he was totally disoriented, but his mind cleared quickly as he went through the litany he used every morning. The war was behind him. Deep breath. He was alive and well. Deep breath. He was safe. Final deep breath. Rocca and Nielsen had won the war, or at least they'd managed to turn the numbing horror of those years into the script for a movie.

His heart slowed to a near-regular rhythm as he swiveled his head and took in the familiar surroundings. Light tan walls, brown and red curtains at the windows, a lobby-sized full-color poster advertising *Free Fire* on the wall. He was in the master bedroom of his Culver City condo, thousands of miles away from combat. Here he was perfectly safe. No one could come in or out, unauthorized. The round-the-clock security guards kept out anyone who wasn't on Erik's visitor list, and his list was only two people long. Tony and Allison Rocca.

Erik crossed the room in five quick steps and slapped savagely at the button on the dainty, rose-patterned alarm clock. He really ought to replace it soon. It was a continual reminder of his brief but painful marriage to a rising young actress named Daniele Renee. Daniele had been long gone when Erik and Tony had gotten together again four years ago, and Erik had seen no reason to mention her. He knew that Tony would be supportive and sympathetic, but there was nothing to gain by rehashing the whole mess. He'd made a mistake and now he was paying for it.

It was already past seven. He was due at the office at eight-thirty. Erik pulled on his slippers and hurried down the hall past Jamie's room. He was currently using the room for an at-home office, but it could be converted very quickly when his son got well enough to come home.

The moment Erik opened the drapes in the living room, his cat appeared, a big, white angora he'd christened Al. Erik had found him on the doorstep last January and no one had responded to the lost cat notice he'd put in the paper. By then, Erik had grown to like Al.

"Want some fresh air, Al?"

Al streaked out the second Erik opened the sliding glass door. Erik's tiny balcony overlooked the children's pool, but it was deserted at seven in the morning. Erik had chosen this particular condo so that Jamie could be close to the pool. The staff doctor at Pine Ridge, an expensive, private institution for autistic children, had reported that Jamie seemed to show interest in his swimming classes.

Erik left Al in the sun, washing his face, and went into the kitchen. He poured yesterday's coffee in a *Free Fire* mug and set the timer on the microwave for thirty seconds, just long enough to warm it slightly.

The timer on the microwave rang, and

Erik drank his coffee down at a gulp. Then he took Al's cat food out of the refrigerator and heated it in the microwave for forty-five seconds. When the timer rang, Al trotted into the kitchen right on cue. He knew Erik's routine. The first ring of the timer was for Erik's coffee, and he didn't bother to come running for that. But the second ring was his, and he always appeared just as Erik set the plate of warm food on the floor.

It was time to take his morning shower. Erik filled a bowl with fresh water, set it on the floor next to his purring cat, and headed for the master bathroom. The unlimited supply of hot water had seemed like heaven when he'd first moved in. To make things even more perfect, the cost of the hot water was covered by the monthly homeowner's fee, and Erik treated himself to long, marvelously relaxing showers anytime he wanted. Perhaps his lengthy showers were a reaction to the miserable conditions in combat. Only a minimum of cleanliness had been possible, and relaxing showers were non-existent. And before that, during Erik's childhood in Minnesota, the old electric water heater in the farmhouse kitchen had been too small to provide more than a quick scrub before the spray turned cold. Whatever the reason, the master bathroom shower was one of Erik's favorite places.

It was seven forty-five by the time Erik drove out of the complex. He stopped to wait for a group of middle-aged women joggers to cross Overland Avenue, heading toward the running track at West Los Angeles College. One of them was his downstairs neighbor, Mavis Perkins. She was a Beverly Hills lawyer, the quintessential career woman, and she left for work each morning dressed in the height of fashion. Erik could have lived for several years on what she spent for her designer wardrobe, her hairdresser appointments, and her visits to the nail boutique. But this morning Mavis looked like a refugee from a thrift store in her baggy purple sweatpants and grubby orange T-shirt. She'd told Erik that she was jogging for her appearance, but she certainly didn't care about her appearance while she was jogging. It didn't make sense, but Erik had given up trying to figure out women.

Erik turned the corner at Jefferson Boulevard and followed it past the new business parks that had sprung up almost overnight. As he drove east, the area grew more industrial, offices giving way to small factories and warehouses. He turned left on La Cienega and took the Fairfax cutoff. The traffic was a mess, as usual, and Erik was running late. He'd planned on eating breakfast out, but now there wasn't time. He settled for a quick stop at a Winchell's Donuts to pick up two maple bars for Tony, two cinnamon twists for himself, and a cup of coffee to go.

The rest of the drive was easy, and Erik managed to swig down the stale coffee and eat both cinnamon twists by the time he turned on Hollywood Boulevard and parked in the Schwartzvold lot. He opened the office door at precisely eight-thirty to find Tony pacing the floor, clutching a copy of their proposal for *Video Kill.*

"There's a couple of maple bars in here with your name on them." Erik put the bag on the desk and headed toward the coffee pot with the single-minded purpose of a true addict.

Tony followed him. "Did you hear the news this morning?"

"Nope."

Erik took his cup from the drainboard and wiped it meticulously before he filled it. It was a basic difference between the two men. Erik washed his coffee cup every night before he left the office and Tony hadn't touched sudsy water since the last time Allison had dropped in.

"And you didn't take time to read the paper?"

Tony was grinning broadly now, and Erik turned to look at him.

"That's right. I didn't take time to read the paper. What's with you, Tony? You're acting like a cat with a mouthful of feathers."

"Come with me and I'll show you."

Tony grabbed Erik's arm and steered him into the reception area. Since they had no need for a secretary, it held two matching couches, a long wooden coffee table for spreading out papers, and a television monitor with a DVR on top. Tony pushed Erik down on the nearest couch and turned on the television to play the recording he'd just made. The stabbing last night had been almost identical to their first scene in *Video Kill*, and he could hardly wait to see Erik's reaction.

3

Allison Rocca was wearing the apron Tony had given her two years ago when they had first moved to their new house in Studio City. It was a chef's apron, much too large for her, with ribbon ties that wound twice around her small waist. Tony had personalized it with one of his messages, most of Tony's gifts had messages, and Allison's apron said MY BUNS ARE PERFECT in bold red letters.

She opened the refrigerator, a gleaming steel model with a built-in ice maker, and took out a Tupperware bowl filled with potato salad. Everything in the kitchen was new, from the six-burner gas range top to the double ovens and industrial-sized microwave built into the wall. The appliances would have put many restaurant kitchens to shame, and Allison felt a bit intimidated by the matching copper pans hanging on a metal rack over the butcher block work center and the variety of specialized utensils in its neatly divided drawers. Her most successful entrees were made with packaged ingredients and Campbell's cream of mushroom soup.

The party yesterday had been catered, but Allison had provided the potato salad. It was made from her mother's recipe, and Allison had spent hours cooking potatoes, peeling hard-boiled eggs, and reading the Cuisinart instruction booklet to identify the proper attachments to chop everything up into the right-sized pieces. Allison's potato salad had been the hit of the party. Even the woman from the catering service had asked for her recipe.

Allison got out a lovely bone china plate and put a scoop of potato salad on the side, decorating it with three ripe olive slices and a sprinkle of Hungarian paprika. She was taking lunch to her mother today. Helen Greene's appetite was failing and Allison was determined to come up with something that would tempt her.

As Allison stood back a bit to survey her work, she brushed back her naturally curly, reddish-blond hair. Since she'd allowed it to grow past shoulder length, it often got in her way. Brushing it aside with the back of her hand was a nervous gesture she'd developed lately, right along with tapping her fingers against the arm of the couch and jumping visibly every time the phone rang. She reached out to rearrange an olive slice and nodded in satisfaction. The potato salad not only looked appealing but also was made with sour cream dressing, a good source of calcium. Since her mother also needed a high concentration of protein, she arranged choice slices of turkey, rare roast beef, and ham in an overlapping design, topping each slice with a sprig of fresh parsley, rich in iron, from her greenhouse herb garden. She added a radish rose and a few crisp carrot curls, then frowned as she realized that yesterday's guests had eaten the last of the kaiser rolls. There was no way she'd spoil her mother's plate by adding a slice of Tony's Bunny Bread.

Tony's favorite brand of bread was snowy white and tasteless, so fluffy that he could squash a piece into a marble-sized ball. Tony called these pellets "bread pills," and Allison couldn't hide her disgust when he rolled them between his fingers and popped them into his mouth. Tony regarded bread primarily as a vehicle to keep peanut butter off his fingers, and he had never understood Allison's rhapsodies over brioche, pumpernickel, dark rye, and sourdough.

Allison opened the freezer door and smiled as she spotted a package of brown 'n' serve whole wheat rolls. When she smiled, Allison's pretty girl-next-door face turned into an object of stunning beauty. The transformation was almost magical as her brown eyes sparkled with golden highlights and her highly defined cheekbones lost their severity.

When Allison had been an aspiring actress, long before she'd married Tony and given up that ambition, she had once been chosen for a deodorant commercial on the strength of that transformation. She'd been solemn for the first shot, breaking into a sudden smile as she'd held up the sponsor's product. The director had told Allison that her appeal was subliminal. A woman watching the commercial might think that she'd be beautiful, too, if she used the sponsor's deodorant.

As Allison turned on the oven to preheat, she wished again that she could make a decent loaf of bread. After two abysmal failures that might have been hilarious if they'd happened to anyone else, Allison had tabled her attempts at bread making for times when Tony was out of town. She still remembered her first flop, and her delicate ivory complexion took on the bright rosy hue of embarrassment. She had mixed up the dough exactly as the recipe had directed and kneaded it with strict adherence to the instructions. Everything had gone along perfectly until she'd placed the dough in a warm place to rise for a few hours. Then she'd dashed out to pick up some crew socks for Tony, and while she was waiting for the clerk to ring up the sale, she'd run into her former agent. Would Allison please join her for lunch? There were some people she simply *must* meet.

The restaurant was a show biz spot where people greeted each other in exclamations. *Darling! You look stunning! It's been simply ages! How marvelous to see you again!* There was the usual flurry of near-miss kisses, the point of contact aborted at precisely the last second by a common concern for makeup. Allison found herself wedged in a two-person booth with four people. One of them was the same director who'd done her deodorant commercial. Was she still working? How about a high-budget toothpaste commercial? There was a casting call in an hour if she was interested. He'd take her in personally and introduce her, right after lunch.

When Allison had arrived home after the casting session, which had turned out to be nothing but a cattle call, she'd found Tony pacing the floor impatiently, waiting to take her to dinner. They were meeting several big names and it was a command appearance. Could she be ready to go in ten minutes?

Allison had been ready, they'd driven to the restaurant, and she'd spent the evening talking to the wife of a man who'd later turned out to do nothing for Tony's career. Allison had forgotten her rising bread dough in the rush, and when they'd returned home, shortly before midnight, she'd tumbled into bed without even changing into her nightgown.

Tony's voice had roused her the next morning. Was she growing something in the oven? There was a white, pulsating mass in there that looked like it was trying to ooze out the door.

Allison had let out a genuine cry of alarm and rushed to open the oven door. Her bread dough! She'd forgotten all about it! As the cold morning air had hit the warm yeasty mass, it had given a dying sigh and deflated, leaving huge, stringy patches of gloop all over the inside of the oven. When Allison had tried to clean up the mess with a wet sponge, it had spread like paste, taking total possession of the oven. Tony had

63

sat at the kitchen table and laughed, sipping his coffee and making references to *The Sorcerer's Apprentice.*

An entire year had passed before Allison had worked up the nerve to try it again. Her second attempt had showed no tendency to rise at all, so she'd popped it into the oven anyway, hoping for the best. Tony had come home just in time to see her take her loaves out of the oven, two squat, brown bricks that fell from the pan with a solid thunk. He'd laughed at the dismayed expression on her face and cracked one of his usual jokes. Why didn't she bake a couple more batches so they could build a fireplace? Allison had smiled good-naturedly, but she had given up on the fine art of bread making.

Allison's face grew solemn as she thought of her husband. Things had changed since they'd moved into their expensive new house, and just last week, when she'd tried to discuss the distance that was growing between them, Tony had shrugged it off. He'd insisted that Allison was looking for a problem where none existed. Everything was fine. She was probably depressed because of her mother. He'd feel the same way, in her position.

Allison knew Tony was partially right. Visits with her mother were emotionally draining, and it took all of Allison's strength to smile and keep up a stream of amusing chatter while she sat in a chair by the bed and watched her mother slowly die. Some afternoons, when Allison came home from the convalescent center, it took hours to shake her feelings of depression and helplessness. She seldom went out anymore, preferring to stay by the phone in case her mother suddenly took a turn for the worse. She watched endless hours of television, switching from channel to channel, hoping for something intriguing enough to take her mind off the woman who lay dying in Bel Air thirty-five minutes away.

When Helen Greene had first gone to the doctor, sixteen months ago, Allison had refused to accept the diagnosis. She'd urged her mother to go for a second opinion, a third opinion, and then a fourth. After the fifth specialist, her mother had stopped all that nonsense. Helen Greene knew she had terminal cancer and she didn't need more doctors to confirm it. Allison would just have to accept the inevitable.

Helen had stayed in her own home for as long as she could, and then sold the house to pay her medical expenses at the convalescent center. The sale had gone through a year ago, and Allison suspected that her mother's money had run out. When she had questioned Tony about it, he'd told her to let him worry about supporting the family.

In many ways Tony was an old-fashioned man. He had handled their finances from the start, and Allison admitted that it was probably wise. She'd never been good at budgeting. She knew their elaborate home was a financial drain. The mortgage payment was high, but Tony had told her to leave that to him. He'd said that in show biz you had to spend money to make money.

They'd moved into their new house right after *Free Fire* had been released. Tony had been sure his future as a screenwriter was assured, and they'd opted for the top-of-the-line, four-bedroom Colonial at Studio City Estates. They had spent the previous eight years of their marriage in a tiny Los Angeles apartment, and neither Allison nor Tony had anticipated the upkeep that was necessary on such a large home. There were gardeners, pool maintenance men, a pest control service, and, over Allison's objections, a weekly cleaning crew. Allison still felt guilty about the cleaning crew — she'd been raised to believe that a woman should take care of her own house — but Tony had insisted. To alleviate her guilt Allison went into a flurry of dusting and vacuuming before the crew arrived so they wouldn't think she was a bad housekeeper.

While she waited for the dinner rolls to brown, Allison switched on the kitchen television. The announcer was saying something about a stabbing in Hollywood and she half-listened as she tidied up the kitchen. In the middle of the report, she took the rolls out of the stove, wrapped two of them in aluminum foil, and put everything into a basket for carrying, including the pan of double-fudge brownies she'd picked up at a local bakery. Even if her mother didn't eat them, she could dole them out to the nursing staff.

Methodically, Allison locked up the house. There were four sets of sliding glass doors leading to the pool area, two side doors, one double front door, and the attached garage door. Then she got into the silver convertible that Tony had bought her for her last birthday and backed carefully out onto the circular driveway.

Allison didn't think of the news flash again until she was walking up the brick steps of the convalescent center. The newscaster had said something about a disc the killer had left at the scene. Now she wished that she'd listened more carefully. The whole thing reminded her of the movie idea that Tony and Erik had pitched last year.

Tony was on the phone with Alan Goldberg, and Erik half listened as he paged through their *Video Kill* treatment. He was still sickened by the account he'd seen of the murder. Sharee Lyons, the young victim, had been stabbed repeatedly. The thought of the killer planning the whole scene, setting up his video camera on a tripod in the bathroom, and cold-bloodedly capturing her death was gruesome.

Erik remembered the morning, almost two years ago, when Tony had first approached him with the *Video Kill* idea. Both men had been intrigued with the possibilities. Erik recalled using words like *promotable* and *high concept* as they'd settled down to work out the logistics. It had been fun spicing up Tony's "hot" idea with bits of evocative dialogue guaranteed to sell the project. Then it had been pure fiction, a wild flight of fancy. Now that their idea had become a grisly reality, it had turned into something else altogether, something revolting, something evil, something that Erik wasn't prepared for at all. He felt almost as if their idea had been stolen and violated in some unspeakable way.

Tony laughed, and Erik tried to concentrate on the one-sided conversation. He caught phrases like *If we're lucky, he'll do it again* and *Let's just hope the police don't catch him right away.* Naturally, Erik was glad that Cinescope was interested in *Video Kill.* He certainly could use the money. But Tony seemed to be totally ignoring the fact that a brutal crime had been committed.

Erik barely noticed as Tony said his good-byes and hung up the phone. He didn't look up until he felt Tony's hand on his shoulder.

"What's the matter, Erik? Are you turning squeamish about doing this movie?"

"Of course not." Erik frowned. "It's your attitude, Tony. You're completely forgetting a girl was brutally murdered and the killer is loose. It's a cause for alarm, not celebration."

"The Killer Is Loose?" Tony began to grin. "*Cause for Alarm?* You really ought to take up writing movie titles, Erik."

Erik made a disgusted face. He knew Tony was trying to distract him with jokes, but it wouldn't work this time.

"All right. They're movie titles. So what? I still object to your attitude, Tony. Here we are, using this girl's murder for our own ends, and you're, well, you're so damn happy about it!"

Tony cocked his head to the side and gave

Erik a long, level stare.

"Aha! I think your sense of Lutheran morality is kicking up again."

"That's not it." Erik sighed deeply. "I want to sell *Video Kill* every bit as much as you do, but I can't believe you had the audacity to tell Alan that we're hoping the killer will strike again."

"Did I say that?" Tony looked stunned. "Oh, hey, I didn't mean it *that* way! I mean, I wasn't thinking about the murder itself. I was just excited about what it would mean to us."

Erik gave in. Tony looked genuinely contrite.

"All right, Tony. We all say things we don't mean. I just don't think we should gloat over this thing, okay?"

"Sure. Honestly, Erik. I wish that actress hadn't been killed, but she was. And even if we do take advantage of it, that can't change what's already happened. Right?"

"Right. Did you say Sharee Lyons was an actress?"

"Yeah. She'd been to a couple of cattle call auditions, but she hadn't landed anything yet. I guess that part was on before I recorded it."

After a beat of uncomfortable silence, Tony got up and headed back to his own office. Erik shut off the television and went to his laptop. There was work to do. He still had to make a couple of changes in the fourth act of Alan's detective script and print it out.

As Erik worked, his sense of outrage faded a bit. It was common for L.A. girls to claim they were actresses whether they were or not. If you drove down Sunset and talked to any hooker on any street corner, nine times out of ten she'd tell you she was just doing tricks on the side until she got her big break in show business. Sharee Lyons could have been out earning the rent last night when she'd picked up some weirdo. There were a lot of sick people on the streets.

"Erik?" Tony stuck his head in the doorway and shifted from foot to foot, a sure sign that he had a problem. "Alan called me back. He wants us in his office for a meeting at three."

"Fine. We can take this script in at the same time."

"Yeah, that's what I told him. Look, Erik, I probably ought to leave well enough alone, but I think it would really improve our chances if we could get the press to use the name 'Video Killer.' I've got a buddy at the *Times* who owes me a favor, but I won't cash it in if you've got objections."

Erik thought it over for a moment and then he shrugged. "Go ahead, Tony. The publicity can't hurt."

"It's really all right with you?"

Erik nodded. "Whatever."

"Erik?"

"Hmm?"

"I sent flowers. Anonymously. I figured we might look like ghouls if we put our names on the card."

Erik stared at Tony's earnest face and started to laugh. There were times when Tony had absolutely no sensibilities, but his heart was in the right place.

4

Alan Goldberg was in a rotten mood when he buzzed his assistant on the intercom. He'd spent the past forty-five minutes arguing with his uncle in Hawaii and he still refused to go ahead with the *Video Kill* contracts. If their option ran out while the old man was dragging his heels, someone else would be sure to snatch it up and make the profits that could have been theirs.

There was a click as his assistant came on the line, and Alan spoke before she could even ask him what he wanted. "Would you believe it, honey? *Video Kill*'s the hottest concept to come along in years, but the old man says it doesn't reflect the quality inherent in the Cinescope image. He actually told me it was cheap exploitation! And this from the man who made *Attack of the Giant Slugs*!"

"I'm sorry, sir. He's not in at the moment. Could I take a message?"

Alan caught his assistant's verbal cue. Whenever she called him "sir" that meant someone was waiting to see him. He switched on the closed-circuit television and scanned the reception area. Jerry Dietman from the accounting department was there. And accountants never had good news.

"Get rid of Jerry, honey. And come in here with your personnel roster. We've got a lot to do."

A moment later his assistant opened the door and stepped in. Alan motioned to the chair next to his desk, and she sat down.

"What did you tell Jerry?"

Alan's assistant smiled. "I said you were tied up with an emergency situation and it might be quite some time before you could get back to him."

"Good girl!" Alan reached out to run his hand up her silk-clad leg. He grinned when she uncrossed her legs and moved closer. "Later, honey. Right now I need you for something else. Who's the best composer we've got under contract?"

"For feature or episodic?"

"Feature."

"Drama or comedy?"

"Drama. Heavy drama. Lots of murder and suspense."

Alan's assistant flipped through the personnel roster expertly. "There's Ralph McCabe, but you usually give him the tear-jerkers. You know, the kind of *Love Story* thing where one of the principals dies while the violins weep?"

"Right." Alan nodded. "We just bought a disease-of-the-week movie about Parkinson's. I'd better save him for that. Who else have we got?"

"The Bassingers. You like them, but I hear they're having some problems. According to their secretary, he's got something going on the side and she's threatening to leave him."

"Okay, forget the Bassingers. There's always a hassle when a team splits up. Who else?"

"How about Ronnie Gruber? He's had three months off and his secretary says he's chomping at the bit."

"Gruber's good. I'll go with him. Now, let's talk about art directors."

Alan's assistant flipped the pages in her roster. "Hertzel's available, but he just came back from the Betty Ford Center and it might be a good idea to wait and see if it took."

"Right. How about Ellen Payton?"

"Ellen's just winding up on that Civil War bio-flick, but she's scheduled for surgery just as soon as the picture wraps."

Alan nodded. "Oh, yeah, let's not forget to send flowers. Who else have we got?"

"Stewart Scott's between projects and his contract's got six months to run. You used him on that last espionage film, didn't you?"

Alan smiled. "He's perfect. Put him down. I've already decided on Tom Steiner to direct. He's through with his last film, isn't he?"

"It wrapped last Friday and he flew out that night for a month's vacation in the Bahamas. His wife's still in town, but his secretary booked two seats on the plane and arranged for a suite at the Paradise Island Casino Hotel."

Alan thought for a moment and then he smiled.

"That means he's been there for almost a week. He gambles, doesn't he?"

"That's what I've heard. Mostly baccarat. Rumor has it he dropped over fifty thousand the last time he was there."

"Then his wife ought to be doubly grateful that I'm calling him back early." Alan chuckled. "Make connections for him on the first flight back to L.A. I want him in my office by ten tomorrow morning at the latest. If he asks, you can tell him that he'll be directing Cinescope's new feature about the Video Killer."

"But . . ." Alan's assistant looked puzzled. "I thought your uncle nixed the project."

Alan nodded. "He did, but I'll talk him around. I'm just putting my team together in advance."

"And since everyone you're calling in is already under contract, there's no money expended?"

"You've got it. I always said I had the smartest assistant in the biz."

"And I always said I worked for the smartest boss in the biz."

Alan watched appreciatively as she got up and walked toward the door. She stopped and smiled as she caught him staring.

"Could I make a suggestion?"

Alan nodded. His assistant seldom offered unsolicited advice, but when she did, it was good stuff.

"How about using Lon Michaels for director of photography? I know it's not really his type of project, but your uncle knows Lon won't do anything but quality films."

"That's brilliant. But will Lon do it? I barely managed to talk him into doing the *Jubee* trilogy."

"I have great faith in your persuasive abilities. Perhaps you could invite him in as an adviser, just until you find the right man, of course. And then if you can't find another director of photography, he'll just have to step in, as a personal favor to you."

"Dynamite! Get Lon on the phone for me right away. And thanks for the suggestion, honey."

"You're welcome, but that wasn't the suggestion."

Alan raised his eyebrows in a question as she walked back to his desk and put her lips to his ear. A few whispered words and he began to grin.

"*That's* your suggestion?"

"That's it. Of course, now might not be a good time if you want those calls placed right away."

"The calls can wait." Alan pulled her down on his lap. "Uncle Meyer would have a stroke if he heard me say it, but there are some things even more important than making movies."

Lon Michaels was preparing for a scene in *Return of the Jubees,* the final movie in the *Jubees* trilogy. Just as soon as he'd finished setting up the lighting and cameras, Marvin Friedman would come in to direct the scene. Since it was one of the hottest days of the year and the temperature on the set was well over ninety degrees, Marvin was waiting for Lon's call in the air-conditioned trailer parked outside the soundstage.

"Miss DeMarco? Could I have full frontal, please?"

One of the identically costumed Jubees turned to face the camera. "You're uncanny, Lon. How did you know this one was me?"

Lon laughed. "That's easy. Your left ear sticks up a little higher than your right."

Miss DeMarco reached up to feel her pointed pink ear. "I never noticed that before, but how about the rest of us? You can't tell us all apart, can you?"

"Yes." Lon nodded. "Mr. Thielen's fur is pinker right over his chin, Mrs. Jackson has a curly whisker next to her eye, Miss Evert's tail has a little white spot near the tip, Mr. Heller's paws are worn smooth on the outside, and Mr. Bromley has a nose that tilts to the left. Now, let's get back to business. I don't want to keep you under these lights any longer than I have to."

Lon made a minor adjustment in the camera angle and squinted through the lens. Six pink, furry Jubees were seated in a circle on the forest glade set. The trees towering over them appeared gigantic even though they were actually medium-sized pines in wooden pots. That was because not a single Jubee exceeded forty-two inches in height. The Jubees were played by little people.

Cinescope had originally planned to hire children, but that was much more expensive. Child actors fell under social welfare rules. The length of their workday was severely curtailed, licensed tutors had to be hired so schoolwork could be done between takes, and the studio had to pay for a child welfare supervisor to sit in attendance at all times to watch for any infraction of the rules. It was much easier and cheaper to use little people.

Lon was adjusting the lights when the phone rang. A moment later, his assailant signaled for him to take the call.

"Not now, Susan." Lon waved her away. "Take a number and I'll call back after I finish this setup."

His assistant, a pretty brunette in her twenties, shook her head and put her hand over the mouthpiece. "It's Mr. Goldberg, Lon. I told him we were in the middle of lighting a scene, but he says he needs to talk to you immediately."

"Okay, I'll be right there." Lon turned to his camera operator. "Bring up the kicker on Mr. Bromley's head about half an f-stop and see what you can do about side-lighting that big log to make it more three-dimensional. Then shut down the lights and crank up the air-conditioning. We don't want our Jubees to melt into pink puddles on the forest floor."

There was a burst of laughter as Lon walked off the set. The cast really liked him. He treated them like the professional actors they were, and he didn't pat them on the head the way the director did. Lon was one of the few people in the industry who seemed genuinely concerned for their comfort. On the first day of shooting he'd ordered the carpenters to cut five inches from the legs of their personalized director's chairs so their feet could touch the floor.

Lon took the phone his assistant handed him and leaned against the wall. He hoped this wouldn't be a long conversation.

"Hi, Alan. What can I do for you?"

Alan countered with a question of his own. "When is this Jubee thing wrapping, Lon?"

"Marvin thinks ten days, but I'd give us twelve to be safe. Why?"

"Did you hear about the video-recorded murder last night?"

Lon frowned. Surely Alan hadn't called just to discuss this morning's gruesome news story. "I heard about it, Alan. My assistant used to live in that building and she's pretty shaken up over the whole thing."

"Right. Do you know anything about the

treatment we optioned last August from Rocca and Nielsen?"

"You'll have to refresh me, Alan. Something about a serial killer, wasn't it?"

"Right. It's called *Video Kill,* and the concept ties in perfectly with the murder last night. I'd like you to think about doing it."

"Me?" Lon was shocked. "Look, Alan, I really think you'd do better with someone who's had more experience in the murder-suspense genre."

"Maybe, but I still want you. This one's a guaranteed blockbuster, and I can make you a very good deal."

Lon was silent for a moment, trying to think of a way out. The details of the murder had sickened him and there was no way he wanted to be associated with a project that capitalized on it. At the same time Alan Goldberg wasn't the type of man to take outright rejection lightly.

"Alan, I'm flattered you thought of me, but I'm not sure I could do it. You're talking to the guy who was fired from a slasher film for being too sensitive."

"What does *that* mean?"

"It means the sight of blood makes me sick. Even *fake* blood."

Alan laughed. "That's what I thought

you'd say. Okay, Lon. I'd never ask you to make a commitment on something you didn't want to do. How about helping us as an adviser? Just until we zero in on the right man for the job? I'd consider it a personal favor."

Lon knew he was being suckered in, but there wasn't much he could do about it. "Of course, Alan. I'd be glad to help."

"Great! I'll put the rest of the team together today, and we'll all meet on . . . uh . . . just a second, Lon, and I'll check my schedule."

There was a click and Lon was put on hold. A few seconds later Alan came back on the line. "Tomorrow's clear for me. Can you be in my office tomorrow morning for a ten o'clock meeting? Unless you're shooting, of course."

"No, I'm free." Lon sighed. Alan had a copy of their shooting schedule and he knew they had a late call tomorrow. "Your timing couldn't be better, Alan."

There was a frown on Lon's face as he walked slowly back to the set. What he'd told Alan was perfectly true. He'd never been any good at blood and guts, and now that he recalled the details of Rocca and Nielsen's treatment, he was positive he didn't have the stomach for it. His forte had always been comedy and light romance.

"Bad news, Lon?" Susan looked concerned as she handed him his clipboard.

"What? Oh, no, Susan. Everything's fine. Will you ask the Jubees to take their places? I'll run a final check before we call for Marvin."

Lon was still deep in thought as the Jubees took their positions on the set. He'd seen through Alan's machinations and he was sure that the search for the right cinematographer would be halfhearted. For some totally unfathomable reason, Alan seemed determined to use him for *Video Kill*. It didn't make sense, but Alan Goldberg was God at Cinescope and what God wanted, God got. Lon knew he'd have to come up with one hell of a good recommendation for a substitute cinematographer, or he'd wind up doing the blasted thing by default.

5

Sunday, July 11

It was so quiet that Brother could hear the Rain Bird sprinklers click on in the front yard of the six-bedroom Tudor across the street. The sputtering noise disturbed his concentration, so he got up to shut the window, switching on the air-conditioning instead. One week had passed since he'd filmed the initial scene of his project, a week spent in meticulous preparation for tonight's work.

As Brother turned to look out the window, he noticed that the wind had picked up slightly. The yard was well illuminated with the carriage lights his mother had loved. They were on a photoelectric switch that turned them on at dusk and off at dawn. As he watched, an advertising circular skittered across the neatly mowed lawn and came to rest against the base of the huge coral tree that marked the edge of his mother's property. Brother watched it flutter in the wind, snared by the thorny bark of the tree. It was a nice image, worthy of Lon Michaels. Perhaps he'd use it someday. Brightly colored paper struggling ineffectually against an immovable object and then a slow dissolve to a similar human struggle. Woman against man, perhaps?

There was a sudden gust of wind from the opposite direction and the paper tore free, leaving a ragged, triangular-shaped shred on the thorn. Brother smiled. This, too, could be used. A second gust was violent enough to rattle a window in his mother's section of the house. The sound reminded Brother of his obligations. He hadn't checked the downstairs lately, and it was possible the cleaning woman had neglected to close a window.

Brother pulled open his center desk drawer and got out the front door key. He used it so seldom, it was unnecessary to carry it on his key ring. Then he locked up his own wing of the house and used the outside stairway to the side yard, where a winding flagstone path led him through his mother's English rose garden.

The formal garden held only unpleasant memories for Brother. His mother had ordered the bushes from England and had hired an English gardener to design and landscape the area. She had often boasted that the design was identical to the garden at Windsor, on a slightly smaller scale, of course, and she'd taken tea there at precisely four every afternoon. Brother still remembered how he'd rushed home from school to bathe and dress for the occasion. From four to four forty-five, Brother had been required to sit on his mother's white garden furniture and make exceedingly polite conversation while they sipped Earl Grey tea, his mother's favorite, and munched on dainty sandwiches that were as dry and tasteless as wedges of cardboard. Even now, years later, he cringed when he thought of those ordeals. Thank goodness he'd devised a way to escape them!

When Brother had gone to England to attend Oxford, a family tradition, he had discovered that there was more to a formal tea than watercress sandwiches and a correctly steeped pot of Earl Grey. There were also hot buttered scones with a variety of tasty marmalades and English trifle, a huge glass bowl filled with choice berries, cake, excellent brandy, and rich whipped cream. Perhaps, if his mother had varied her menu, he might not have resented playing Little Lord Fauntleroy. But, as a result of those mandatory teas, he still had a deep-seated hatred for things that were English.

Brother hurried through the formal garden without noticing whether the gardener was still following his mother's standing instructions. The roses could grow wild for all he cared. When he arrived at the front door, he was slightly winded. As he unlocked the door and pulled it open, warm light from the interior spilled out to meet him. For a moment Brother was disconcerted, but then he remembered the new timer system he'd ordered last week. The electrician must have hooked it up while the housekeeper was there.

Since the lights were on in the living room, Brother started his inspection there. The windows were locked up tight and everything appeared to be in order. He stopped for a moment to look at his mother's portrait hanging over the mantel. It had been done in England, when she was a child. The artist had painted her in the gardens at Danslair, her family estate, and she was wearing a tailored forest-green riding habit. She was staring slightly to the left and she was solemn faced, as if anticipating the duties that would await her as an adult. A small brass plate set into the bottom of the frame was inscribed with the words ELIZABETH SMYTHE-CARRINGTON, AGE TEN.

The portrait was slightly askew, and as Brother reached up to straighten it, the lights switched off. He stood in the inky darkness for a moment and then groped his way to the doorway. A lamp went on in his mother's bedroom, and Brother felt his heartbeat accelerate. The new timer was completely unnerving. It was almost as if his mother were still alive, leaving the living room to go to bed.

Brother walked down the hall to his mother's bedroom and picked up the flashlight she had always kept beside the bed. Luckily, the batteries were still functional. She must have replaced them right before she died. If he knew where the electrician had installed the mechanism, he could switch the timer to manual, but it would be quite a task to locate it in the dark. He'd just have to check the rest of the windows with what his mother had stubbornly called her "torch."

After Brother checked the bedroom windows, the light in his mother's bathroom went on, so he checked that, too. While he was there, he noticed that the cleaning woman had done a poor job of polishing the mirror. There were streaks on the surface of the glass. Brother took a tissue and wiped off the streaks. He supposed it really didn't make any difference now, but old patterns were difficult to break. His mother had always been very strict with her employees and insisted on immaculate surroundings.

As Brother made his rounds of the other rooms, he noticed that the cleaning woman was becoming lax without his mother's supervision. He considered writing a detailed memo with a list of corrections, but as he progressed from room to room, he decided that he had no choice but to fire the woman and hire a replacement. He was muttering angrily to himself by the time he climbed the stairs to his own quarters. Now he'd be forced to conduct interviews with housekeepers and check their references when he should be concentrating on his important work.

Brother poured himself a small cognac and sipped it, attempting to clear his mind of anything except the scene he was soon to film. Tonight's star could easily play the role. She was a seasoned veteran of a half-dozen low-budget movies, and she'd dropped out of the business to marry into money. Now, after a ten-year absence from the screen, she was in the process of making a comeback. Brother had seen her latest film. She'd played a cameo role in an immensely popular science-fiction feature, and in his opinion, her five minutes on the screen was the only bright spot in the movie.

A current newspaper was spread open on his desk, turned to the society page. His star was hosting a charity gala this evening, and even though the security would be tight, Brother had devised a way to get inside the gates of her Bel Air mansion. When the party was over and everyone had gone home, Tammara Welles would give the finest performance of her life.

Tammara Welles was excited. The gala she'd arranged was turning out to be the charity event of the season. The party people had turned the rolling green lawns of the mansion into an amusement park. One section contained the games of chance, and it was doing a booming business. People were standing in line to try their luck at the shooting gallery with its pop-up targets that were shaped like animals. No one seemed to mind the five-hundred-dollar donation, as long as the proceeds went to charity.

"Tammara, darling!" Mrs. Irving Jacobs rushed up and actually kissed Tammara's cheek. Tammara stiffened reflexively, but she quickly covered by smiling warmly. Barbara Jacobs was new money, so new that she hadn't yet learned to kiss the air in the typical show biz greeting. There were rumors that Barbara had been Bouncy Babbs, a stripper in Vegas, before she'd married Irving Jacobs.

A photographer was headed their way, and Barbara quickly rubbed her handkerchief over Tammara's cheek.

"Sorry, Tammy, I got a little lipstick on you, but it's gone now. I'm such a ditz about those things. My, but isn't this exciting? I've had my picture taken three times already!"

As soon as the photographer took his picture, Barbara backed away.

"I've got to run, Tammy. Irving's going to meet me at the Tunnel of Love. Since he's been taking those vitamin shots, I've got a seventy-year-old tiger by the tail!"

Tammara laughed. At least Barbara didn't have a phony bone in her body. And that was more than she could say about most of the women who were here tonight.

The girl at the booth on the left was making cotton candy, and Tammara stopped to watch for a moment. It reminded her of the Boone County Fair in Iowa. In July, more years ago than she cared to remember, she had ridden to the top of the Ferris wheel and pretended that she owned the land as far as she could see. Now her dream was possible. All she had to do was mention her childhood wish to her husband and he'd buy the whole damn county for her.

The girl at the next booth was selling corn dogs and Tammara's mouth watered. For a moment she almost gave in to the impulse, but she reminded herself that corn dogs were definitely not on her diet. An over-weight actress couldn't expect to get any good parts.

As Tammara wandered past groups of smiling celebrities, she noticed that everyone seemed to have captured the spirit of the evening. Mrs. Geoffrey Bennington, an intimidating old dowager with a particularly acerbic tongue, had actually hiked up her skirt to her thighs and hopped aboard the carousel. Tammara watched in fascination as she rode around and around, sloshing champagne on her expensive hand-beaded skirt, sitting astride a snow-white charger that had been captured forever in the act of rolling his emerald-green eyes.

Even though her husband was rich, Tammara was still awed by the fact that many of her guests had more money than they could likely spend in one lifetime. Little Shirley Kranowski from Luther, a farm town in the central part of Iowa, had worked all summer at the local Rexall drugstore to earn the money for her high school prom dress. The dress was long gone now, but there was still a lot of Shirley Kranowski left in Tammara.

"Hi pretty lady. You look even prettier than you did fifteen years ago."

Tammara whirled around and smiled her first real smile of the evening. It was Lon Michaels.

"Lon!" Tammara threw her arms around him and hugged him tightly. She divided the people in show biz into two categories, fake and real. Lon Michaels was real.

Just then a waiter passed by with a tray of champagne, and Lon reached out to take a glass. "May I buy you a drink? It's got to be better than that awful stuff we drank at our first premiere."

"It is. A very classy lady ordered this champagne. It's Taittinger."

Lon whistled. "Over fifty bucks a bottle at the discount places. How many cases did you order?"

"I'll never tell, but I guarantee there'll be some left over. What are you working on now, Lon?"

"The last film in the *Jubee* trilogy, but it'll only go another week or two. Then, I'm not sure."

"If there's a part in your next one for me, will you put in a good word?"

"That goes without saying." Lon touched the rim of his glass to hers. "To our next feature together."

Tammara laughed. "A guaranteed blockbuster, where Tammara Welles is brilliant and Lon Michaels makes her look even better."

Tammara closed her eyes in anticipation as she took the first sip. She loved champagne. Without thinking, she finished the first glass much too quickly and immediately took another. It was best to be photographed with a full glass. An empty one implied heavy drinking, and she certainly didn't want to be publicized as a lush.

"Come on, Lon. I'm sick of making the right impression on the right people. Let's ride to the top of the Ferris wheel and hide from the world."

Tammara awoke from a deep sleep. By the illuminated face of her bedroom clock she saw it was three in the morning. Something had startled her awake.

She sat up in bed and groped for her glasses. She'd worn contact lenses for years, but her eyes had been allergic to the permanent wear kind and she had to take out her lenses every night to let them soak in their little trays of cleaning solution. As she got out of bed, she staggered slightly on her way to the window. She must have had more champagne than she'd thought. She felt woozy and light-headed as she raised the window and looked out at the deserted grounds.

The amusement park was still there. The party planners had arranged to come and pick up their equipment in the morning. The stands and booths were illuminated by a string of bare light bulbs, and now, at three in the morning, their shadows were harsh and surrealistic. Tammara watched for signs of movement, but she knew it was impossible for anyone to come over the fence without setting off the alarm. Their security system was the best that money could buy.

Just when Tammara had made up her mind to go back to bed, the sound she'd been hearing registered in her mind. It was the sound of water running, and it was coming from the east lawn, where the party people had set up the Tunnel of Love. They must have forgotten to turn it off.

Tammara had her hand on the telephone to call the groundskeeper before she reconsidered. He was an elderly man, and she didn't have the heart to wake him. She'd watched the party people set everything up and there was no reason why she couldn't shut it off.

Dressing was more difficult than she'd thought it would be. Something had raised havoc with her coordination, and she found she had to sit down on the edge of the bed to pull on her slacks and sweater. Tammara slid her feet into the soft-soled moccasins she used as bedroom slippers and got up again with difficulty. It would be so easy to just crawl back under the covers and ignore the whole thing. She turned to give her bed a look filled with longing as she went out the door.

Tammara walked down the circular stairway, wondering if she was dreaming. It seemed to take hours to get to the bottom, walk through the hallway, and let herself out the back door.

The grass was wet with night dew, and Tammara felt the moisture seep into the soles of her moccasins as she made her way in what seemed like slow motion across the huge lawn.

The night was quiet, still and peaceful. Not even a dog barked in the distance. The air smelled tantalizingly fresh, much different from the smog of the daytime, and best of all, there was a perceptible chill in the air. Tammara could almost believe that autumn, with its brilliantly colored leaves and cold north winds, was right around the corner.

The water tumbled and roared in the distance, and Tammara walked slowly around the house to the east lawn. The stars wheeled crazily above her, but at last she was there.

Tammara's breath caught in her throat as she saw the Tunnel of Love. The brightly painted boats were circling endlessly, at evenly paced intervals. Red, blue, yellow, over and over again. There was something terribly sad about watching them, but her mind was too foggy to think of the reason.

As she stood, wavering slightly at the edge of the water, she found herself longing to climb inside. She would lean back against the cushioned seat and trail her fingers in the cool, moon-drenched water until the tips of them tingled deliciously.

The little boats stopped, as if they could read her mind, and a man dressed in black seemed to materialize beside her. Now she knew she was dreaming. He bent from the waist in a courtly, old-world bow and held out his hand.

Tammara moved closer to take the man's

hand and he helped her into the boat. There was a video camera clamped to his side, and it jarred her briefly but she quickly dismissed it. Of course there was a camera in her dream. She was an actress. She turned to look directly into the lens and curved her lips in her most inviting smile.

The man, her dream man, climbed in beside her, and the little boats started again. Tammara had the urge to ask who he was, but she didn't want her voice to shatter the fragile shell of her illusion. Instead, she leaned toward her companion, peering intently into his shadowed eyes as the boat carried them steadily toward the tunnel. He was wearing some sort of hood. Only his eyes were visible through the slits. Was it the hood of a falcon? No, that wasn't quite right. A hood like this had been paired with a costume on the racks at the studio. But what kind of a costume?

The boat entered the tunnel, and Tammara found herself in total darkness. She huddled a little closer to the man as her dream began to take on ominous overtones. Now the pulsing hum of the machinery had turned into something frightening, something uncontrollable, like the heartbeat of some predatory, mechanical beast.

There was a bright pinpoint of light, and

Tammara's eyes dilated as she stared into the flame of a silver lighter. At that exact instant her numbed mind dredged out the memory that had eluded her. The hood had been hanging with an executioner's costume. This was not a good dream. She had to wake up.

Tammara cried out sharply in terror as the executioner moved toward her. She heard her scream echo off the walls of the tunnel, but the dream didn't disappear. There was no reassuring burst of light as she reached out in panic to turn on her bedside lamp. There was only the icy shock of the water as her fingers brushed its surface.

Tammara tried to scream again as her groggy mind reeled in terror.

And then executioner's hands were around her neck, strong fingers squeezing, bruising her tender skin. Tammara's glasses slid off, and she heard them clatter as she kicked out with all of her strength. The same padded cushion that had cradled her moments ago now served to smother her pitiful defenses as the executioner's fingers tightened into bands of fiery pain. And then the darkness of the tunnel rolled back to reveal the deeper blackness that claimed her.

6

Monday, July 12

Oliver "Sam" Ladera stood on the crest of the east lawn and watched his men scurry back and forth below. A violent murder. A beautiful actress. And Sam was willing to bet a week's salary that they'd run into the same brick wall again. He didn't know how it was possible to actually record a murder in progress without leaving some visible clues, but the Video Killer had done it once. And Sam had no doubt that this was a repeat performance.

"Do you want us to dust the switch that controls the boats, Chief?" Zeke Jackson, Sam's young black assistant, tapped him on the sleeve to get his attention.

"Go ahead, Zeke, but I don't think you'll get much. The groundskeeper turned off the boats when he spotted Miss Welles."

Zeke nodded. "And the Video Killer probably used gloves again, right?"

"Right."

Sam frowned wearily as Zeke raced off to instruct the fingerprint men. His eyes were bloodshot from lack of sleep and he felt ten years older than his actual thirty-six. He'd been up since the call had come in shortly after four this morning, and he'd gotten a grand total of five hours' sleep in the past two days. His ex-mother-in-law used to tell him that he looked like Sylvester Stallone when he had dark circles under his eyes, and Sam had gone into a rage every time she'd made the comparison. Sure, he had a cleft in his chin like Stallone's. Lots of people had clefts in their chins. It was also true that he had dark hair and brown eyes, but that's where the resemblance stopped. Sam was six feet tall.

"Chief?" A young female officer held out a steaming cup of coffee. "It's fresh. The housekeeper made it when she came in at seven. She asked to make certain we returned the cups. They're lace porcelain, imported from Europe. That's twenty-four-karat gold around the rim, and the roses on the cups are all painted by hand. I'm pretty sure they're close to a hundred dollars apiece."

"Thanks, Judy. Would I be up for a sexual harassment charge if I asked you to collect them and take them back when the guys are finished? I could always ask Donovan to do it but . . ."

Judy laughed. "I'll do it, boss. Donovan's got hands like meat hooks. Besides, I want to take another look inside. I might spot something the guys missed."

Sam sipped the strong brew, not even minding that it had no cream or sugar. It was delicious. Maybe coffee tasted better when you drank it out of a hundred-dollar cup. As he finished the coffee, he looked down and saw his officers standing in tight little groups, handling their coffee cups with the utmost of care. Judy must have warned them. And Donovan, that big Irish oaf, was actually holding his little pinky out in the air.

Sam couldn't help it. He started to shake with repressed laughter. This whole situation was incongruous, L.A.'s finest milling around on this lush, green lawn at the crack of dawn, sipping coffee out of porcelain cups just like they were attending a social function.

Damn, but he missed his ex-wife Katy! His description of Donovan putting on social manners would have driven her into absolute hysterics. A glum expression settled over Sam's face, but it had little to do with the Video Killer. It was missing Katy, not the way she'd been at the end, a desperately unhappy woman who'd wounded him with her sarcasm, but the earlier Katy, the Katy he'd married.

He'd met Katy Brannigan in college. He was there on a scholarship, but he still had to work part-time to earn the money for books and supplies. The student job center had assigned him to the college cafeteria. The day he'd met Katy the menu was a familiar one, rolled turkey roast, mashed potatoes with gravy, grayish-green canned peas, a scoop of stuffing, and ice cream with chocolate sauce and a cherry. Four students helped on the assembly line. Sam had nicknamed them according to function. Knife, Scoop, Ladle, and Plunk. The trays had three compartments, a large one on the bottom for the meat and potatoes and two smaller ones on top for vegetables and dessert.

Sam smiled a little as he relived that day. Everything had gone along like clockwork as the trays were passed from hand to hand. Knife carved the turkey, flopping two slices on each tray. He also added the peas. Scoop put a mound of stuffing on top of the turkey, a ball of mashed potatoes next to it, and a scoop of vanilla ice cream in the dessert compartment. Ladle poured gravy on the potatoes and fudge sauce on the ice cream. Plunk placed a cherry on top of the ice cream, a paper cup of cranberry sauce next to the turkey, and finished off by plunking a roll on the tray.

Sam was serving as Scoop, and he was preoccupied, thinking about an upcoming test. As a result he inadvertently mixed up the routine. He got the dressing on top of the turkey and the ball of potatoes beside it, but instead of reaching for the vanilla ice cream, he dipped the scoop into the potatoes again and put a big mound in the dessert compartment.

Ladle, who stood next to him, noticed the mix-up and laughed. For the first time Sam looked, really looked, at Ladle. Short. Red hair. Freckles. Cute! She gave him a devilish grin, and as he watched with horrified fascination, she deliberately ladled chocolate sauce on the potatoes in the dessert compartment.

Visions of losing his job and not being able to buy his books for next semester flashed through Sam's head. But, just as he was about to open his mouth to call back the tray, Ladle leaned close to whisper, "Don't say anything. I'll bet you a beer that no one'll notice."

Sam's mind worked double time. They probably wouldn't fire him over one little mistake. He'd never made one before, and the risk was definitely worth it because suddenly the thing he wanted most in the world was to sit in a booth at the campus pub with the incredibly blue-eyed Ladle. So he nodded. And Ladle grinned as she passed the tray to Plunk, who topped the mashed potato sundae with a bright red maraschino cherry and a sprinkle of nuts and sent it down the conveyor belt to the cashier.

A lush California blonde, the sorority type, who was wearing a swirling skirt topped off by a skintight pink sweater, showed her student I.D. and took possession of the tray. Then she tottered off in incredibly high heels to join her boyfriend, a handsome, clean-cut fraternity type.

"I've seen her before," Ladle whispered, "and she's always wearing a brand-new sweater. He's just her type except, with him, it's a cashmere sweater. I figure there's an entire flock of goats running around naked because of them."

"Not flock . . . herd."

Sam corrected her without thinking, and then he wished he could take back the words. But she didn't seem upset as she stared up at him.

"Herd? Are you sure?"

"I'm sure." Sam nodded. "I'm taking zoology this semester."

"Okay, I believe you. What's quail?"

She was looking up at him with those twinkling eyes, and Sam's mind went blank for a second.

"Uh . . . covey. A covey of quail."

"How about fish?"

"School. A school of fish."

"Lions?"

"Pride."

"And what's a draft?"

"A draft?"

"Yes, a draft."

Sam was completely stumped. "I don't know. I've never heard of a draft."

"It's the kind of beer you're going to buy me tonight. Watch!"

Sam tore himself away from Ladle's blue eyes to find that the sorority girl was just starting her dessert. Couldn't she see that the "ice cream" wasn't melting? Sam held his breath as the spoon she held dipped down and then raised slowly to her bright pink lips. Her mouth opened. The spoon went inside and came out again, clean. Sam was positive that she'd jump up from her chair any second, but she merely batted her eyelashes once at her boyfriend and then swallowed.

"And now . . . for the second taste."

Ladle's breath puffed out against his ear and Sam shuddered slightly. Ladle seemed very sure of herself, but Sam still couldn't believe his eyes. Surely on the second spoonful the sorority girl would realize that her sundae tasted like potatoes.

The girl laughed at something her boyfriend said, a little tinkle of a laugh, and then her pink lips opened again. No reaction. And again. Still no reaction. After a few minutes of spooning and laughter and chattering, the dessert compartment was empty and the girl and her boyfriend went out through the swinging glass doors.

"Well?"

Ladle looked over at him triumphantly and Sam shrugged.

"You win, but I never thought we'd get away with it."

"I knew we would," Ladle said smugly. "My mother makes something she calls Mock Apple Pie. The filling is nothing but soda crackers and spices. Not an apple in it. But if you're expecting apple pie, you taste apple pie."

That night at the pub Sam had found out that Ladle's name was Katy Brannigan, the oldest of five children in a noisy, good-natured Irish family. He'd also discovered that he liked Katy Brannigan a lot. By the time they entered their senior year, they were inseparable. It all seemed part of a natural progression when they'd married right after graduation and moved into a small apartment. Sam had landed a good job with the L.A. police force, and Katy had gone to work as a stringer for the *Times,* occasionally getting an actual byline. Their troubles hadn't started until Sam had clawed his way up in the ranks to become chief of detectives.

Even though she knew it was unfair, Katy had resented Sam's meteoric rise. After over ten years of slaving away at the *Times,* Katy was still writing obits and recipes. Looking back on it all, Sam guessed he should have seen the warning signs, but he'd been too busy to notice. It had come as a total shock when Katy had asked him for a divorce.

Katy had told him that their marriage was stagnating. She'd talked it over with a couple of women in her awareness group and they'd helped her to understand. She'd moved directly out of her parents' arms to those of her husband's. She'd never had the opportunity to test her own strengths as a single woman. What about college? Sam had asked. That didn't count, Katy'd insisted.

College was an artificial environment and she'd lived at home the whole time. And yes, she still loved him, but it was criminal to deny herself the freedom to grow and mature as a person, to be recognized as a respected woman in her own right. As Mrs. Ladera, the wife of the popular Los Angeles chief of detectives, she was a total extension of him.

Sam had argued and pleaded in vain, but nothing he'd said could sway her. Their divorce had gone through last month, and the luxury apartment that had been so warm and cheerful had taken on the feeling of a tomb without her. Sam had tried to cover up his despair by throwing himself into his work, but it felt as if all the joy in his life had been packed up with Katy's clothes. Now, eight months after she'd walked out the door for the last time, he still found himself reaching out in the middle of the long, lonely night to touch her.

His eyes hurt, and Sam reached up to rub them. Perhaps he'd feel better if he could get a good night's sleep, but that prospect was pretty dim right now. And it would be nonexistent when he called in the press for this second murder. He'd just have to learn to function on quick catnaps until the Video

Killer was caught. And he'd have to put Katy completely out of his mind.

It was two minutes past seven in the morning when Alan's assistant had answered the phone in his bedroom. To Alan's relief, she'd sounded brisk and businesslike even though she'd been wearing nothing but a pair of high-heeled satin bedroom slippers. Now it was eight-fifteen, and Alan was still sitting on the edge of the bed, talking to Uncle Meyer from Hawaii. By switching the phone from ear to ear, he'd managed to pull on a pair of pajama bottoms.

"Look, Uncle Meyer, I think we ought to go ahead and exercise our option. After all, lightning did strike twice. *Video Kill* is turning out to be one hell of a hot property. Rocca and Nielsen have agreed to write the screenplay to parallel the actual murders, and that makes it more historical than sensational. I just can't see any advantage to waiting any longer."

Alan lit another cigarette, not noticing the one that was smoldering in the ashtray. He couldn't understand why the old man was dragging his feet. Maybe looking at all those grass skirts had addled his brain.

"No, Uncle Meyer, I can promise you that this won't be a cheap exploitation film. I

111

already told you that Lon Michaels is consulting with us, and you know his reputation for quality."

His uncle's next question made Alan wince. "No, Uncle Meyer. Lon hasn't actually agreed to sign on, but he's interested. If you give me the go-ahead now, I'm sure I can get him for you."

"What was that?" Alan held the receiver close to his ear. The connection with Hawaii was worse than usual. "Did you say *sample scenes?*"

There was a pause while his uncle repeated his statement. Alan groaned.

"But we can't *do* that, Uncle Meyer! It's against the Writers' Guild rules. The only way to get scenes from the actual script is to put Rocca and Nielsen under contract."

There was another long burst of words from the receiver. Alan groaned again.

"I know. I know. That's not the way it used to be, but that's the way it is now. I'm in violation if I even *ask* for a sample scene, and Rocca and Nielsen face a possible expulsion from the guild if they agree. If anyone finds out, Cinescope could be in big trouble. That's not chutzpah, Uncle Meyer, it's insanity!"

There was another rapid burst of conversation from the receiver, and Alan motioned for his assistant. In the past fifteen minutes she'd dressed in one of her tailored suits and she looked strangely incongruous in his bedroom.

Alan raised his arm in a drinking gesture and his secretary hurried to the liquor cabinet. She mixed a Bloody Mary and handed it to him. Alan drank it down at a gulp and motioned for another.

"Yes, Uncle Meyer, I realize I'm only the *acting* head of Cinescope. Now, let me see if I've got this straight. You want to see the first three scenes from Rocca and Nielsen on spec. No money. No signed contract. And the hell with guild rules. If you like their work, you want Lon Michaels to call you personally and commit to the project. Then, and only then, will you authorize the contracts. Is that right?"

As his uncle confirmed, Alan took a long swallow of his second drink. Then he made an obscene gesture with the phone that made his assistant collapse on the bed in silent laughter.

"Thank you, Uncle Meyer. You have a nice day, too."

Tony parked in the lot and raced into the back door of the Schwartzvold building. He didn't have time for the "Walk of the Stars" this morning. The Video Killer had struck again. That meant that Alan would be sure to call and he was running late.

"George! Hold the elevator!"

Tony ran across the lobby and got in next to George Sturges, the young attorney who had an office on the fifth floor. As the elevator groaned its way upward, Tony noticed that George was looking at his shirt. He was wearing his new, long-sleeved purple one that said THE PARANOIDS ARE AFTER ME in huge red letters.

"Nice shirt, Tony." George nodded as he got off on the fifth floor. "I've got a couple of clients that could use one of those."

The elevator seemed to take forever to get up to the tower. Tony breezed into the office at eight forty-five to find Erik staring morosely at a paper plate containing two maple bars and two cinnamon twists. An unopened container of Winchell's coffee was leaking merrily away on the desk, but Erik didn't seem to notice.

"Who died? Besides Sharee Lyons and Tammara Welles, I mean." Tony grabbed one of the maple bars and bit off the end.

"I think we did."

Tony stopped chewing and swallowed the piece whole. It stuck a little, but he got it down without choking.

"Alan called at eight-thirty." Erik's voice was funereal.

"He didn't exercise his option?" Tony was flabbergasted. "I just don't believe it! Does he know about the new murder last night? *Video Kill*'s even hotter than it was last week. Alan's crazy if he —"

"Calm down, Tony," Erik interrupted. "He says it's still pending. He just called to lay down some conditions."

"What conditions?"

"The first one is that our screenplay follow the actual murders."

"Yeah. I'm working on that. I've got an appointment with the chief of detectives."

"You actually got an appointment with Sam Ladera?" Erik raised his eyebrows. "That's amazing, Tony. The newspapers say he's not talking to anyone."

"It was easy. Sam and I went to school together. I figure I can get him to tell me the inside story."

"That's one down." Erik still looked glum. "The second condition's not so easy. Alan wants to use Lon Michaels for director of photography."

"What's wrong with that? Lon Michaels does great work! I can't believe Alan actually signed him."

"He didn't. That's the second condition.

Alan's uncle won't go with anybody except Michaels, and Michaels isn't sure he wants to do it. He claims he's not familiar enough with the genre. Alan wants us to talk him around."

"Okay," Tony agreed. "That shouldn't be hard. Lon and I went to school together."

"Is there anybody you *didn't* go to school with?"

"Nobody important." Tony grinned. "You know what they say about birds of a feather. Now, what's the third condition? I know you always save the worst for last."

"Alan talked to his uncle in Hawaii this morning. The old man insists that we turn in three sample scenes of the screenplay before he'll commit to the movie."

"He can't do that! It's against guild rules."

"I know that. So does Alan. He said he explained all that, but the old man's stubborn. He's gung ho on the concept, but he won't buy unless he can read the first three scenes. No sample, no sale."

"So what are we going to do?"

"I don't know." Erik sighed deeply. "I told Alan I'd talk it over with you and call him back. I need this sale, Tony . . . for personal reasons. But breaking guild rules could get us in a lot of trouble."

"Yeah. *If* they catch us."

116

Tony looked at his maple bar and put it back on the plate. He wasn't hungry anymore. Erik might need this sale but not half as much as he did. Six months ago he'd been forced to borrow to pay the bills, and he was in hock up to his eyeballs. The banks wouldn't touch him, and he was already into the Guild Credit Union for the maximum. The only loan he'd been able to get was off the street, and they'd offered him a way to make the payments if he didn't mind doing work that was borderline legal. The "little job" he'd been holding down wasn't something Tony wanted to talk about in polite company, but his back was to the wall. Guild rules? They seemed insignificant compared to what could happen to him if he didn't make his loan payments on time.

"Look at it like this." Tony stood up and paced in front of Erik's desk. "Who'd know about it if we dashed off the first three scenes and delivered them to Alan?"

"We'd know."

"True. And while our consciences might twinge all the way to the bank, we're not about to turn ourselves in to the guild."

"That's true." Erik nodded. "But Alan would know."

"Alan?" Tony shrugged. "Alan's not going to say anything to risk Cinescope's signatory status. He's got more to lose than we do."

"So you think we should do it?"

Erik was clearly wavering. Tony took time to light a cigarette. Then he nodded.

"I vote yes. The risks outweigh the benefits. Even if the guild does find out about it, we'll probably get away with a slap on the wrist and a stiff fine."

Erik sighed deeply and Tony could tell he was still disturbed. Lutheran guilt again. Finally he nodded.

"All right. I'm with you. I just hope this whole thing doesn't blow up in our faces."

"Blow up? *Blow Up?* What a terrific title for a movie! Now, clean up that disgusting brown puddle on your desk and I'll go put on a good pot of coffee."

Erik and Tony waited until the red light stopped blinking over the door of sound stage twenty-six before they pushed it open and went inside. Tony nudged Erik and gestured toward a man dressed in chinos and a designer polo shirt who was sitting in a leather director's chair on the edge of the set.

"That's him, Erik. Lon Michaels in the flesh."

"Really? I never would have guessed it."

Erik grinned as he noticed the back of the cinematographer's chair. It said LON in large gold letters.

Tony nudged Erik as they walked toward the set. "Let me start things off, Erik. You jump in to support whatever I say, even if it's complete bullshit."

"That seems to be my role in life." Erik grinned. "Okay, Tony, you're up first."

Erik stayed a step behind as Tony tapped Lon on the shoulder. He'd wanted to call Lon for an appointment, but Tony had been insistent that they barge right in. It was supposed to give them a psychological advantage. Lon wouldn't have time to marshal his arguments against *Video Kill* if they took him by surprise.

"Lon! Good to see you again." Tony was all smiles. "I'm Tony Rocca, and this is my partner, Erik Nielsen. You may not remember me, but we did a graduate project together at UCLA."

"We did?"

"Professor Truitt, Film Production five-oh-three. It was a short subject about a magic Hula-Hoop."

Lon began to smile. "Of course. You wrote the script!"

"Careful, Lon. The walls have ears. That script was a real turkey, and I would have flunked without your tricky camera work."

"It wasn't *that* bad." Lon laughed. "You know, I just never made the connection with your name before. I saw *Free Fire* and I thought the script was excellent."

"Thank you, Lon. Erik and I really worked hard on it. Now tell me, honestly, what did you think of the camera work?"

"Andy Coyne's a very competent man."

"Same old Lon." Tony shook his head. "I should've known you'd never knock a colleague. Don't you ever get bored, being such a nice guy all the time?"

Lon laughed. "Sometimes. Now, cough up, Tony. You didn't come here just to renew an old acquaintance, did you?"

"Nope. We came here to talk you into doing *Video Kill.*"

"That's what I was afraid of." Lon sighed. "Look, Tony, I've already told Alan that it's not my type of film. I've never done murder-suspense. And now there's another reason. I knew Tammara Welles, and her murder has me rattled. I wouldn't want to be a party to sensationalizing her death."

"Of course not." Erik took up the argument. "Neither would we. We want to concentrate on the personality of the killer and downplay the rest. We want to do *Video Kill* with taste and class."

120

Lon raised his eyebrows. "A serial murder story with taste?"

"That's right." Tony stepped in. "We're trying for less of a murder story and more of a psychological profile. Do you think it can be done?"

"I don't know." Lon frowned slightly. "It's certainly a challenge. Look, guys, I wish you all the luck in the world but —"

"I suppose I shouldn't mention this," Erik interrupted before Lon would turn them down, "but Alan's signed Tom Steiner to direct. You're familiar with his work?"

"Uh, yes."

Lon's slight hesitation told Erik that he was right on target.

"Tony and I are afraid that he's going to turn *Video Kill* into another *Murder On Call*. The original script was quality work until Steiner got his hands on it."

Lon nodded. "I've seen the film. Steiner did the rewrite, didn't he?"

"You bet he did." Erik gave a rueful laugh. "He ditched the original concept and came up with pure blood porn."

"And you're afraid he'll do the same thing with *Video Kill*?"

"You got it. Tony and I just don't carry enough weight to make sure that the film's done the right way. That's why we need you,

Lon. If you demand final cut approval, you'll get it. Steiner'd go on record as director, but you'd actually be running the show."

"I see." Lon smiled slightly. "You not only need my talent, you also need my clout. Steiner, huh?"

"Steiner." Erik and Tony spoke in unison.

"It's tempting to think that I could actually force Steiner into doing quality work."

There was a long pause, and Tony motioned for Erik to remain silent. He'd sold life insurance for a while when he was in college and he knew that the first person who spoke would be the loser. Finally Lon cleared his throat.

"Look, guys, I don't want to make any commitments at this point. I'll be wrapping on this *Jubee* thing in a week or two, and I promise to think seriously about it then."

"That's all we ask, Lon." Tony reached out to shake his hand. "How about lunch sometime soon? We're starting on the script and we'd really appreciate your input."

"You want my suggestions for the *script*? I've been in this business for years and no one's ever asked me to consult on a script."

Tony nodded. "I know it's unusual, but you'd be doing us a real favor. We trust your priorities when it comes to aesthetics. Take the first murder, for example. The stabbing in the shower? We think it would be much more effective to imply the violence, rather than let it all hang out up there on the screen. Is there any way to shoot that scene *through* the shower curtain? Or maybe with backlighting? Or shadows?"

Lon nodded. "That's easy, Tony. You have several options, but I think your best bet might be to use the technique I did in the lake scene in *Carole's Dream.*"

Just then a bell rang on the set, and Lon stood up. "Sorry, guys, I have to run. Nice meeting you, Erik. And Tony, it's good to see you again. Why don't you check with Susan on your way out and set up lunch for next week? Have her pick a day when we're starting late so we'll have plenty of time to talk. In the meantime, I'll run a few tests with low-level color and see what I can come up with."

Tony waited until they were out the door and then he slapped Erik on the back. "He's hooked! You were inspired in there, partner. I never would have thought to ask him to save us from Steiner. Where the hell did you hear that story about *Murder On Call?*"

"From the busboy at Rosie's Bar. It's a big-time studio hangout. The busboy's been there for years and he knows where all the bodies are buried."

123

"How did you get him to tell you?"

"Purely by accident, Tony. We started talking and I mentioned I was a writer. So he warned me to stay away from Steiner."

"Well, I'm certainly glad you brought it up. I think that's what tipped the scales with Lon."

"It helped. But I think your bit about getting Lon to call the shower shot is what really put us over the top. What do you say we reward ourselves with some lunch?"

"Sounds good."

"The studio commissary?"

Tony groaned. "You said reward, Erik, not punish. Let's go to Rosie's Bar. I want to slip your busboy a twenty."

"That's fine with me, but you can keep your twenty. I already tipped the busboy for the Steiner story."

"I figured you did." Tony grinned. "This money's going for new information. I'm going to ask him how to get a better deal out of Alan Goldberg."

7

Tony Rocca sat on a hard wooden bench outside Sam Ladera's door. He'd been sitting on this same uncomfortable bench for more than forty-five minutes. The chief of detectives was holding a press conference in his office and the door was shut. The officer at the desk, whose nametag identified him as Andy Mertens, had told Tony that the conference could run as long as an hour.

Tony spent the time staring at the middle-aged officer, studying him for a possible character in one of his scripts. He was probably in his early fifties, brown hair graying at the temples, and he had hazel eyes that were separated by a classic Roman nose. His shoulders were massive, but he didn't seem overweight. He had the build of a former football player who'd kept in condition. Tony guessed that the big man could move quickly if the situation warranted.

It was while he was looking at Andy's

hands that Tony noticed something curious. Only the top of his left hand and forearm were sunburned. Tony got up and walked around the desk, supposedly to read several notices that were tacked up on the bulletin board. What he was really doing was examining that curious sunburn. Left forearm, left hand, and now that he looked closely, he could see that the left side of Andy's face was affected, too. He thought about it quite a while before he figured it out.

"Excuse me, Andy? Do you live to the north of here?"

"Yeah."

"And do you drive a car that doesn't have air-conditioning?"

The officer looked surprised as he nodded. "That's right. How'd you know?"

"It's your sunburn. Left hand, left forearm, and the left side of your face. You don't get that kind of sunburn at the beach, so I figured you must have driven to work with the morning sun on your left. Then, when you drove home, you had the same left exposure from the afternoon sun. Since your elbow's sunburned, I decided you must have stuck it out the car window, and nobody leaves the window open in the summer if they've got air-conditioning."

"Not bad!" The officer looked impressed

for a second, and then his eyes narrowed. "Are you a plainclothes detective?"

"Nope." Tony grinned. "But I went to high school with your chief and we used to swap detective magazines."

The door to Sam's office opened and a group of reporters trooped out. There wasn't a smile among them. A couple of them were grumbling angrily and no one reached for a cell phone.

"A pretty glum lot, huh?" Andy shrugged as they moved past his desk. "Looks like they didn't get what they wanted."

"Sam's keeping a lid on this thing?"

Andy nodded. "A tight lid. The chief's the only one who's seen those murder DVDs. Everybody's trying to pump him for information. Yours is just a social visit, right?"

"Right." Tony covered his guilt with a smile. "Just tell him the guy who gave him his nickname is out here. Tony Rocca from Hollywood High."

Tony watched as Andy buzzed the inner office. It was true that his visit was social, but he had an ulterior motive. He needed some inside information. The press had covered the murders, but their facts were sketchy. What Tony really wanted was to get his hands on the murder discs.

"Yes, Chief. I've got it." The officer put

down the phone and looked at Tony with a puzzled expression. "He said to tell Mr. Archer to come right in. But I thought your name was Rocca."

"That's right. Archer's my nickname."

"Oh." Andy leaned over the desk. "What's the chief's nickname? You can tell me. I won't pass it around."

"You'll have to figure that one out for yourself." Tony got up and covered half the distance to the door before he took pity on the frustrated officer. "It's really pretty easy, Andy. Just go see some old Humphrey Bogart movies."

Tony pushed open the glass door that had been outfitted with blinds for privacy and found Sam waiting for him. They stared at each other for a long moment. Sam was the first to speak.

"You look the same as you did in high school, Archer!"

"So do you, Mr. Spade."

Tony lied through his teeth. Sam looked as if he hadn't had any sleep in months.

"And you've learned to lie with a straight face. I look like roadkill and we both know it. Help yourself to a cup of coffee and tell me what you've been doing since high school."

Tony walked over to the two silver urns

sitting on a table at the side of the room and poured himself a cup of black coffee. Then he carried it over to the chair in front of Sam's desk and sat down.

"A couple of tours in the Middle East and then back here to UCLA. Right now I'm trying to survive in the movie business. That just about sums it up. Oh, and I'm married, no kids. How about you?"

"College and the police department. I was married, but it didn't work out. She decided she needed a divorce to find herself."

"Bitter?"

"I guess so." Sam shrugged. "After all those years it's hard to get used to living alone. She's a reporter."

"Was she with the group that just left?"

"No. They haven't assigned her to any big stories yet. That was part of the problem. I kept on getting the promotions, and she felt she was just spinning her wheels at the paper."

There was an uncomfortable silence for a moment, and then Sam switched the subject.

"Did you say you were in the movies?"

"Not exactly *in* them." Tony laughed. "My partner and I are writers. The last thing we wrote was *Free Fire.*"

"I saw that! It was good."

Tony smiled. It always gave him a lift to hear that someone had liked his movie. He took a sip of his coffee, wondering how to get the subject around to the murders, and choked slightly. It was the worst coffee he'd ever tasted.

Sam looked concerned. "I forgot to warn you about the coffee. Did you take it from the urn on the left?"

"Uh . . . yeah. I think I did."

"Then you're drinking the press pot. We give them lousy coffee. It's one way to cut press conferences short. Go pour it out and take a cup from the other urn."

When Tony returned to his chair with a fresh cup of coffee, he found Sam watching him with a thoughtful expression on his face.

"I need to talk to someone, Tony. Can I trust you with something confidential?"

Tony took a sip of his coffee and set the cup on the corner of the desk. Sam was right about the coffee. It was considerably better than the first cup, but that wasn't saying it was good. Then he put on his best friendly and nonjudgmental look. Sam probably wanted to talk about his divorce.

"You can trust me, Sam. I don't talk about a friend behind his back."

Sam nodded, and Tony sat back, prepared

to listen to the long, sad story of a failed marriage. Instead Sam took off on another tack altogether.

"I should have guessed you'd go into something with film. You were always hustling to get money for matinees. Remember how we used to cut history class to make the two o'clock feature at the Grand?"

Tony nodded. Sam was working up to something in a very circuitous way. He'd just have to sit patiently and wait for him to get there.

"Tony? This may sound a little bit off the wall, but are you a Hitchcock fan?"

"I wouldn't call myself a fan, but I had a class on Hitchcock films once. Why?"

"And you don't get freaked out by blood and violence, do you?"

"No. I don't like it, but I saw plenty of gory scenes in combat. What's this about?"

"Do you remember those Hitchcock films well enough to compare them to other films?"

"I think so." Tony had reached the end of his patience. He met Sam's eyes squarely. "Stop quizzing me and spill it, Sam. What are you fishing for?"

There was a tense silence, but finally Sam seemed to make up his mind.

"I've got a big favor to ask you, Tony. Just

say no if you don't want to do it and we'll forget it. Okay?"

"All right, Sam. What is it?"

Sam took a deep breath and sighed. "Will you watch those videos we found at the scene and tell me what you think?"

Allison sat in a chair at her mother's bedside, crocheting yet another afghan. Her mother had rallied a bit when she'd first come in, but after a few minutes she'd dozed off. The only sound in the room was her mother's labored breathing and the soft whish of the yarn as it passed through Allison's fingers.

Crocheting was a relatively new hobby for Allison. She'd started shortly after her mother had taken up residence at the convalescent center. It provided just enough challenge to be interesting, but the granny square pattern that Allison followed was the simplest one she'd been able to find. It didn't require counting stitches, and that meant she could pick it up and put it down whenever she chose, without losing her place.

Allison completed one more square and tied off the yarn. She had almost enough for another afghan. It would be her eighth, although none of them were completely finished. She still had to crochet the squares together with something called a joining stitch. That was complicated, and Allison didn't want to enroll in a class to learn to do it. The squares would just have to sit in their plastic bags in the closet until she either learned the stitch or farmed them out to someone else to finish.

This month's afghan was rainbow-colored, and Allison got out the red yarn to start another square. There were seven tiers to the squares in the rainbow colors. She always remembered them by something she'd learned from Miss Parry, her fourth-grade teacher. The rainbow's name was Roy G. Biv., red, orange, yellow, green, blue, indigo, and violet.

As she started on the next row, Allison realized that she remembered quite a few of Miss Parry's mnemonics. The Great Lakes were HOMES, Huron, Ontario, Michigan, Erie, and Superior. The notes on the lines in the treble clef were "Every Good Boy Does Fine." And the notes on the spaces spelled out the word FACE. Perhaps she should try out for a quiz show.

Her mother made a slight sound in her sleep, and Allison glanced over at her. It was painful to watch Helen Greene sleep. Her mouth sagged open slightly and her thinning white hair was plastered to her forehead. Her body was so wasted, it barely made a bulge under the sheet that covered her. She was becoming a living skeleton.

Allison blinked back tears. She'd heard people say that death held no dignity, and now she knew what that meant. Her mother's facial hair was growing as a side effect of the chemotherapy. Helen Greene, who had always been flawlessly groomed, was now growing a beard of white straggling hairs. What if her mother should see herself in a mirror? She'd be so appalled she might give up and die!

Angrily, Allison flung down her crocheting and ran out to find the head nurse. For the money the convalescent center charged, they ought to at least shave her mother's chin. As she headed down the hall, Allison began to have other suspicions. Her mother was sleeping much more lately. Were the nurses doping her up so they wouldn't have to tend her so closely? She'd seen the exposés on nursing homes across the country. Sometimes a patient was sedated just so the nurses could have an easy day.

By the time Allison reached the head nurse's office, her legs were trembling and her mouth was set in a straight line of anger. That anger grew into a rage as she caught sight of Miss Stanley at her desk, sipping a cup of coffee. How dare this woman lounge around when her mother was dying?!

"Hello, Mrs. Rocca." The nurse smiled and motioned her in. "I'm just on my afternoon break. Would you like to join me for a cup of coffee?"

"No." Allison was so upset she forgot to be polite. "My mother is growing a beard!"

Miss Stanley nodded. She was quite used to handling upset relatives. "And you think we're being negligent by not removing it, especially at the prices we charge. Is that right?"

Allison felt the wind knocked out of her sails. She barely managed to nod.

The head nurse smiled and indicated a chair. "Sit down for a minute, Mrs. Rocca. Of course we'll remove your mother's facial hair if you insist, but there's a reason we haven't done so yet. Are you interested?"

"Well, yes. Of course." Allison sank down into the chair.

"Your mother has been extremely uncomfortable for the past twenty-four hours. There's been a change in her analgesics. We've had trouble adjusting the dosage. That's why she's sleeping so much. And waking her just to remove her facial hair seems counterproductive. When her medications are adjusted and her condition has stabilized, we'll certainly do it."

"Oh." Allison nodded, but she still felt she had to explain. "I know it's not medically important, but my mother has always taken pride in her appearance. I just, well, I thought she'd give up completely if she saw how she looked."

"That's a good point, Mrs. Rocca. And it's one of the reasons that there are no mirrors in our patients' rooms. If they ask for one, of course we'll bring it, but we make sure they look their best before we do."

A great weight of guilt dropped on Allison's shoulders. She'd suspected the worst, and instead, she'd found that Miss Stanley was merely concerned for her mother's comfort. Tears came to her eyes and she found she was unable to blink them back.

"That's all right, Mrs. Rocca." The nurse's voice was so very kind that Allison cried harder. "You're under a great deal of stress, and I really insist that you sit here and have a nice hot cup of coffee. Dr. Naiman doesn't agree with me, but I find coffee is soothing. Cream or sugar?"

"Both. Thank you, Miss Stanley."

"It's Doris. Do you mind if I call you Allison? It's such a pretty name."

Allison nodded. Doris Stanley was a lot

nicer than Allison had expected her to be. By the time Doris had brought her coffee, she felt so much better that she ventured a slight smile.

"I notice you're making a new afghan." The head nurse smiled back. "You must have dozens by now."

"Eight, but they're not finished. The squares are all done, but I haven't learned how to crochet them together."

"Oh, that's the easiest part. Why don't you bring everything with you next week and I'll teach you. Your mother should be more alert by then and we'll lay it out on the floor in her room. She might enjoy watching us."

After Allison had finished her coffee, she took a quick peek at her mother and left for the day. For the first time in months her smile reached her eyes. She felt good as she walked through the lobby and down the steps where she stopped to call Tony. She had punched out the first two digits of his office number before she remembered what Tony had written in the note he'd left for her this morning. He was out doing research on the murders and he wouldn't be at the office until after five. And he'd be working until midnight again.

Allison's spirits were somewhat dampened as she got into her car, turned on the radio, and listened to the traffic report. The freeway was a mess due to a twelve-car collision. She'd have to take the Sepulveda Pass to get home and that took twenty minutes longer. She put on her favorite Vivaldi CD to relax her and pulled out of the parking lot. She could tell Tony about the afghan tomorrow, if she saw him. Now that she thought about it, he probably wouldn't be interested anyway. The fact that she was about to learn a new crochet stitch was pretty insignificant compared to the important movie he was writing.

8

Erik drove home as the sky was beginning to darken. He'd stopped at Tito's Tacos and eaten one of their special enchiladas verdes, pork with green chili sauce. It was hot and spicy, and it would keep him awake for the work he had to do tonight.

While other people might be experts on the expensive Los Angeles restaurants, Erik considered himself a cheap-food connoisseur. He knew the menu and price list of every cut-rate eatery in Culver City. Since Erik had grown up on his mother's farm cooking, he insisted that his food be well prepared and plentiful. No nouvelle cuisine for him. A hand-painted china plate containing nothing but paper-thin slices of meat, an asparagus tip, three teaspoons of sauce, and a grape sliced in twelve pieces left him cold. The one time Erik had tried it, he'd stopped for a Big Mac on the way home.

Tito's, the restaurant Erik had chosen

tonight, was right up at the top of his list along with the Roll & Rye Deli for their pastrami burgers. There was also Dinah's, great for strawberry pancakes, and whenever Erik was in the mood for a platter-sized steak, he went to Petrelli's on Sepulveda Boulevard.

Erik got into his car and turned left on Overland Boulevard, traveling past Sony Studio's main gate. Living in a condo within walking distance of a studio practically guaranteed that he'd never work there. Erik would have to spend two hours on the crowded freeways every day, driving to Cinescope, which was on the other side of the pass. Erik knew he could move to the valley for an easier access to Cinescope, but then Rocca and Nielsen would be sure to sell something to Sony. You couldn't outsmart fate.

A gorgeous blonde raced across Overland, from the fitness center to the singles apartments on the other side of the street. She was wearing a pink leotard that left absolutely nothing to the imagination. Erik frowned as he hit the brakes and waved her on. Tony might accuse him of being a prude, but Erik still felt that there was a place for an outfit like that and it certainly wasn't in the middle of a busy street.

As he waited for the light to change at Overland and Jefferson, Erik snapped open his briefcase to make sure he had the notes he'd done for the first scene of *Video Kill*. Tony had called in at noon, after his interview with Sam Ladera, and reported a total failure. He hadn't been able to get any facts that weren't already in the papers. Naturally, Erik had been disappointed, but he'd urged Tony to hurry back so they could block out the scene. Tony had hemmed and hawed on the phone and finally admitted that he was tied up for a couple days. Personal business. Erik should take the time off and enjoy himself for a change.

There had been no way Erik could go home in the middle of the day, so he'd stayed at the office and compiled all the information they'd been able to get. The work he'd completed was on a flash drive in his briefcase, and he intended to start blocking the first scene tonight, on his personal computer.

Erik turned left and pulled up to the guard's kiosk on Sunshine Lane. The condo complex had an automatic gate-opener and every homeowner was given a magnetically coded card. The system was great when it worked, but the arm on the gate was broken again.

"Erik Nielsen. Apartment seven fourteen."

The words were out of Erik's mouth before he realized that the woman in the kiosk was Norma, his favorite security guard. She'd been really helpful when he'd moved in, giving him the name of a plumber when his sink needed fixing and answering all his questions about the complex. Norma was just about his only friend among the four-hundred-odd residents of Sunshine Lane.

"What are you doing here, Norma? I thought you didn't work weekends."

"I'm not supposed to." Norma smiled and pressed the button to open the gate. "The night man called in sick, so they called me to come in at the last minute. Oh, Erik? There was a special delivery letter for you. I knew you weren't home, so I told the postman to leave it in your box."

Erik thanked her and drove down the tree-lined street to his garage. He parked in his numbered space and stopped at the mailbox on his way upstairs. His heart thudded hard in his chest as he read the return address on the special delivery letter. It was from Dr. Sanders at Pine Ridge.

The moment he'd unlocked the door and switched on the lights, Erik ripped open the envelope. A relieved smile spread across his face as he read the first few sentences. Jamie was definitely making progress. He had actually tried to talk when he saw Erik's video of the L.A. Zoo.

Al was rubbing up against his legs, meowing pitifully, and Erik scooped him up on his way to the kitchen. He opened a can of cat food and shoveled half out on a paper plate. Then he poured himself a beer. He was about to go back to the living room when he noticed that Al was eyeing his food with distaste.

"Oh, boy, have I got you spoiled!" Erik was sure that Al smiled as he bent down to pick up the plate and warm it for a few seconds in the microwave. "Is this better?"

Al licked his hand as he set the plate on the floor, and Erik grinned. His mother used to say that it was impossible to own a cat. The cat consented to live with you, but only if you went out of your way to please it. Now, as Erik watched Al eat, he had an idea. He hurried to get the video camera he'd purchased last month and shot a full minute of Al, digging into his food. He'd already told Jamie that they had a cat and this would give him the opportunity to see Al.

Erik had spent the past three weekends shooting videos to send to Jamie. The first one had been of the planes at L.A. International Airport. The second had shown the neighborhood kids swimming in the condo pool. Last Sunday he had recorded the animals at the zoo. Erik carried his beer to the living room and sat down in his recliner to finish the letter.

Dr. Sanders had a suggestion. Erik should appear at least once in each video. It would give Jamie the opportunity to see his dad any time he wished, simply by watching the videos. It might also lead to greater recognition on Erik's monthly visits. If these weekly videos worked for Jamie, Dr. Sanders would incorporate them in the school's general therapy program. Other parents would be encouraged to make videos to keep in visual touch with their children.

Erik was smiling as he carried his briefcase into the office and turned on his computer. He was doing the best that he could for the son that only he had wanted. Daniele had been nearly hysterical when she'd found out that she was pregnant. Thank God she'd told him instead of going straight in for the abortion she'd arranged. It had taken a large sum of money to buy Daniele's promise to have Jamie and then give him to Erik at the time of the divorce. He'd borrowed the money from the teachers' credit union, and it had taken him ten years to pay it off, ten years of scrimping and saving every penny of his miserable salary as a high school English teacher. He'd been at the end of his rope when Tony had located him and suggested they write a screenplay about their experiences in combat.

The computer beeped, and Erik put in the flash drive he'd brought from the office. He owed Tony a lot, and it was unfair to be mad at him just because he'd needed to take a few days off. Tony'd had a rough time lately with his money problems and Allison's depression over her mother's illness. Erik was well acquainted with Tony's work habits. Tony put off the actual writing for as long as possible, letting everything mull over in his mind. Then, when a deadline was staring him in the face, he worked like a demon for twenty-four-hour stretches and turned out brilliant work. In their three years together Erik had learned to accept his partner's writing habits and adjust to his crazy time schedule.

The screen on his computer glowed brightly, and Erik adjusted the contrast. Then he opened the file and started to work. It might take him a week, but he'd block out the first scene himself, without Tony's help. They could always revise it later. He wouldn't put any more pressure on Tony to keep regular office hours. The first three scenes would be done in time. Rocca and Nielsen had never failed to meet a deadline yet.

Tony stood at the foot of the bed, squinting through the viewfinder on his video camera. It was a few minutes past nine at night, and Tony could tell that everyone was tired. He'd shot seventeen takes on the last scene and it still wasn't up to par. They'd catch it tomorrow, when everyone was fresh.

"Okay, kids. That's a wrap for tonight."

Tony watched as Tina, the blonde, and Ginger, the redhead, untangled themselves on the bed and stood up. Tina reached for her robe and slipped it on, not bothering to tie the belt. They'd already seen everything that she had to offer.

"Thank God that's over!" Tina massaged the left side of her tush and groaned. "I'm getting a cramp."

"A cramp's nothing compared to how you'll feel tomorrow night." Bobby, the male lead, leered at her. "Have you read the next scene?"

It took a minute for Bobby's innuendo to sink in. When it did, Tina turned to Tony with alarm. "He's kidding, isn't he, Tony?

When I signed on for this thing, they told me I wouldn't have to . . . you know."

Tony laughed. Tina looked truly indignant.

"Bobby's putting you on, Tina. You don't have to 'you know.' The next thing we shoot is the bathtub scene."

"You creep!" Tina glowered at Bobby. "It's a good thing this is only soft porn!"

"All right, children. Stop squabbling." Tony opened his gym bag and started to pack up his equipment. "Tomorrow, same time, same place. I'm going to step up our schedule until we get this thing wrapped up. Oh, yeah, do you two girls have a ride home?"

"You mean because of the Video Killer?" Tina looked a little nervous.

"That's right. It's not exactly safe out there on the street."

"Bobby's giving us a ride until my car's fixed," Ginger said. "You don't have to worry about losing your cast, Tony."

"I really wasn't worried," Tony quipped. "So far he's murdered only actresses, and the way things went tonight, you two girls aren't in any danger at all."

Ginger picked up a rubber duck from the bed and bounced it off Tony's head, but all three of them were laughing as they went out the door.

147

After they had left, Tony quickly checked the bedroom and bathroom for forgotten items. The maid came in every morning, and he didn't want to leave any incriminating evidence. The Traveler Motel might not be the top of the line in the world of accommodations, but the management would still object if they knew he was shooting a porn flick in one of their rooms.

There was a wet towel on the bathroom floor. Tony tossed it over the rack and straightened the bed just a bit. He wanted to give the impression that this room had been used in a perfectly normal manner. Then he put his miniature video camera in his gym bag and opened the door, hanging out the sign for the maid to come in the next morning. This was Tony's fourth film, and he'd used a different motel each time. The first three were already being distributed, and Tony hoped no one would ever find out that he'd produced, written, directed, and filmed them. He'd had little choice in the matter. It was a way to repay his loan, and he still had to finish this one before his debt was paid off.

Tony walked down the block and around the corner. His car was parked on a side street, three blocks away. He got in and drove toward Hollywood, stopping on the way to pick up a Whopper and fries from the first Burger King he passed. By the time he got to his office, he'd already eaten the French fries, and he finished the Whopper in the parking lot. Then he tossed the trash in the Dumpster and went in the back door of the Schwartzvold Building to ride the creaky elevator up to the thirteenth floor.

The office was deserted and the coffee was stone-cold. Tony made a fresh pot and sat down at his desk. He was tired, but there was work to do, and he couldn't expect Erik to do it all. Erik probably assumed he'd been spending his day away from the office goofing off. He had no idea that Tony was working a double shift on the porn so he could finish it fast and devote all his time to *Video Kill.*

Tony took a legal-sized pad from his center desk drawer and picked up his pen. He stared at the blank yellow page while he sipped coffee and geared himself up. It was time to think about the murder scenes Sam had shown him. When he'd leveled with Sam and told him about the movie they were writing, Sam had laid down some ground rules. Tony wasn't to tell anyone he'd seen the murder videos, not even Erik. He was to maintain that their script was a fictionalized account until *after* the killer

149

was caught. He had to keep several specific facts secret. Sam needed them to eliminate the sickos who would turn themselves in, claiming to be the Video Killer.

Tony had been flabbergasted. People turned themselves in for murders they didn't commit? Sure, Sam had told him. It happened frequently. When he'd worked on the L.A. Strangler case, over thirty people had claimed they were guilty. That was why the police held back some critical information to use as a test to weed out false confessions. If it wasn't reported in the media, only the real killer would know that he'd held the knife in both hands to stab his victim or, in the case of the Video Killer, that he'd worn black gloves and an executioner's hood.

Naturally, Tony had agreed to Sam's conditions. He'd called Erik right there from Sam's office and told him that Sam had been no help at all, that they'd have to wing it on the script. He still felt like a rat for lying to Erik, but it couldn't be helped. Erik would understand when the killer was caught and the whole thing came out.

Tony sighed as he blocked out the opening. The video had begun with a forward tracking as the killer had climbed the stairs to Sharee Lyons's apartment and gone

150

inside in the darkness to wait for his victim. It was suspenseful and very creepy. Then there had been another forward tracking shot down the hall to the bathroom. Now that he recalled the details of the first murder, Tony shuddered. He thought he'd seen every conceivable act of violence in combat, but this had been different. Sharee Lyons hadn't been killed in a passionate frenzy. It was quite the opposite, and that had made it even more horrifying. The Video Killer had carefully calculated his every movement to present the best shot for the camera. He'd directed the whole thing, and the fact that he'd actually murdered a woman to get the scene he wanted had been totally irrelevant to him. It was monstrous.

Sam had been right on the money to compare the first disc to *Psycho.* Hitchcock had shot the shower scene in much the same way. Sharee Lyons had even resembled Hitchcock's actress, Janet Leigh. There was only one critical difference. Miss Leigh had walked off the set after the scene was finished.

The second murder disc was also patterned after Hitchcock. It was the Tunnel of Love scene from *Strangers on a Train.* Tammara Welles had been a ringer for Laura Elliott, Hitchcock's star.

151

Was the Video Killer a professional film-maker? Tony wasn't sure. Handling a video camera was something almost anyone could do adequately. The newer, expensive models were so fully automatic that all you had to do was aim and the camera did the rest. There were hundreds of classes offered at high schools and colleges to teach film technique. The videos looked professional, but they could be the work of a talented and well-trained amateur. But was it possible for one man to record a gruesome murder as he, himself, committed it?

Tony considered the logistics. It was one thing to stage a murder with actors. Then the filmmaker could direct the scene from behind the camera, reshooting as many takes as he needed. But the Video Killer had done everything himself. In only one take. With no editing. On top of all that, he'd taken part in the action. It seemed impossible, but Sam had been certain that the Video Killer had worked alone. Could he be wrong? Tony had to see the DVDs again to make sure.

Tony picked up the phone and dialed the number of Sam's high-rise condo on Wilshire. Sam picked it up on the first ring.

"Sam? This is Archer. Can I see those DVDs again? As soon as possible?"

"Sure, Tony. You can see them now if you like." Sam sounded alert. "I'm just sitting around here going crazy, waiting for the telephone to ring."

"You think he'll do it again?"

"That's my guess." Sam sighed. "We've got a full force out there, but we have no idea where. Or who. Or even when."

The surprise showed in Tony's voice. "You already know *when* Sam. Sunday night. He's established a pattern."

"That's the writer in you talking. Twice is not a firm pattern, especially when you're dealing with a psychotic. For all we know he might hit on a Tuesday, at high noon."

"But that's not what you're betting on, is it, Sam? I'll wager five bucks that you've already called up the reserves for Sunday night."

Sam hesitated for a moment and then chuckled. "You win, Tony. It's all I've got to go on. Unless you've come up with something new?"

"Just one thing. Are you a hundred percent positive the Video Killer worked alone?"

"I'm not a hundred percent positive of my own name. Why?"

"I just went through the logistics. It's pretty complicated to commit a murder and film it at the same time. That's why I want another look at those discs. If the camera pans or changes focus when the Video Killer's on screen, he's got an accomplice."

"Okay, let's check it out now. Your place or mine?"

"Why don't you come here? Thirteenth floor, Schwartzvold Building. I've got a fresh pot of coffee, and there's nobody here but me."

"Fine. I'll transfer my calls to your number and drive right over. What time is it?"

"It's after ten."

"Good!" Sam gave a sarcastic laugh. "If I hurry, I'll be between rush hours. See you in fifteen minutes."

Tony felt a little pang of conscience as he cleared his desk. He'd promised Erik he would hurry with the outline, but blocking out the first two scenes would be a lot easier after he'd seen the murder discs again. Erik would just have to wait.

As Tony hurried into the tiny kitchenette to put on a fresh pot of coffee, he caught sight of his reflection in the mirror over the sink. His eyes were puffy and his skin was sallow. Working nonstop was taking its toll. Since it had been hot in the motel room, his T-shirt was rumpled and sweat stained. The homeless on skid row probably looked

154

better than he did.

Tony finished making the coffee and grabbed a fresh T-shirt from the stash he kept in the cupboard. Then he hurried to the bathroom to wash up. Less than five minutes later he was shaved and dressed in a crisp, new royal blue T-shirt that said I NEVER COULD READ SUDOKU in red glitter letters. At least he looked better. Now it was time to do something to feel better.

Tony ran back to his office and grabbed the bottle of amphetamines he kept for emergencies like these. He gulped down a fifteen-milligram upper and made a mental note to get more on the street tomorrow. Using illegal stimulants was dangerous, but there was no way he could keep up this pace on coffee alone.

Munchies. He ought to put out some kind of food to have with the coffee. Tony raced to his Day-Glo orange file cabinet and pulled open the third drawer. Allison had filed his emergency food supply as a joke. The hanging file under "S" marked SNACKS contained a package of Chips Ahoy and a box of Ritz Crackers. There was also a can of sardines, three chocolate bars, and a jar of Cheez Whiz. He arranged them all on the table in the reception area and set out two coffee mugs, a jar of Cremora, and a

container of sugar. The upper was just starting to hit. It made his hands tremble slightly,
but he felt much more alert as he rode down
in the old Otis and waited in the lobby for
Sam to arrive.

9

Lon smiled as he posed the fully articulated mannequin in the shower stall he'd ordered from the prop department. He was working late at the studio, shooting the test footage he'd promised for Erik and Tony. Lon enjoyed test shots. He often ran experiments with the new equipment that appeared on the market. He'd developed numerous techniques that would bring out the best of its qualities. Often the results were amazingly good, but most producers preferred to stick with standard equipment and conventional techniques. They simply had no imagination. Anything out of the ordinary, no matter how impressive, was suspect. At least Tony and Erik seemed eager to try something new and different. And they'd promised him he'd be in sole charge of the photography. It was a golden opportunity to do something different, something artistic, and perhaps even radical. Lon found himself wishing he could be a part of their *Video Kill* project, but something held him back. It wasn't just the subject matter; he knew he could deal with that if he had to. It was a deep-down reluctance, some sort of psychological block that he couldn't seem to overcome.

He had just finished setting up his shot when there was a knock at the door. Before he had time to call out, Diana Ellington opened it and stuck her head inside.

"Lon, darling! You're working late."

"So are you, Diana. Night shooting?"

Diana sighed and shook her head. "Dubbing. Will you invite me in? Or am I interrupting the genius at work?"

Diana smiled and swept her long eyelashes up to reveal her best asset, what people in the trade called her "bedroom" eyes. They were dark and widely spaced, creating a startling contrast with her delicate English peaches-and-cream coloring. One film reviewer had coined the phrase "bedroom eyes in a schoolmarm's face." And she was certainly using them on him tonight.

Lon laughed and motioned her in. "I'm just running some tests, Diana. Nothing critical. Coffee?"

"God forbid! I've been swilling the horrid stuff all day. I'd much rather have a nice, tall gin and tonic with a squeeze of lime. I'm into preventive medicine these days."

"Preventive medicine?"

"Lon, darling . . ." Diana gave him a smoldering look. "Tonic is quinine water. For malaria, you know? I can be almost certain I'll never come down with it."

Lon laughed. "Very cute, Diana. Unfortunately, Cinescope didn't see fit to equip me with a bar."

"Oh well." Diana sat down on a stool near Lon's test set. "We'll just have to pop out to the Polo Lounge when you're through for the night. Go ahead, darling, finish up your work. Is there anything I can do to help?"

Lon shrugged. "Well, you could stand in for my mannequin if you don't mind being stabbed in the back with a rubber knife."

"I don't mind." Diana slid off the stool, giving Lon a flash of lovely tanned thigh. "It's certainly not the first time I've been stabbed in the back in this business."

Lon shot several takes, but it was difficult to keep his mind on his work. Diana had said she'd been dubbing, but she was dressed to kill in a baby blue silk dress that came barely to midthigh. And she was wearing full makeup. Most actresses who were scheduled for dubbing wore old comfortable clothes and no makeup. Diana looked smashing and extremely provocative. Although they'd worked together on a project in the past, she'd never dropped in on him at work before. It was clear she wanted something from him. There was only one way to find out. Lon cut the lights and picked up his jacket.

"Let's go, Diana. My hands are beginning to shake. It might be the first symptom of malaria."

Diana slid off the stool and moved so close that Lon could feel the heat from her body. "Perhaps, darling. But then, it may only be me."

Tony and Sam sat on the couch watching the television screen. They were on their third or fourth pot of coffee — Tony'd lost count. They'd finished all the food except for one sardine that was staring at them, glassy-eyed, from the open tin. It was midnight and they'd watched the Sharee Lyons murder scene twice.

"You were right, Sam." Tony clicked off the television. "I couldn't find anything to point to an accomplice. When the killer's on screen, the camera's stationary."

"And you still think he's doing Hitchcock?"

Tony nodded emphatically. "There's no

question in my mind. The footage we just saw was pure Hitchcock, I'll swear to it. I'm just amazed that the killer pulled it off with his self-imposed limitations."

"You mean the fact that he's working alone?"

"Yeah. It would take a hell of a lot of planning, Sam. He has to know Hitchcock, inside and out. And he's got to be damn good with that camera."

Sam poured himself a little more coffee and dumped in plenty of Cremora and sugar. "Do you think the Video Killer could be someone who actually worked for Hitchcock?"

"He'd be too old. Hitchcock died thirty years ago and this guy's strong and athletic." Tony clasped his hands together. They weren't shaking as much now, but the upper he'd taken an hour ago had almost worn off. "I just don't know, Sam. It's like I said before, he could be a professional or he could be a very talented amateur. That's not much to go on."

Sam nodded ruefully. "If this were Fargo, North Dakota, it would be a lot easier. You can't even walk down the street in L.A. without bumping into a director or a producer or a cameraman. And as far as videos go, forget it. They've taken the place of snapshots. Half the guys on the force have videos of their kids on their cell phones."

"Forget the video aspect." Tony tried to put some energy in his voice. "Let's concentrate on the victims. Female. Both of them. And did you notice how much Sharee Lyons looked like Janet Leigh in *Psycho*?"

"Sure." Sam nodded. "And Tammara Welles was a ringer for Laura Elliott in *Strangers on a Train*. I already thought of that, Tony. I'm planning to go through all Hitchcock's films to identify the female victims, and then I'll try to contact any actresses who resemble them. It's a big job, especially since Hitchcock made twenty-five feature films."

"You're only counting the American ones, Sam. He also made twenty-eight British films for a total of fifty-three. And that doesn't count the special sequences he did for other directors."

Sam sighed. "I can't do it alone, Tony. That's over a hundred hours of watching films, not to mention the time it'll take to identify the look-alikes. And I don't dare bring anyone in to help me while this whole thing is still under wraps."

"Why all the secrecy, Sam? There must be a couple of guys in the department you can trust to help you."

"Not really." Sam sighed. "That's how leaks happen, Tony. The only way to keep a secret in the detective business is to keep your mouth shut. I've already broken that rule by bringing you in."

Sam looked so depressed, Tony couldn't stand it. The least he could do was offer to help. Sam had done him a big favor by showing him the murder scenes and giving him permission to use what he'd seen in his script.

"Since I'm already on the inside, maybe I can do something. I know a guy who has a complete collection of Hitchcock films, including the ones that were never released in America. I'll have him dupe them and then I'll write out a plot synopsis and a list of the female victims. I still remember a lot from class, Sam, and I might even be able to dig up my notes. Once you have my list of movie victims, you can figure out some way to warn the actresses without giving too much away to the media."

"Spoken like a true friend." Sam smiled for the first time that night. "Archer does the legwork and Sam Spade gets the credit. How soon do you think you can get that list for me?"

"A week or two, maybe less."

"Thanks, Tony, I'd really appreciate that."

Sam looked a little more cheerful as he stood up and yawned. "You didn't spot anything new on the DVDs tonight, did you?"

"Not really." Tony frowned. "All we know is that he's great with a camera, and he's got a style that's almost the same as Hitchcock's except, well . . ."

"Except what? Spit it out."

"Except I gotta admit it's great footage, Sam. Head and shoulders above Hitchcock's. I know the Video Killer's a real sicko, but he's the best filmmaker I've ever seen!"

Lon opened his eyes as Diana got out of bed and slipped on a robe. "Where are you going?"

"You'll see, darling. I'll be back before you can miss me."

Lon sat up and arranged the pillow behind his head. He was smiling. Diana still hadn't told him why she'd taken him to her place and practically raped him, but he wasn't complaining. This sort of thing hadn't happened to him very often and it sure as hell beat working.

There was a satisfied grin on Lon's face as he reviewed the evening. They hadn't bothered to go to the Polo Lounge. Diana had decided it would be too crowded. She'd suggested her place instead. And then, the moment she'd unlocked the door, she'd wiggled out of her dress, kissed him passionately, and led him to the bedroom. Why? Lon knew Diana wasn't the type to sleep around with just anyone. Rumor had it she favored only those few select men who could make a real difference in her career. But why him? And why now?

"Here, darling." Diana appeared in the doorway with two tall, frosted glasses. "I've brought you the cure. Unless you don't have those symptoms anymore."

Lon took the glass, set it down on the table next to the bed, and reached out to part her robe. "I've still got them, but I don't think the cure is in this glass."

"Insatiable!" Diana laughed and got into bed, snuggling up close to him. She ran her hands down his body and moved in a way that made him gasp. Then they began again, slowly this time, touching and rubbing and tonguing the places that caused the most exquisite pleasure. Many minutes passed before Lon sat up again and took the first sip of his drink.

"Okay, Diana, let's talk. I don't want to give the impression I'm ungrateful, but I'm sure you didn't invite me here because you were crazed with passion at my good looks or my charm."

Diana put on such a look of grievous injury that Lon almost laughed out loud.

"Lon, darling! How can you be so unfeeling? Do you really believe that I had an ulterior motive for this interlude of passion we shared?"

"Cut! Print it! You're a wonderful actress, Diana, but the cameras just stopped rolling. The sex was great. I loved every minute of it, and I'd like to do it again, anytime. But what do you *want*?"

Diana sighed. "Either you're a hard case, or I'm losing my touch. Truth?"

Lon nodded. "Truth, Diana."

"I want one of the leads in *Video Kill.* I'm getting typecast, playing nothing but diplomats' wives and uptight society ladies. I'd die for the chance to do something different. How about it, darling? I know you're on the project."

"Then you know more than I do." Lon shook his head. "I haven't made any commitments, Diana. It's a real pity, but I'm afraid you expended all your energy tonight for nothing."

"But you *will* sign on eventually, won't you, Lon?" Diana looked worried. "It could be so perfect for both of us. I'd love to work with you. And we'd have so many opportunities for more nights like tonight. You *did* enjoy it, didn't you?"

Lon grinned. "You know I did. Are you giving me an incentive, Diana?"

"Perhaps." Diana flashed her famous smile as Lon got out of bed and began to dress. "Will you promise me you'll at least *think* about it?"

"I promise." Lon finished dressing and turned to look at her. "By the way, Diana, do you know Rocca and Nielsen?"

"The team that's writing *Video Kill*? No, I don't think I've ever met them."

Lon leaned down to kiss her lightly on the forehead. "Don't bother to show me out, Diana. I know the way. And if you ever have the chance to meet Rocca and Nielsen, jump at it. You three have a lot in common."

10

Sunday, July 18

Twilight had deepened into the lengthening shadows of night. Brother's desk lamp cast a bright circle of light in the darkness of his workroom. He was in the process of casting just the right actress for the segment he was taping tonight, and he'd narrowed his choices down to two, both listed in the Academy Players Directory. The first actress was best known for her part as a tycoon's mistress on a popular prime-time drama. The desk lamp threw a circle of warm yellow light on her face as Brother studied her publicity photo. She was the right age for the part, and she fit the physical description of the character. But there was something inherently wrong with casting her. She was too blatantly sexual. He needed someone who was sensual and yet refined.

With a sigh, Brother flipped to the second candidate's picture. This actress was in her early twenties with a smooth, unlined face. She was definitely an ingénue, and it would create all sorts of problems to cast her as an older woman. Neither of the two candidates would do.

As he had done so often in the past, Brother asked himself how an expert would handle the problem. Which actress would Lon Michaels choose for tonight's critical role?

The familiar technique worked, and Brother smiled as he flipped through the directory and found the perfect woman for the role. The face that stared back at him from the printed page had the right natural coloring and bone structure. She was perfect for the part. This veteran actress would give her finest performance tonight, under his expert tutelage, one that people would remember for years to come.

Brother marked the page and closed the directory. The actress he'd chosen had just completed a PBS drama and the wrap party was tonight. Brother would be ready and waiting for her when she came home to her beach house after the party was over.

One more check of his equipment was in order, and then he was ready. Now there was nothing to do but wait. To pass the time he planned to rewatch the Englishman's work and compare it to his own.

The screening room, as Brother now called it, was the small bedroom that had once been the nursery. The room had been his for four years and then it had belonged to his sister, Victoria, for a brief period of time. When Victoria had died, at four months of age, his mother had removed the crib and all the baby furniture. It had been used as a storeroom until he had turned it into his screening room.

Brother flipped on the high-resolution monitor. Then he pressed the fast-forward control to find the scene he wanted. As he watched the images flash on the screen in rapid motion, he leaned back in his leather armchair and let his mind wander. He really needed to have this room repainted. The pink walls with their dancing white teddy bears were no longer appropriate. He still remembered the flurry of activity in the children's wing when the decorators had arrived to "do" the nursery for his sister. And the rage he'd felt when his mother had announced that he was moving to a nice, big room of his own. She had started calling him "Little Brother" then, and before he'd known what was happening, he was no longer his mother's baby.

■ ■ ■ ■

Brother had wanted to go to the park, but Nanny was downstairs with mother, and she didn't have time to take him. And now Papa wouldn't take him, either. Papa couldn't come home anymore. Nanny had told him that Papa was in heaven. Someday he'd go there, too. Then they'd all be together again, but for now, it was just Brother and Mother and his dumb baby sister.

It was lonely upstairs, with only Baby Victoria for company. Since she was taking a nap, he had to be very, very quiet. He knew the maid was supposed to be upstairs with him, but she'd left right after Nanny had gone downstairs. If he stood on his chair, he could see her standing on the bottom step of the outside stairs, talking to the gardener from next door. She was smoking a cigarette, but that was their secret. The maid brought him cookies if he didn't tell on her.

Brother got out his trucks and started to play, but it was no fun alone. He was trying to be a good, big boy like Nanny said, but the trucks slipped out of his hands and crashed into the nursery wall. And then Baby Victoria was crying, and he knew

Nanny would be mad if she found out why. He pushed open the door and ran to the crib to tell his sister to be quiet, but everything he said just made her cry harder.

Baby Victoria's face was red and her mouth was open wide. There were no teeth in her mouth. She was ugly and stupid. Brother stood by the crib and stared down at her in exasperation. She should go back to sleep. If she went back to sleep, no one would know he crashed his trucks into the wall.

There was a pillow on Nanny's cot, and Brother put it over his sister's noisy, wide-open mouth. Now no one could hear her. Her legs kicked against the blankets, and he laughed as he watched them. The harder he pushed down on the pillow, the more her feet kicked. This was much more fun than playing with his trucks.

After a long while her feet stopped kicking. Carefully he raised the corner of the pillow to peek. Baby Victoria wasn't crying anymore. Now she was very quiet.

There was the sound of a door slamming downstairs and Brother put the pillow away and ran back to his playroom. He was building a tower with his blocks like a very good boy when Nanny came back upstairs.

Brother came back to the present with a jolt when the scene he wanted flashed on the screen. He hit the stop button on the remote control and backed up the video just a bit. Alfred Hitchcock had gained a reputation through false pretenses. Brother would expose him for the charlatan he was by reshooting Hitchcock's famous death scenes the way they should have been done.

It was late by the time Brother finished watching the scene he was filming tonight, but he needed everything fresh in his mind before he left. There were no second chances in the cutting room for him. He had to stage this scene perfectly, the first time around, so that he could leave the video for the police. Their evidence room vault was the safest place in town to store his discs. No studio bigwig could pull him off this project. It was his. His alone.

Brother still remembered the time, ten years ago, when Lon Michaels had been working for a major studio. Everyone in the industry knew that Lon was the best cameraman in the business, but he had been over budget. Lon had argued that the excellent footage he'd already shot more than made up for the delay and the extra expenditures. Unfortunately, the studio didn't agree. Two men had come into Lon's office while Brother was there to confiscate the reels of film. Legally, Lon's film belonged to the studio and there had been nothing he could do to reclaim it. Another cameraman had completed the film and Lon's work had been ruined.

Brother had learned a valuable lesson from Lon's misfortune. He'd vowed that such a catastrophe would never happen to him. His wonderful scenes with Sharee Lyons and Tammara Welles were under the armed protection of the police. No studio in town could touch them or alter them in any way. And, best of all, the detective in charge had decided to keep the content of his masterpiece from the press. If people in the industry knew the full scope of Brother's project, the no-talent jealous ones might try to stop him from completing his work.

As Brother reached for his briefcase of equipment, the clock on his workroom wall began to chime. He was late! Brother grabbed his things and rushed down the stairs. As he locked the outside door behind him, a smile crossed his face. Diana Ellington had told Lon Michaels she'd die for the lead in his next movie. That rumor was all over town. And everyone knew that she'd slept with Lon to try to get the part. Life was ironic. Tonight Diana would discover that she'd landed the part she craved so much even though she'd seduced the wrong man.

Diana Ellington stifled a yawn. She wanted to go home and crawl into bed, but it was Sunday night and she'd been edgy all day. The Video Killer had struck on the past two Sundays and she was afraid to leave, alone. The party would last all night. Perhaps she should curl up on the couch on the set and stay right there until morning.

"Was that a yawn, sweetie? The party's just starting."

Diana froze as a commanding hand took her elbow. It was Ian Jasper, Hollywood's golden boy producer. She turned slowly, using her eyes to their full advantage to give Ian a smoldering look as he whirled her around and embraced her. If she could get Ian to take her home, she wouldn't have to worry about being alone.

"Ian, darling, I was just thinking of leaving. I'm dubbing in the morning and I simply have to get to bed."

"With or without me?"

Diana shivered a little as she gazed up into

his craggy face. Ian was well known for bedding actresses and then creating juicy parts for them in his next feature, if he liked them enough. Lon Michaels might come through with a part for her in *Video Kill,* but there were no guarantees in this business and it always paid to have more than one iron in the fire.

"What a tempting thought," Diana breathed, snuggling a bit closer. "But, Ian, dear, from the look on your companion's face, I assumed you were otherwise engaged for the evening."

Ian laughed as he followed Diana's gaze. The starlet he'd brought to the party was standing in the corner with a glass of champagne, staring at them malevolently.

"Engaged? That word has negative connotations, darling. Marietta may have certain expectations, but I'm sure she wouldn't object to a threesome."

Diana managed to keep the interested expression on her face even though her hopes plummeted. There would be no opportunity to talk to Ian about a starring vehicle if Marietta were there.

"Ian, dear." Diana smile up at him, "I'm afraid I never did learn to share with good grace. Let's take a rain check until you can devote all your energies to me."

Ian glanced over at Marietta again. She had been a bit possessive lately, and his arms tightened around Diana.

"I'll stay at the party until eleven, and then I'll take Marietta home. That'll put me at your house no later than midnight. Can you make a dry martini? One where the vermouth is only a fleeting memory in the mind of the gin?"

"I can make the driest martini in existence." Diana smiled. "To be completely honest, my vermouth bottle's been empty for years."

Ten minutes later Diana was in her white Jaguar, using her cell phone. It took ten rings but finally a sleepy voice answered the phone. Her agent, Marsha Weitz, grasped the situation quickly. Yes, she knew all about Ian Jasper. Diana should dress in a blue negligee. It would set off her coloring perfectly. To make a dry martini the way Ian liked it, she needed to stop by Malibu Liquor to buy Boodles, Ian's favorite gin. Diana should also pick up green cocktail olives, the kind stuffed with garlic. As far as the rest went, Diana should resist slightly, just enough for Ian to think he was making a conquest. Diana would have no trouble with Ian Jasper. Thank God it wasn't that schmuck, Bernie you-know-who!

Diana felt great as she hung up the phone. She stopped at Malibu Liquor and bought everything she needed, and then took the Pacific Coast Highway north. The moon was so bright on the ocean that she could see the dial on her watch. It was only ten-thirty. She had an hour and a half until Ian arrived — plenty of time for a relaxing bath and a complete makeover. She could hardly wait for her performance to begin. Seducing Ian could be the biggest break of her career. She'd indulge every one of his fantasies, and by the time he left her beach house in the morning, he'd be planning a marvelous showcase movie for her.

The house was dark as Diana pulled up in the driveway. She must have forgotten to turn on a light. Diana put her car in the two-stall garage and left the garage door open for Ian. Parking on the street was impossible here. Cars lined the shoulder of the highway twenty-four hours a day. She'd been lucky to find a beach house with a double garage.

Diana was fumbling for her house key when she noticed that the connecting door to the kitchen was already unlocked. She hesitated, her hand on the knob. Should she call the police to have them check out the house? No, that was silly. She was overreacting to the publicity about the Video Killer. It was true that both victims had been actresses, but they'd lived in the city, miles from here. She was perfectly safe. If she called the police, they might still be here when Ian arrived, and that would put a real damper on her plans. Firmly Diana turned the knob and pushed open the door. Moonlight streamed in the kitchen window, making a ghostly white rectangle of the refrigerator. Everything was exactly the way she'd left it. The teapot was still sitting in its cozy on the counter, and her cup, half empty, was beside it. No one was here. She was paranoid, that was all.

Even though she told herself that there was nothing to fear, Diana snatched a stainless steel chopping knife from the holder on the counter. It was heavy and sharp; the saleslady had told her it was perfect for dicing onions and celery. She gripped it tightly in her hand as she went into the living room to switch on the lights. Everything was fine there, too. No signs of an intruder. Diana began to feel a little foolish about her paranoia, but she methodically checked out the other rooms. She'd order a photoelectric timer for the lights tomorrow. There was something terribly unnerving about stepping over the threshold into a pitch-black room.

The last room Diana entered was her bedroom. She gave a little cry of dismay as she glanced at the antique clock on the dresser. Ian would be here in forty-five minutes. Her check of the house had taken much longer than she'd thought. A relaxing interlude in the bath was out. She'd barely have time for a quick shower.

Diana slipped out of the red silk jumpsuit she'd worn to the wrap party and left it crumpled on the floor of the dressing room. Her maid would take it to the dry cleaners in the morning. Then she put on a plastic cap to preserve her hairstyle and took the quickest shower in history.

In less than ten minutes Diana was seated at her lighted makeup table, dressed in her very best blue peignoir set. She'd allot twenty minutes for her makeup, and then she'd prepare the martini pitcher. Everything had to be ready by the time Ian arrived. Marsha had told her that Ian hated to be kept waiting. Women were supposed to wait for him, not the other way around.

Diana had just finished curling her eyelashes when she noticed a blurry movement in the shadows of the master bedroom. Since the door to her dressing room was open and only a dim light was on by the bed, the room was in partial darkness. For a moment she considered running back to the bathroom, where she'd left the knife, but that seemed silly. The window in the bedroom was open slightly and the curtains had probably fluttered in the ocean breeze. Instead, she picked up her eyeliner and concentrated totally on drawing the fine even line at the base of her eyelids to emphasize her "bedroom eyes." It was a technique that a studio makeup expert had taught her. When she had finished with the eyeliner, she glanced back at the spot where the shadow had been, but it was gone now. The breeze must have shifted.

Diana used a sable brush to highlight her cheekbones with the special blusher that was responsible for her "peaches-and-cream" complexion and dusted powder over her lip gloss for the "schoolmarm" look. She had just raised her brush to give her hair a final touch-up when the moonlight streaming in the dressing room window was blocked out by a looming black shadow.

Diana tried to whirl around, but her chair wouldn't move. Then, before she had time to do more than gasp, she felt something tighten around her neck. As she struggled, desperately clawing at the cloth that was strangling her, her eyes stared in panic into the mirror. A striped silk necktie was cutting into the flesh of her neck.

She had to have air! Diana grabbed frantically at the dark shape behind her, but she couldn't reach. Her mind screamed in panic, but she was unable to make a sound. Ian would save her! He'd be here any second! Please, God! Please!

But there was no sound of a car in the driveway. No flash of headlights against the windows of her bedroom. And then, as her vision grew dim, she saw it. The red light of a video camera recording her death. Just as it had recorded Sharee Lyons and Tammara Welles.

Diana's legs kicked out reflexively, a last bid for life-giving oxygen. The heel of her satin slipper caught the leg of the makeup table. Bottles of lotions and multicolored powders shattered on the glass surface, but all Diana heard was the high-pitched ringing in her ears. She was not aware when her legs slowed and stopped kicking, when her arms ceased to flail at the empty air. She was perfectly still. Her lifeless "bedroom eyes," bulging grotesquely toward the mirror, saw nothing at all.

Ian Jasper was a half hour behind schedule

as he drove up to the Malibu beach house and parked in the garage. He gave the engine on his Lotus Elise an extra rev before he shut it off; it was due for another monthly tune-up. He lowered the garage door with the control on the wall, not wanting his car to be spotted. He'd told Marietta he was going to a late meeting. There was no sense antagonizing her if this thing with Diana didn't work out.

There was no answer to his knock at the door. Ian knocked again, impatiently. He had expected Diana to be watching for him to drive up.

Ian let himself out of the garage and walked around the side of the house, peering in the windows. The kitchen was clearly deserted. It was also clean, with the exception of a teapot and a cup. That was a plus for Diana. Ian hated messy women. He walked around the side of the house and ducked under a trellis covered with bougainvillea, one of California's reasons for weekly gardeners. The damn stuff grew like a weed, and it had to be pruned constantly.

The drapes were open in the living room, but no one was there. Ian could see the bottle of Boodles sitting on the bar, along with two glasses and a jar of olives. Diana had definitely been expecting him. If he found her asleep in the bedroom, he wouldn't bother to tap on the window to wake her. He also wouldn't bother to contact her again. There were no second chances with Ian Jasper.

Diana's bedroom had French doors leading to a rear patio. Ian peered in through the sheer curtains and saw that the bed was unoccupied. Since Diana's car had been in the garage, he knew she was home. He'd take a look in the dressing room, and then he'd give up and go back to Marietta. She knew the drill, and she'd be waiting up for him.

The lights of Diana's dressing room were on, but it had an impossibly high window. Ian told himself he should give up and go home, but this whole thing bugged him. He'd never met a woman who hadn't greeted him enthusiastically, even when he was hours late. Perhaps something was wrong. Diana could have fallen, getting out of the shower, and injured herself.

A three-step utility ladder was leaning up against the side of the house. Ian felt a bit silly as he climbed it. He was going to a lot of trouble for a one-night stand, but Diana had really gotten under his skin. He couldn't help feeling that something was very wrong.

As Ian peeked into the dressing room, he

had to grip the sides of the window to keep from falling. Diana was sprawled in the chair at her dressing table and she was undoubtedly dead. Her face was bloated, and her tongue protruded from her mouth in a swollen lump. Ian retched and scrambled down from the ladder, almost falling in his haste to get away from the sight. It wasn't until he was back in his car again, squealing away from her beach house, that his heart rate began to return to normal and he could think clearly.

Ian pulled over to the side of the highway and lit a cigarette with shaking hands. He wanted to run, to forget what he'd seen, but that wasn't the smart thing to do. It was possible he'd been spotted at Diana's. Then he'd be a suspect in her murder. He had to call the police right away and tell them exactly what he'd seen through Diana's window.

Allison sat upright in bed, started out of a deep sleep. Her heart pounded wildly in her chest and her hands felt icy as she clasped them together. Was this the aftermath of a nightmare or had something else awakened her?

She listened intently, but there was nothing to alarm her. The neighborhood Pekingese was barking again, but that was normal. And she could hear the creaking of the roof as the Santa Ana wind blew in from the north. That was normal, too. Then she heard it, and she instinctively knew it was a repeat of the sound that had intruded on her sleep. There was someone moving around downstairs.

Allison reached for the revolver Tony kept in the drawer of the night table. He'd insisted that she learn how to use it for precisely this reason. With the gun in her hand, she quietly tiptoed to the top of the staircase and listened.

Another noise. It sounded like someone had opened the refrigerator door. Allison crept down the stair on silent feet and peeked around the corner of the kitchen doorway. Tony was there, making a huge sandwich at the counter.

"Tony! You scared me half to death!"

Tony whirled around and grinned as he saw his wife standing there with the gun. Sheepishly, he put his arms in the air. He was holding a loaf of Bunny Bread in one hand and a pickle in the other.

"Don't shoot, lady. I just came in to rip off your ham and Swiss. I'll make you a sandwich if you holster that weapon and sit down at the table."

Allison laughed and put the gun on top of the refrigerator. Suddenly she was ravenous, and it was no wonder. She hadn't felt much like eating alone. Dinner had been a can of water-pack tuna, eaten at the counter. She tossed Tony a loaf of deli rye for her sandwich and then she caught sight of the kitchen clock.

"It's after three in the morning? Oh, Tony . . . you must be exhausted. Were you at the office all this time?"

"Guilty." Tony hacked off a wedge of ham for Allison and plunked it on a piece of rye bread. "I've been working for hours, blocking out the first scene. I probably should have sacked out on the couch at the office to save time. I have to be back there at eight in the morning to meet Erik."

Allison felt a tiny flicker of doubt as she gazed at her husband. She'd called the office twice tonight, but no one had answered the phone. There were some people who could ignore a ringing phone and go right on working, but Tony was not one of them. Tony couldn't even walk past a ringing phone at a restaurant without picking it up. And tonight wasn't the first time she had called the office and failed to reach him. She knew it was a standard ploy for husbands to say they were working late at the office to cover their infidelities. Did Tony have a mistress? Allison had deliberately avoided confronting Tony in the past because she wasn't sure she could cope with the truth, but perhaps she was doing her husband an injustice. He might have a reasonable explanation of why he hadn't answered the phone.

"Did you take time out for dinner, Tony? I called the office but no one answered."

"Not really. I just had a quick fast-food burger. What time did you call?"

"Once at a little after seven and again at eight."

Tony thought fast. He'd been holed up in the motel room with the porn crew when Allison had called.

"You must have just missed me, honey. I stopped by the health club for a massage. My back was killing me. And then I caught a Whopper at Burger King. Was it anything important?"

"No." Allison shook her head. "I just wanted to talk, that's all."

"We'll talk now. I've got almost five hours before I have to leave again."

Tony slathered ketchup on her sandwich. Allison hated ketchup, but she decided not to object. Tony would insist on making her another sandwich, and that would take time.

Even though he'd claimed he had five hours, Allison knew that four was more accurate. It was three o'clock now, and he'd have to get up at seven. He needed at least a half hour to wake up, shower, and grab a fast cup of coffee before he started on the thirty-minute drive to the office. If they didn't get to bed soon, Tony's four hours would be cut down even more.

"Let's eat this fast and go right to bed," Allison suggested. "We can talk there."

"Talk?" Tony grinned at her. "Talk isn't exactly what I'd prefer to do in bed."

Allison subtracted another hour from Tony's projected sleep total, but she felt so relieved, she gave him a big smile. If Tony had spent the evening with another woman, he certainly wouldn't want to make love to her now. As all her suspicions faded away, she made a mental note to call Erik in the morning and tell him that Tony wouldn't be in until late.

Thirty minutes later they were in bed, but neither of them was happy. "I'm sorry, honey." Tony put his arm around Allison and hugged her tightly. "I guess I'm just too tired."

"Of course." Allison hugged him back. "Go to sleep, Tony. I love you."

"Love you, too."

As Tony's voice faded off into silence, Allison had all she could do to hold back her tears. She told herself she was being ridiculous. Tony was tired. It was nothing more than that. She'd be tired, too, if she worked the kind of hours Tony had been putting in lately. It didn't mean anything. He still thought of her as a desirable woman, didn't he?

Allison tried to relax and count her blessings. Most women would envy her position. Here she was in a cocoon of the finest silk sheets, lying in a king-size bed with matching bedroom furniture that had been especially designed for her. The master bedroom suite was lovely. The whole house was perfect, including the landscaped yards and the grotto swimming pool and spa. This house was a mansion compared to the modest suburban house where she'd grown up. She should be thankful and thrilled that Tony had chosen it for her. And every married couple had sexual problems once in a while, didn't they?

The branches of the huge palm tree outside their bedroom window were creating intricate patterns in the moonlight. The velvety blackness was studded with sparkling stars. It was precisely the kind of gorgeous, romantic California evening that was described in travel brochures, bringing tourists to Southern California in droves. Night-blooming jasmine mingled its musky perfume with the warm night breeze, and Allison took a deep breath before she closed her eyes. Lying here, beside her peacefully sleeping husband, Allison had never felt so rejected or so terribly alone.

11

Monday, July 19

It was exactly nine-thirty in the morning when Tony got into the elevator at the Schwartzvold Building. George Sturges was right behind him. He hollered for Tony to hold the doors while he quickly checked his mailbox. Then he dashed into the elevator, which was making little upward bumping motions, trying to defeat Tony's persistent hand on the door. George was wearing an orange warm-up suit, which made his normally ruddy face even redder.

"I hate jogging!" George winced as he reached out to press the button for his floor. "My boss took it up last month and now every junior partner has to jog. Give me a good laugh, Tony. Let's see your shirt."

Tony pulled open his jacket and let George read his shirt. This morning he was wearing a glaring red T-shirt with black lettering that said I MASH POTATOES WITH MY FEET.

"I don't get it, Tony."

"It's a comment on my ancestry, George. I'm half Irish and half Italian."

George was still laughing when he got out on the fifth floor. Tony got out with him. The elevator was making some strange grumbling sounds, and he didn't want to get stuck between floors. Ten minutes later after he'd trudged up the remaining eight flights of stairs, Tony arrived at his office to find Erik glued to the television.

"Sorry I'm late." Tony headed straight for the coffeepot. "Allison tricked me into sleeping an extra hour and the elevator started acting funny, so I climbed up from five. Did you find the papers I put on your desk? I got the first scene all blocked out."

Erik nodded, but Tony noticed that he didn't look happy.

"I saw it. We can talk about that later. Right now I want you to watch an interview I recorded."

Tony hurried to the kitchenette and came back with a steaming cup of coffee. Erik handed him a Winchell's sack, and Tony sat down on the couch and bit into a maple bar. It was slightly stale, but it tasted good anyway. He was starving. If he remembered correctly, his ham and Swiss was still sitting on the night table by his side of the bed. He had fallen asleep without eating it. He'd also fallen asleep before doing anything else. Tony's face flushed slightly as he remembered. He'd have to make some time for Allison. He loved her and he wanted her, but there never seemed to be time for anything but work.

"You didn't hear the news this morning?"

Erik was staring at him and Tony swallowed a mouthful of breakfast without chewing. "He struck again?"

"That's right." Erik nodded. "I've got the interview with Sam Ladera."

"What are you waiting for? Play it!"

As Tony watched the publicity stills of the newest victim, he gasped out loud. It was Diana Ellington! When they'd met with Lon Michaels, he'd suggested casting her as one of the victims in *Video Kill.*

"Whoa!" Tony reached out and stopped the recording. "You didn't mention our casting ideas to anyone, did you?"

"You mean about using Diana Ellington? No, I didn't. And I called Lon this morning. He doesn't remember telling anyone, either. How about you?"

"Not a word." Tony shook his head. "This is freaky, Erik. I don't like it."

Tony sat silently as he watched the rest of the interview. If the Video Killer was run-

194

ning true to form, there would be another murder disc to watch. He had to see Sam right away. Tony was positive it would be another Hitchcock segment. But which one? Suddenly Tony had it. Diana Ellington looked a lot like Barbara Leigh-Hunt in *Frenzy.*

"Well?" Erik looked glum as he switched off the television. "Looks like we've got the third scene, but it makes me sick, Tony. Do you want to start blocking it out?"

"Not just yet." Tony got up and headed for the door. "I think I'll try talking to Sam Ladera again. Maybe he'll give me some information this time."

"Let's talk about your blocking, first. Do you realize we haven't worked together on this thing for the past week?"

"I know." Tony sighed. "Just write up the first scene the way I've got it outlined, Erik. I'll be back in time to talk about the next one with you."

"No." Erik was firm. "We're supposed to be a partnership here. I've already written the first scene. It's on your desk."

"You have?" Tony was astonished. "But how could you write it without my blocking?"

"I blocked it myself when you didn't come through. And I think I did a good job."

"I'm sure you did." Tony backpedaled a bit. He could tell Erik was upset. "I'll tell you what, Erik . . . I'll sit right down and read it now if you'll run down and get me another maple bar. I'm starving this morning. And when you get back, we'll hash it out together."

The moment he heard the elevator doors close behind Erik, Tony picked up the phone. His first call was to Sam to arrange a meeting. The next was to his friend in Van Nuys to get him to hurry on that copy of his Hitchcock collection. Then he settled down to read Erik's first scene. It was good. Probably the best thing Erik had ever written. Erik had done a super job of portraying a fictional killer, but it wasn't the way the murder had actually happened. Now he had to figure out some tactful way to tell Erik that they couldn't use any of it.

Kathleen Brannigan, she'd taken her maiden name back after the divorce, stood in front of the glass wall that separated the editor-in-chief from the rows of desks that belonged to ordinary reporters. She could see her reflection in the glass, and she knew she looked especially good this morning. She had dressed for this interview in a dark green suit, molded perfectly to her size-8 figure. The saleslady at Prada had convinced her to part with almost three weeks' salary by telling her that this particular shade of green set off her eyes and highlighted her glistening auburn hair. There had been no way Katy could resist such persuasion when she knew that the saleslady had probably assisted such luminaries as Meryl Streep and Anne Hathaway in this very dressing room. It was a well-known fact that scores of famous women in Los Angeles passed through the distinctive glass doors on Rodeo Drive to shop for their extensive wardrobes. The clothes inside were expensive and chic.

Mr. Morgan looked up and smiled at Katy. It was well known that he appreciated a good-looking woman, but he didn't give promotions on that basis. He still thought his female reporters should stick to society, food, and fashion. He was usually fair but not especially tactful. If Bill Morgan thought a reporter had turned in a sloppy piece, everyone in earshot knew it. That was the reason Julie Thompson, Katy's closest friend on the paper, had nicknamed him "Billy Goat Gruff."

This morning, when Katy had checked her mailbox and read the summons to appear in Bill Morgan's office, she'd been terrified that she would be fired. Julie had calmed her fears. If Billy Goat intended to fire Katy, he'd do it at her desk, in front of all the other reporters. Katy had been at the paper long enough to know that.

Then Julie had advanced her theory, and it had been Katy's turn to laugh. Julie had been sure that Billy Goat was going to put her on a new assignment, something to do with the Video Killer.

"Me?" Katy had been dumbfounded. "That's impossible, Julie. I've been assigned to the health section for five years now. There's no way he'll assign me to anything more important than booster shots."

"Oh no?" Julie had retorted. "His hotshots are coming up empty-handed on the Video Killer story. And it's your ex who won't talk to the press. I think Billy Goat figures you've still got some pull with Sam."

"But I don't!"

"He doesn't know that. Right now Billy Goat's in a panic. I'm so sure I'm right, I'll wager lunch. If Billy Goat fires you, I'll take you to lunch at Spago. And if he assigns you to the Video Killer story, you take me."

Katy had agreed after a glance at her bank balance. Lunch was expensive at Spago. Now her heart was beating fast as she opened the door and stepped into the glass-walled cubicle. If Mr. Morgan asked her to work on the Video Killer story, she'd come right out and tell him that she and Sam weren't even on speaking terms. She would not, under any circumstances, crawl to Sam for a story. And she wouldn't try to trick him into giving her information, either. She had her integrity.

"Katy. It's always a pleasure to see you." Bill Morgan gestured toward the straight-backed chair in front of his desk. "Is everything all right in the health section?"

"Just fine, Mr. Morgan." Katy sat down and tried to look more poised than she felt.

"Good. How far ahead are you?"

Katy thought fast. "Unless bubonic plague strikes the rich and famous, I'm approximately a month ahead."

"Good. I'm pulling you for a month, Katy. I need you to work on a special project. Let me tell you up front that if you bring in something good, I'll promote you to the city desk."

Katy felt her knees start to shake. Could Julie's far-fetched idea be right?

"I'm talking about the Video Killer story, Katy. Since you've met quite a few members of the police force socially, it might be easier for you to get them to open up a little. Of course, I wouldn't want you to compromise any relationship you may still have with your ex-husband, but it seems to me you have an advantage over my regular crime boys."

"Oh, Mr. Morgan, I . . . I . . ."

Mr. Morgan leaned forward and stared straight into her eyes, and suddenly all Katy's resolve about honesty and integrity evaporated. The city desk. He wanted to move her to the city desk. She'd been trying to break into real news for years!

"I know it's asking a lot, Katy, and I can understand why you wouldn't want to use your former status for the purpose of getting the story. But some paper out there's going to get the scoop. And I want that paper to be us."

Katy nodded. She didn't trust herself to speak. Mr. Morgan was offering her a shot at the big-time, and there was no way she could turn it down on simple scruples. She'd go down to the police station right after lunch. Everyone said that Sam was still in love with her, so it should be easy to win his confidence again.

"Well?"

Katy managed to keep calm. She was wise enough to know that Mr. Morgan was dangling a carrot in front of her nose. This was the time for negotiation, and Katy knew how to play that game.

"If I get the story, would my promotion to the city desk mean the usual salary hike?"

"Of course."

"And I'm free to work on this assignment any way I choose as long as I get the goods?"

"Absolutely."

"Fine, Mr. Morgan." Katy smiled genuinely for the first time since the interview had begun. "It's a deal. I'll turn in my extra columns and get started right away."

Katy waited until she got inside the ladies room before she let out a whoop of excitement. She knew the only reason Mr. Morgan had given her this opportunity was because she was Sam's ex, but lots of people moved up the ladder by using their connections.

She dumped her purse out on the counter, found her cell phone, and used it to call Spago. And she didn't even wince when she had to use Sam's name to secure those last-minute reservations. Then, when her hands had stopped shaking and she thought she looked solemn enough, she went up to the third floor and stopped at Julie's desk.

"I'm through. Let's go to lunch now." Katy waited a beat for the tension to build in Julie's face. Then she laughed and bent down to whisper in her ear. "It's on me!"

Erik sat in the chair across from Tony's desk and glared at him. "Are you saying I did a bad job?"

"No, of course not. It's very well written, Erik, a lot better than I could have done. But it's, well, it's just not right!"

"What the hell does *that* mean?"

Tony lit a cigarette and took a deep puff to stall for time. He knew he was doing a bad job of explaining things to Erik, but it couldn't be helped. Erik would just have to write the scene over the way it had really happened. It was critical to the Video Killer story.

"Look, Erik, your way just isn't realistic enough."

"My way isn't realistic?" Erik's mouth dropped open. "Jesus, Tony! I read your blocking, and your killer's straight from central casting in that phony executioner's hood. And to make it even more hokey, you have him doing Hitchcock's shower scene. You think *that's* realistic?"

"Calm down, Erik. I see your point." Tony did his best to pacify Erik. "Look, your way would be perfect under any other circumstances, but I know he wore the hood. And

I also know that the first murder was a *Psycho* remake."

The moment the words were out of Tony's mouth, the expression on Erik's face changed. "Good God, Tony! Did you actually get a look at that murder video?"

Tony thought fast. He'd have to talk his way out of this one. "Don't be an asshole, Erik. Sam's turned down everyone who asked for a private viewing, and that includes his boss, the chief of police. What makes you think he'd show it to me?"

"I notice you avoided my question, Tony." Erik looked suspicious. "Give me a simple yes or no. Did you or did you not see that murder video?"

Tony sighed. Erik was pinning him down like a lawyer. "Okay, Erik, I'll give you a solemn Italian oath. I swear on my mother's grave that I didn't see it."

"Fine, Tony, except your mother doesn't have a grave. She's still alive."

"Yeah, well . . ." Tony looked sheepish. "If my mother were dead, I'd still swear on her grave. Now, can we drop this idiotic cross-examination and get to work?"

"Not until you've answered my questions. If you didn't see the murder video, where did you get all this inside stuff about the killer?"

This time Tony had his answer ready. "I'll tell you, but you have to promise not to laugh."

"All right. I promise."

"I was sitting here last night staring at the computer screen. I knew I had to block out that scene and nothing was coming. You know the feeling?"

Erik nodded.

"So I decided to try to think like the Video Killer. I got out that picture of Sharee Lyons and asked myself what made her special. Why would I choose this particular girl? Then it came to me. She was an actress and she looked just like Janet Leigh. And the press reported she was killed in the shower. That's when I came up with using *Psycho.*"

"You didn't think the whole thing was far-fetched?"

"Sure I did. But then I pulled the other file, the one with the picture of Tammara Welles. Don't you think she looks like Laura Elliott?"

"Who's Laura Elliott?"

"The actress Hitchcock killed off in *Strangers on a Train.*"

Erik frowned. "I don't think I saw it."

"Well, I did. And take my word for it, the resemblance is there."

"How about Diana Ellington?"

"The first murder in *Frenzy.* She's a dead ringer for Barbara Leigh-Hunt, if you'll pardon the pun."

Erik winced. Tony's sense of humor had been pretty insensitive lately. "So you want us to write a Video Killer whose motivation is remaking Hitchcock?"

"Why not? It's a hell of a gimmick, even if I'm wrong. Now, can we please write the damn thing the way I've got it blocked out? As a personal favor to me?"

Erik looked surprised. Tony never asked for favors. "Well . . . okay. I'll give in to your superior intuition this time. But get the blocking done ahead of time from now on. I worked for almost a week on that scene, and now we can't use any of it."

"I will. Why don't you start on it and I'll see what I can dig up on Diana Ellington's murder. If I don't get back before you leave, put what you've done on my desk."

"You're leaving *now*? You just got here, Tony!"

"I realize that, Erik, but there are a couple of things I've got to do. Allison's mother is worse and I promised to stop by at the convalescent center."

The irritated expression on Erik's face was immediately replaced by one of concern.

"I'm sorry, Tony. Does it look bad?"

"It doesn't look good. I'll give you a call and fill you in. And Erik? I promise I'll have the other two scenes blocked out by the time you need them."

"Don't worry about it, Tony. I'll be fine if you can stay just one scene ahead of me. And tell Allison . . . oh, hell. What can you tell someone at a time like this?"

"Chin up, keep a stiff upper lip, and things will look better in the morning, I guess. None of them do any good."

"Right." Erik nodded. "Good luck, Tony. Remember that Allison's mother has rallied lots of times before."

As Tony got into the elevator, he realized that he should have been an actor. He'd convinced Erik with that story about Allison's mother, but he didn't feel good about it. That was twice he'd lied to his partner in less than five minutes. He really wanted to go back and level with Erik, but he couldn't. There was his promise to Sam to keep, and he was already ten minutes late to see the third murder disc.

Allison smiled as she put down the phone. It was her first smile of the morning since she'd heard about the Video Killer's third victim, Diana Ellington. Allison had met her in an acting workshop once. Thank

206

goodness the call from Doris Stanley had been good news, not bad. Allison didn't know how much more bad news she could take.

The head nurse had been cheerful. Allison's mother was doing very well this morning. She'd even eaten a large breakfast. The chemotherapy seemed to be having a positive effect, and since Dr. Naiman would be running some tests today, could Allison skip her regular visit and come in early tomorrow instead?

Naturally, Allison had agreed. It was nice of Miss Stanley to call and tell her. But now the day stretched out with nothing to do except crochet or watch television. She supposed she could call one of her old friends and suggest lunch, but she didn't really feel up to socializing. And Tony was busy. He'd told her he'd probably be home very late tonight. Allison glanced at the kitchen calendar, but there was nothing that she had to do today. Then she noticed the date and gasped. Today was their wedding anniversary.

Allison grabbed her purse and car keys and ran out the door. She had to shop for a present for Tony. Luckily, she'd seen the perfect gift in a boutique not far from the house. It was a beautiful gold cigarette lighter with a little notch on top. When the end of a cigarette was inserted in the notch, the lighter flamed automatically. Since Tony was always complaining about lighting a cigarette when he was using the computer and then getting his fingers back on the wrong keys, it would be perfect for him. Allison still remembered the time he'd typed a whole scene in *Free Fire* with his right hand off by one row and they'd spent hours deciphering words like *bpdu cpimt* and *casia;tu* and *jamd gremade*.

In less than an hour, Allison was back at the house. The boutique had engraved the lighter with the phrase Allison had chosen. YOU LIGHT UP MY LIFE. Tony would groan at her syrupy sentiment, but she knew he'd love it anyway. Now she'd call Erik at the office to see if Tony had mentioned anything about their anniversary.

The phone rang seven times before Erik answered. He sounded harassed.

"Hi, Erik. It's Allison. I hope I didn't catch you in the middle of something."

"You did, but that's okay. I was just looking for something on Tony's desk and it took me a while to uncover the phone."

Allison laughed as she imagined the mess that Tony's desk must be in. Both Erik and Tony were lax when it came to filing. Before her mother had gotten so sick, she'd gone every Monday to help them. The papers were probably knee-high by now.

"Listen carefully, Erik. I'm about to make you an offer you can't refuse."

"Oh? What's that?"

"I'll drive in to do all the filing on Monday if you guys will buy me a hot dog. The only people I've talked to lately are nurses and doctors, and I'm sick of it all."

"I can understand that." Erik's voice was warm and reassuring. "But there's no need to bribe me with the filing, Allison. I'll buy you lunch anytime."

"Then Monday's okay?"

"That's fine with me, but Tony's tied up on Monday. He's having lunch with someone at the studio."

"You're free?"

"I'm free."

"Good. I'll come in anyway, we can go to lunch, and then we'll meet Tony back at the office later. Is he there, Erik? I need to ask him a question."

"He's left already, Allison." Erik sounded puzzled. "How's your mother?"

"She's doing much better. I talked to the head nurse this morning and she's responding well to the chemotherapy. They're running more tests today, but things look better than they have in a long time."

"That's wonderful, Allison. Tony was all upset about it this morning. So you're going to see her this afternoon?

"No. They've asked for no visitors. I'll have to wait until tomorrow."

There was a long silence, and Allison could hear the tinny sound of another conversation bleeding into their line. It was so faint she couldn't make out the words. Finally Erik spoke again.

"What's going on, Allison? Tony told me your mother was worse and he had to go visit her."

"But that's not true, Erik! I talked to the head nurse not more than an hour ago. I don't understand why Tony would tell you . . ." Allison stopped in midsentence and laughed. "Oh, now I get it."

"Get what?"

"Today's our wedding anniversary, Erik."

"Your anniversary?" Erik felt his anxiety slide away. He'd blown the surprise Tony had planned for Allison last year by saying the wrong thing over the phone and now it seemed he'd done it again this year. "I'm sorry I said anything, Allison. Now I know why Tony gave me that story."

Allison laughed. "He's probably on his way home right now. I'd better hurry and make myself pretty. Where shall I meet you for lunch on Monday?"

"We could go somewhere nice."

"I'd rather go somewhere not-so-nice. You're always bragging about your little neighborhood finds. Take me to one that makes a great hamburger."

Erik thought for a moment. "Donny's has great hamburgers if you're up for grease."

Allison laughed. "Grease is one of my favorite foods. Does Donny's have chili?"

"Four alarm, maybe five."

"That settles it. Tell me where and when, and I'll meet you."

"Okay. One o'clock at Donny's Bar and Grill at the corner of Fairfax and La Cienega. You can recognize it by all the graffiti on the wall. And, Allison? You'd better wait in the car for me. Donny's isn't exactly a restaurant. It's more like, I'm not sure of the polite way to say it."

"A meat rack?"

"What's that?"

Allison giggled. "Sometimes I wonder about you, Erik. You've been out here for years, but you're still a Minnesota farm boy at heart. A meat rack is another name for a pickup joint."

"Nice phrase. I like it. Donny's is definitely a meat rack. Most of the women in there look like streetwalkers, but I can't tell for sure with the styles right now. For all I know they could be investment bankers. Uh, Allison? Now that I think about it, maybe Donny's isn't such a good idea after all. It's not exactly your kind of place."

"Don't you back out now!" Allison scolded him. "Donny's sounds exciting, and I promise not to go in until you get there. Just look around the parking lot for the lady with the rose in her teeth."

"You wouldn't!"

"You'll just have to wait and see."

A few more minutes of light banter and Allison hung up. It was almost twelve-thirty, and Tony could be home any minute. She was smiling as she raced to the closet to put on her very best outfit. She wanted to look nice for Tony's surprise. Whatever it might be.

12

"Everything looks fine, Erik." Dr. Trumbull wrote a notation on Erik's chart and looked up with a smile. "Your lungs are clear . . . this time."

Erik smiled back. He liked his new doctor. One of the things that really burned him about going to the V.A. hospital was the way they kept switching his doctors. It was a lottery, but this time he'd lucked out. Dr. Trumbull was young and he didn't mince around with medical terminology. He called Q fever by its common name, not some multisyllabic medical term that no one but a doctor could pronounce.

"So how are the headaches?"

"Worse." Erik didn't mince around, either. "The pills you gave me aren't working."

"And the blackout periods?"

"Just as bad, but the psychiatrist told me not to worry. You've got his report there, don't you?"

Dr. Trumbull nodded. "He seems to think that the blackouts are your way of dealing with the trauma you experienced in the war. Some of the front-line vets I've treated have flashbacks and nightmares that turn them into basket cases for months at a time. You have a bad headache with a blackout, and you're back on your feet again the next morning. You're lucky, Erik. It could be much worse."

Erik nodded, but he didn't feel lucky. In fact, he felt another headache coming on. It was a good thing he'd finished up his work at the office.

"Let's try something different for the headaches." Dr. Trumbull pulled a packaged sheet of pills from his desk. "There's a new drug on the market they want me to test. How do you feel about becoming a statistic?"

"I'll try almost anything. Does it have any side effects?"

"You mean like gaining two hundred pounds?" Dr. Trumbull smiled as he handed Erik a sheaf of papers to sign. "We haven't found any side effects so far, but the test group has been pretty small."

"I'll try it." Erik signed his name to the papers and exchanged them for the packet of pills. Then he noticed the name of the drug. "Mezo . . . what?"

"Mezopropathalomine. I call them zonkers because that's what they do. Take one every time you feel a headache coming on. It'll knock you out in about thirty minutes and keep you out for an hour or more. It should block out all the pain and leave you rested. Now, run down to the lab and do the drill for them and come in to see me in two weeks."

The lab didn't take long. Erik rolled up his sleeve for a veteran nurse who looked a little like Louise Fletcher in *One Flew Over the Cuckoo's Nest* and let her take his blood pressure. Then there were the usual blood and urine samples. The nurse was efficient, and within ten minutes Erik was through. He left the building and took a deep breath of the air outside. He hated the smell of a hospital. Then he walked quickly to the parking lot and retrieved his car. He had to hurry if he wanted to beat the traffic on the freeway.

As Erik pulled out of the lot and drove past the beautifully kept lawns, he tried not to glance toward the psych building on his right. Its locked wards were directly across the quadrangle from the Wadsworth Theater. Erik had seen enough of the Wadsworth to last him a lifetime. He had stared at its entrance for a solid month from a barred window in the psych building.

The strain of a broken marriage and a son with serious medical problems had taken its predictable toll. Erik had managed to hold himself together until the divorce was final and he'd sent Jamie off to Pine Ridge. Then he had suffered what the doctors at the V.A. hospital had called acute stress syndrome. The memories of those painful months, spent in the confines of a locked room, were something that Erik was determined never to experience again. For months after he'd been released with a clean bill of health, he'd worried that Daniele would find out about his breakdown and wage a custody battle, but he'd eventually realized that his ex-wife wasn't remotely interested in Jamie. In all the years that Jamie had been at Pine Ridge, she'd never even called to ask about his progress.

The San Diego Freeway was already crowded, but Erik hopped on anyway. At least it was moving. It took him thirty minutes to navigate the six-mile stretch to Culver City, and several times he fought the urge to get off and take Sepulveda, which roughly paralleled the freeway. Whenever he'd taken Sepulveda as an alternate route in the past, he'd always seemed to get behind cars turning left, across traffic. A five-cycle wait at a stoplight was much more frustrating than crawling along on the freeway.

As he turned in on Sunshine Lane, Erik pulled straight up to the guard kiosk. The residents' entrance was still blocked off with white-and-orange sawhorses. Norma waved and pressed the button to raise the gate.

"The gate's still broken?"

"Nope." Norma grinned. "It's broken again. They fixed it this morning, but some lady in a Cadillac drove right through it."

The neighborhood kids were out playing ball on the street, and Erik stopped to let them finish pitching before he drove through. The boy at bat was about Jamie's age. Perhaps they could become friends when Jamie came home.

It took Erik less than five minutes to park his car, look through the mail, and feed Al, who'd obviously spent a grueling morning holding down the rug. There was nothing in the refrigerator that looked interesting enough to eat, so he called out for a pizza. Erik had the delivery boy at Chris's Pizza well trained. He knew that the word *tip* was an acronym for "To Insure Promptness." Since Erik had the reputation for tipping generously, his pizzas were always delivered piping hot, just out of the oven.

Erik poured himself a beer and sat down in front of the television set to wait for his food to arrive. Al padded in and jumped up to nestle on his lap. The afternoon sun streamed into the living room, and the scene was domestic and tranquil. He'd just gotten a new medication for his headaches, Jamie was showing improvement, and the first scene of the screenplay was practically finished. Erik tried to convince himself that everything was fine. There was no reason to sit here feeling like the other shoe was about to drop.

Katy checked her appearance in the rear-view mirror and added a touch of blusher to her cheeks. Sam would like her new suit. Green was his favorite color. And she was wearing her hair long and loose, the way he'd always preferred it. It would be difficult to see Sam again and even more difficult to ask for a favor, but it would be worth it in the end. She had decided to come right out and tell Sam the truth. She'd say that Billy Goat had assigned her to the Video Killer's story, that it was critical to her career at the paper, and that she'd be very grateful for any help he could give her.

"Mrs. Ladera!" Andy Mertens, the desk

sergeant, looked up as she approached, and his florid face crinkled in a broad smile of greeting. "What are you doing here?"

"Hi, Andy." Katy smiled back, even though she had to squelch the impulse to say that she was no longer Mrs. Ladera. "I came to see Sam, if he's available."

"Well, he said no more visitors, but . . ." Andy hesitated. The chief had left strict orders, but Katy wasn't exactly a visitor. And everyone in the department knew he'd been in a blue funk since his divorce. He'd just started to act halfway human again when this Video Killer thing hit. Maybe seeing her would be good for the chief.

"Hang on a couple of minutes, Mrs. Ladera. There's some lady reporter with him right now, but she won't last long. He's already kicked out three today. Everybody wants a story on the Video Killer, and the chief's getting real touchy about it. Personally, I think he's about ready to blow his stack, and you know what that means."

Katy nodded. Sam's temper was slow to build, but when it reached the point of no return, there was always a fiery explosion. She certainly didn't want to be the one who pushed him over the edge with her questions about the Video Killer. Perhaps it would be smart to think of an alternative plan.

"I'm guessing it won't be more than five minutes." Andy gestured toward Sam's office door. The voices inside were growing louder. "Would you like a cup of coffee while you're waiting?"

"No, thank you, Andy. I'm well acquainted with the kind of coffee you make here. It hasn't gotten any better, has it?"

"Not really." Andy grinned, showing the gap between his front teeth. Just then the door to Sam's office opened and a pretty blonde rushed out. Katy recognized her immediately. It was Jessica Clarke, the award-winning syndicated columnist. She was frowning and her face was very red. She hurried past Katy, noticed her notebook, and turned to speak to her.

"If you're here for a story, you'd better forget it. He almost bit my head off!"

"I'm not here for a story." Katy smiled sweetly. "I'm just his ex-wife."

"Ex-wife?"

Katy nodded.

"Well, I can certainly understand why you divorced him. That man is an absolute bear!"

As soon as she left, Andy stood up. "I'll tell the chief you're here, Mrs. Ladera. And don't worry. I'll calm him down a little before I send you in."

Andy was gone for a full five minutes, time enough for Katy to come up with a good cover story. She'd wanted to be up-front with Sam, but this wasn't the time for honesty. If he found out she was here for a scoop on the Video Killer, he'd be sure to explode. Finally the office door opened and Andy motioned to her.

There was a smile on Katy's face as she passed through the doorway, but she quickly sobered when she caught sight of Sam. He looked awful. Her first instinct was to rush to put her arms around him, but that was crazy. They were divorced, and Sam wouldn't let her hug him anyway.

"Hello, Sam."

"Katy. What can I do for you?"

Katy stood, waiting for him to motion toward a chair, but he didn't, so she sat down anyway. He was as stubborn as always. This was going to be more difficult than she'd thought.

"I've got a problem, Sam, and I was hoping you'd help. Billy Goat gave me a new assignment today and —"

Before she could finish her sentence, Sam interrupted her. His voice was sharp and impersonal. Did he really hate her that much?

"If it has anything to do with the Video Killer, you can turn right around and leave."

"It doesn't!" Katy felt a telltale blush spread over her cheeks. "It's a Sunday supplement thing on lady cops. Look, Sam, I know the only reason I got this assignment is because I'm your ex-wife. Billy figured the connection would get me in. I don't like this any better than you do, but if you'll let me do a couple of interviews, I'll be out of your hair in no time."

"Lady cops?"

"Right. Please, Sam? I'll be really embarrassed if I have to go back and tell Billy that you kicked me out of your office."

"You're sure Billy didn't send you to fish for anything else? Like information about the Video Killer?"

"Oh, Sam!" Katy put on her best injured expression. "You know Billy. He'd never send a woman on an important assignment like that!"

"I guess that's true." Sam smiled slightly. "Are you still doing the health section, Katy?"

"Yes, but you're the only one who knows how difficult that is. I still can't spell *penicillin.*"

This time Sam's smile was fuller. "I always thought the arts were more your style. What happened to that sculpture class you were going to take?"

"The same thing that happened to the painting class. I bought all the supplies and then I chickened out. That reminds me, is all that unused canvas still in the storage locker?"

"It's still there. Do you want it?"

"No, I just wondered, that's all. How about the potter's wheel and the loom?"

"They're right next to the folk dance costumes and the classical guitar."

Katy looked up at Sam sheepishly and was relieved to find that he was still smiling.

"There's ten years of my life in that storage locker, Sam. All the projects I started and didn't finish."

"Yep. Just like our marriage."

"Come on, Sam. I . . ." A lump rose in Katy's throat and she blinked back tears. This was ridiculous. The last thing she wanted was for Sam to see her crying.

"Sorry, Katy." Sam was the first to speak. "I guess I just miss you sometimes."

"I . . . I miss you, too, sometimes."

Katy blinked hard. The tears were still threatening. This was precisely what she wanted to avoid. Thinking about her marriage with Sam always made her cry, and part of her wished for a reconciliation. She told herself it was impossible. If they hadn't worked out their problems in ten years, starting over wouldn't accomplish much. She was better off alone, wasn't she?

"Well?" Katy stood up and deliberately put a smile on her face. "What do you say, Sam? Do I get to interview those lady cops?"

"Sure." Sam stood up, too. "I'll set up something for you right away if you want to start this afternoon."

"Thanks, Sam." They were walking to the door, and without thinking, Katy reached up to hug him. She felt Sam's surprise and then his arms tightened around her. It felt good. Very good. Katy stepped back quickly before it could feel any better and reminded herself that this was business. Newspaper business.

"Ask Andy to get you settled in one of the interrogation rooms. I'll see who's available."

"Thanks again, Sam." Katy paused at the open doorway. Then she reached up quickly and touched the side of his face. "You look like Stallone again, Sam. Please get some sleep."

When Tony turned on Ventura Boulevard,

he was whistling. So far, everything was going great. He'd spent an hour in Sam's office, going over the new murder disc, and he was definitely right about the Hitchcock thing. Last night's victim, Diana Ellington, was a ringer for Barbara Leigh-Hunt. And the segment had definitely been patterned on *Frenzy,* right down to the tie that the killer had used to strangle her. The murder disc had been chilling, even more so than Hitchcock's scene, and in Tony's opinion, the actual filming had been brilliant. He'd left Sam with the promise to hurry on the list of Hitchcock's victims, and now he was heading home to enlist Allison's help. She didn't know it yet, but she was going to be his research assistant. It would be easy to convince her. She adored Hitchcock movies.

Tony pulled up in a loading zone and rushed into a small shop on Ventura. The sign on the window read PATTI'S POPCORN. Allison was a sucker for popcorn and he'd take her a little gift along with the movies.

"May I help you, sir?"

A pretty brunette was manning the counter. She looked good enough to be a movie star. Most native Californians did. Tony had once heard a theory about that. Their mothers had been the prettiest girls from cities all over the country who had come out here to break into the movies. Naturally, there weren't enough roles for everyone, and some of the pretty would-be actresses married the handsome boys who had also come out here to break into show business. They'd had pretty babies together. Now the pretty babies had grown into a whole new generation of gorgeous young adults, and that's why Californians were so good-looking. The whole thing sounded a little like the old story about why firemen wore red suspenders, but this girl certainly seemed to lend credence to the theory.

"I need an assortment of popcorn." Tony looked at the display case. There were twenty-six varieties. "Uh, I guess your twelve-pack will do."

"Certainly, sir." The girl pulled out a carton with twelve dividers. It looked like a giant hat box. "Which flavors would you like?"

"Chocolate, butterscotch, cherry, lemon . . . what's that blue one?"

"Blueberry, sir. It's our new flavor of the month."

"Okay. Throw some of that in. And make up the rest with your favorites, all except the licorice. There's no way I can eat black popcorn."

The girl laughed. "I know what you mean. It looks like the stuff we used to pop over the campfire. Would you like this gift wrapped, sir?"

Tony nodded, and watched the girl wrap the whole package in red cellophane and top it with a big red bow. Allison would love it. Then he handed the girl his charge card and hoped Visa hadn't canceled it yet.

Fifteen minutes later Tony pulled into his driveway and opened the garage door. Allison's car was parked inside, and that meant she was back from visiting her mother. He got out of his car and didn't bother to lower the door. He couldn't spend much time here with Allison. He had to be at the motel in less than an hour to work on the porn movie.

"Hi, honey, I'm home!"

Tony walked into the living room to find Allison sitting on the sofa, watching a talk show on television. She was dressed in a blue dress that looked new to him until he remembered that he'd given it to her for Christmas last year.

"Oh, Tony!" Allison jumped up and raced across the room to hug him. "You had Erik completely fooled with that story about visiting Mom, but I caught on right away. I knew you were planning a surprise for our

227

anniversary. I'm so glad you didn't forget."

Tony thought fast. His anniversary? Uh-oh! It was a good thing he'd stopped by to pick up the popcorn.

"Of course I didn't forget. I've got two presents for you this year. Unwrap the big one first."

Tony grinned as Allison tore the cellophane off the popcorn. She looked inside the box and laughed.

"I love it! What's that blue kind?"

"The girl said it was blueberry. They're all labeled. Now open the box, honey. Except I'd better warn you that I have an ulterior motive for this present."

"Hitchcock films?" Allison's face lit up in excitement as she read the titles on the DVDs. "This looks like a complete collection. What's the ulterior motive, darling?"

"One of the theater arts alumni called me a couple of months ago. They're compiling information about Hitchcock for a project and I promised to make them a list of plot synopses and the names of the actresses who played Hitchcock's female victims. They sent the DVDs by messenger this morning and, well, I don't have time to do it. I thought maybe you might . . . ?"

"Of course I will!" Allison drew out *The Trouble with Harry* and gave Tony a radiant

228

smile. "Do you think we could make copies of these before we give them back? I've always wanted a Hitchcock collection, and there are a couple of films here I've never seen."

"That's your present, Allison. I already arranged it with them. You can keep the DVDs when you're through. There's only one hitch. They're in a real hurry for that list."

"How much of a hurry?"

"A couple of weeks. What do you say, honey? Can you do it?"

Allison counted the DVDs and then she smiled. "Of course I can do it. I was just sitting here wishing for something to do. It's the best anniversary present you've ever given me, honey. Now go open yours. It's that little box on the table."

Tony unwrapped the small package and grinned when he saw what was inside. It was a new lighter, and it couldn't have come at a better time. He'd lost his last one somewhere between the parking lot and the office, and he hadn't been able to find it.

"See that little notch? You just hold your cigarette there, and it lights automatically. I thought it would be perfect when you're working on the computer."

Tony got out a cigarette and tried it. It worked perfectly. Then he read the inscription and laughed.

"*You light up my life?* Oh, Allison, that's terrible!"

"I know." Allison giggled. "It was the worst pun I could think of. Do you like it?"

"I love it!" Tony swept her into his arms and kissed her. "I just wish I could take the night off so we could go somewhere fancy for dinner, but I have to get back to work. Alan's uncle won't cough up a contract until we do some more work on the movie."

"It's all right, Tony." Allison hid her disappointment behind a smile. "Thanks to your present I have something to do. How long can you stay before you have to go back to the office?"

"I've got forty minutes, maybe forty-five."

"Then I know just what we can do to celebrate!"

Allison was about to suggest they hop into bed when she remembered Tony's failure last night. Her sexy smile faded and she raced to think of an alternative. Tony's problem last night had been simple exhaustion, she was sure of it, but he wasn't any more rested today. The last thing she wanted to do was risk another failure.

"You sit here and relax." Allison dropped a kiss on the tip of Tony's nose. "I'll be right back with a surprise."

It took Allison less than five minutes in the kitchen, but when she came back Tony's eyes were closed and he was snoring softly. She almost hated to wake him, but she wanted to give him some sort of a celebration before he had to go back to work.

"Tony? Darling?"

Allison spoke softly, but Tony's eyes opened immediately. He looked startled, then delighted to see her.

"Must'a dozed off. Sorry, honey."

Allison smiled as she set down the platter she was carrying and let Tony pull her into his arms. After a long, wonderful moment, she pulled free.

"I made your favorite sandwiches. Bunny bread, marshmallow fluff, and chocolate sauce. And Gelson's found that red cream soda you're always talking about. They still make it in a couple of bottling plants in the South."

"Honey, this looks like heaven!" Tony lifted a sandwich and took a big bite. A little of the chocolate sauce dribbled down his chin, but he caught it before it dripped on his T-shirt.

Allison picked up her own sandwich and munched. She'd cheated. Her sandwich was on Bunny Bread so it looked the same from the outside, but it had peanut butter in place of the marshmallow fluff and strawberry jam as a substitute for the chocolate sauce.

It took only a few minutes to finish their sandwiches. Then Tony picked up his bottle of red cream soda and pulled her to her feet.

"There's an old Southern tradition with drinks like these. You have to finish the last swallow in bed."

Allison grinned as he led her to the bedroom. "But, Tony, you've never even been in the South."

"Close enough." Tony turned her around and unzipped her dress. "We live in Southern California."

Allison's smile grew wider and wider as Tony undressed her. It reached radiant proportions when he took off his own clothes and joined her in bed. She'd been a silly fool to worry about sex. Tony was about to prove that they didn't have any problems at all.

13

Sunday, July 25

Christie Jensen put on her very best smile as she spotted Mr. Brother walking up to the ticket booth. This afternoon he was dressed in blue denim, and the effect was wonderful. He looked sporty and casual, but elegant just the same. His jacket was stylishly cut and matched his pants perfectly, not like the new-looking jackets and old faded jeans most men wore. His shirt was a muted blue, and Christie realized she'd seen this particular outfit before, probably in the window of one of the exclusive men's shops.

"Hi, Mr. Brother. I didn't expect to see you today. We're showing reruns."

"I noticed that, Christie. What happened to the *R*'s in *Rear Window?*"

Mr. Brother smiled and gestured toward the marquee. The big plastic letters spelled out PEAP WINDOW — HITCHCOCK.

"Oh, that." Christie looked apologetic.

"We have a lot of trouble with the letters, Mr. Brother. They break. I heard Steve say he doesn't have a single good *R* left. They've all turned into *P*'s."

"Then you had better not screen *Rope* until you buy new letters. Everyone will think it's a film about the Catholic Church."

It took Christie a second, but she got it. She laughed and Mr. Brother smiled. Joking with him made her heart do little flip-flops under her new red sweater. Would today be the day he finally asked her for a date? She crossed the fingers of one hand and just as quickly uncrossed them again when she realized it was a ridiculously childish gesture. Mr. Brother always threw her completely off-balance, unlike the other men she dated.

As Mr. Brother took out his wallet to pay for his ticket, Christie noticed the label on the inside of his jacket. It had perfectly embroidered initials for Dolce & Gabbana. Christie had priced a shirt for her father last Christmas, but it had been much more than she could afford. She'd ended up with the usual bottle of aftershave lotion instead.

Mr. Brother slipped a five-dollar bill through the glass cutout, and Christie's fingers brushed his accidentally as she took the money. She jerked back and a blush stained her cheeks. What if Mr. Brother thought she'd done that on purpose, but he didn't seem to have noticed. At least he was still smiling. Her hands shook slightly as she punched up the sale on the computer and the ticket printed out.

"Here's your change, Mr. Brother." Christie pushed a dollar and two quarters back through the cutout, followed by the computerized ticket. "Enjoy the movie. Everyone says it's wonderful. Have you seen *Rear Window* before?"

At first Christie thought Mr. Brother wasn't going to answer. He had already turned away toward the entrance, but he took a step back when he saw that there was no one in line behind him.

"I've seen it many times. What do you think of it, Christie?"

It was her chance! The chance she'd been waiting for! Christie was so nervous, she was almost tongue-tied.

"Well, to be completely honest, I haven't seen it yet. I have to stay in the booth until after the feature starts, and then I'm supposed to help out at the concession counter. Do you think I should see it?"

"Definitely. It's an interesting piece of work if you ignore the moral implications."

Christie nodded. She didn't have the foggiest idea what Mr. Brother was talking about, but at least he was talking. And to her!

"It sounds wonderful, Mr. Brother."

"Wonderful? Not quite the word I'd use, Christie. Psychologically revealing, perhaps. Just remember that what Stewart sees is a projection of his own desires. And he never becomes conscious of the connection between what he sees and his personal life. He remains completely unaware of the parallel."

Mr. Brother stopped. He seemed to be waiting for a reply. Christie knew she had to say something. But what?

"I, uh, I'll be sure to watch for the parallel." Christie stared at him in awe. "Are you a movie critic, Mr. Brother?"

The question had popped out before Christie could stop herself. Why had she asked a stupid thing like that? Now Mr. Brother had stopped smiling.

"I'm sorry, Mr. Brother. I didn't mean to be personal. It's just that you seem so, so knowledgeable."

Christie sighed in relief as Mr. Brother smiled again. She'd almost blown her chances to smithereens. He obviously didn't like questions that were the least bit personal.

236

"Thank you, Christie. I'm not a movie critic, although it's true that I'm knowledgeable about film. I've made a detailed study of Hitchcock's work."

Christie noticed that Mr. Brother's expression changed as he talked to her. She could see his eyes narrow and begin to gleam with excitement. What had she done? If she knew, she'd do it again.

"Christie?" Mr. Brother hesitated slightly. "Could you turn your face slightly to the left? That's it!"

"What is it, Mr. Brother?" He was staring at her so intently, Christie felt her palms grow damp.

"I hadn't noticed before, but you bear an uncanny resemblance to Irene Winston, the victim in *Rear Window.* Are you an aspiring actress?"

Christie felt a blush rise to her cheeks. For the first time Mr. Brother was actually looking at her, studying her with obvious interest. She had kept the secret from her parents, but she'd been taking acting classes for almost a year now. Her mother and father disapproved of actresses, so naturally Christie hadn't mentioned the small part in the popcorn commercial she'd done. She'd almost died last week when her father had seen the spot on television and commented that the girl looked just like her.

"Well, yes." Christie did her best to look dedicated. "I know there are thousands of girls who want to be actresses, but I still have my dreams."

"Excellent! I have something to discuss with you, Christie. Are you working to-night?"

"Uh, no. Tonight's my night off."

Christie regrouped hastily. She was slated to work, but she could always call in sick or something.

"Is there somewhere we could meet?" Mr. Brother gave her a smile that melted the last of Christie's natural reserve. "At eight-thirty tonight?"

"Oh, yes. I'll give you my address."

Christie could barely contain her excite-ment as she printed her address carefully on the back of an old ticket stub and handed it to him. Her family was going to a cousin's wedding in San Diego tonight, and since it was a Sunday night, they'd been reluctant to leave her alone. Her father had made her promise to lock all the doors and windows, and he'd even given her the money to take a taxi home from work. Normally, Christie would have taken the bus and pocketed the extra money, but all the girls in her acting class had been nervous about the Video Killer, and they'd made Christie nervous, too. She was doubly glad she had a date with Mr. Brother tonight. At least she wouldn't be alone.

"Well, I see you have more customers coming." Mr. Brother glanced around to see three ladies approaching the ticket booth. "Until tonight then, Christie. If you can perform the scene Irene Winston does in *Rear Window,* I can almost guarantee that your dream of becoming an important actress will come true."

Mr. Brother nodded and then he was gone, heading toward the entrance of the Bijou. Christie's face was radiant as she greeted the three older women who moved up to the front of the window.

"Three for the matinee, ladies?"

Christie could barely contain her euphoria as she counted out the change and gave the ladies their computerized tickets. Then she tapped her foot impatiently, waiting for the feature to start so she could close the window. She'd watch *Rear Window* from the projection booth and study Irene Winston's part. Mr. Brother knew a lot about film. Perhaps he was a talent scout. Or a big producer. If Lana Turner had been discovered at the lunch counter in Schwab's drug store, there was no reason why she couldn't get her big break right here in the ticket booth at the Bijou. As Christie closed the shutter on the window and raced up to the projection booth, she was sure that tonight would be the luckiest night of her life!

Tony sighed in exasperation. This was the fourteenth take and the scene still didn't work.

All three of Tony's actors wore disgruntled expressions as they sat up on the bed and separated.

"Maybe if you let Bobby take over with the camera and you crawled in here?"

There was a wistful expression on Tina's face, but Tony ignored it. The girls were always trying to put the make on him, and he'd been firm about ignoring their advances.

"Forget it, Tina. I told you before, I'm a happily married man. What's the matter with you two girls today? Tina, you're just lying there like a board. Lick your lips or tremble with desire or something. And the same goes for you, Ginger. You're both supposed to go crazy with passion when you catch sight of Bobby."

"Go crazy with passion over *that*?" Tina flicked her finger, and Bobby quickly covered himself with the sheet. "Don't be ridiculous, Tony. I'm not that good of an actress and neither is Ginger."

"You can't blame me for that." Bobby frowned at the girls. "They act about as sexy as dead kittens."

"Okay, okay, stop blaming each other and concentrate on your lines. Bobby, try to be convincing. Think about something else if the girls don't turn you on. And girls? If Bobby doesn't come through, pretend. This scene isn't going to be much of a turn-on when you two look like you're going to the dentist."

"The dentist?" Ginger laughed. "Now *that's* sexy, Tony. Did you know those chairs tip all the way back? One time, when I was the only patient in his office, my dentist . . ."

"Let's take a break." Tony interrupted what he knew would be a long, raunchy story and pulled a crumpled pack of cigarettes from his pocket. This afternoon he was wearing a mustard-yellow T-shirt that said AUTO EROTICISM DOES NOT MEAN I'M IN LOVE WITH MY CAR. "Anybody else want a cigarette?"

"Tina and I brought our own. You don't mind, do you?" Ginger reached out and grabbed Tony's lighter. "This is a great lighter, Tony. I've seen them in the stores, but I never had the chance to try one before."

Tony watched as Ginger held the end of the hand-rolled cigarette to the little notch on his lighter. Almost immediately the distinctive musky-sweet odor of marijuana filled the small motel room. Tony wasn't wild about the idea of his cast smoking pot while they were working, but maybe it would help. It seemed that everything was going wrong today.

"Tony? Have a hit."

Even though he shook his head, Ginger passed the joint to him. He took a drag automatically and held the smoke in his lungs. Good grass. Maybe it would knock him out of his depression.

Bobby was telling the girls a joke when Tony stood up and walked to the window. It was growing dark, and there was a steady stream of headlights outside. Sunday night in Los Angeles. Would the Video Killer strike again tonight?

Suddenly Tony wished for open spaces where the air didn't smell like exhaust fumes and violent crime was something that only happened in other, faraway places. A ranch. He'd always wanted a ranch somewhere in the foothills. Lots of land with a trout stream running through it and a house built in the lee of a hill. It wouldn't have to be fancy. No gardeners or landscapers required. All he needed was a comfortable old ranch house somewhere in the high desert, sturdy enough to keep out the elements.

What would Allison think of living out in the wilds? Tony wasn't really sure. She'd always been a city girl, and she might miss the bright lights and the convenience stores.

One of the girls came up behind him, Tony didn't bother to find out which one, and handed him the joint. He took another hit and passed it back. Why was he so damn depressed today?

Mentally, Tony catalogued his problems. First there were the lies. He'd lied to Erik because of the murder videos. And to Allison to cover up his moonlighting porn job. Tony knew Allison was hurt and puzzled by the way he'd pulled away from her, but he couldn't tell her about the terrible financial crunch they were in. She had enough problems dealing with her mother's terminal illness, and there was no way he'd burden her with any more worries.

Tony pulled out his packet of uppers and washed one down with a swallow of beer. He knew he was abusing the damn things, but his back was to the wall, and it was the only way he could stay alert enough to meet all his commitments. He'd contracted to complete this film to repay his loan. And he'd promised to block out *Video Kill* for Erik. And he'd agreed to act as an adviser on the murder videos for Sam. On top of all that, he had to try to be there for Allison to lean on. Somehow he had to accomplish everything, even though there weren't enough hours in the day, and when he finally got a chance for some sleep, he was either so wired he stared up at the ceiling or so exhausted he practically passed out. Tony felt as if he were trapped on a speeding roller coaster with no way to get off.

"Hey, Tony, are you all right?"

Tony whirled around as Ginger put a hand on his shoulder. For a moment he'd forgotten that he wasn't alone in the room.

"Can we do something that's not in the script? I just thought it up. Bobby's going to be a dentist, and I'll be his patient. I'll seduce him, and then Tina's going to be the dental assistant who catches us and gets into the act. What do you think?"

"Sure." Tony shrugged. Ginger's idea was a lot better than the script. "Go for it, Ginger."

Twenty minutes later Tony had the scene on disc. It was very good, probably the best thing they'd done so far.

"Okay. That's a wrap." Tony walked to the wastebasket and dropped the script inside. "Let's take a break while Ginger thinks up the next scene."

Ginger gasped in surprise. "You mean we're not going to follow the script anymore?"

"Nope. Your ideas are a lot better than the guy's who wrote this script."

"Wait a minute." Bobby scratched his head. "I thought *you* wrote it."

"I did. From now on Ginger works up the scenes, and I'll see there's a bonus in it. What do you want, Ginger? Extra money?"

"Well, money's always nice." Ginger looked thoughtful, and then her face lit up. "But I'd rather have that nifty lighter of yours. I love the inscription. I'll work out the rest of the scenes if I can have your lighter for a present. Is it a deal?"

Tony hesitated. The lighter was his anniversary present from Allison. It wouldn't be right to give it away, but he didn't have time to rewrite the script.

"Okay . . . you've got a deal."

Tony fought down his feelings of guilt as he tossed Ginger the lighter. He'd pick up another one tomorrow morning before Allison noticed this one was gone. He told himself that she'd never know the difference, and he'd just saved himself hours of work.

Katy Brannigan darted into a space in the fast lane and earned a blast on the horn from the car behind her as she fishtailed slightly. She still wasn't used to the quick steering on her new car. The old Ford she'd driven up until two months ago had been as staid and steady as a truck.

She was driving a red Mazda MX-5, the car she'd bought for herself after the divorce. It was a good car, even *Consumer Reports* said so, but Katy had come to the unhappy conclusion that it wasn't right for her. All the women in her therapy group had recommended a sports car. They'd told her about the sense of freedom a high-powered engine would give her, the fantastic maneuverability, the sexy single image she'd project in a fast, two-seater luxury car. The MX-5 was touted as the top of the line, and Katy admitted that it had never given her a speck of trouble mechanically. But owning the car meant that she had to tailor her lifestyle to fit her vehicle.

Katy loved to wear fancy hats when she got dressed up, but her new car didn't have enough headroom. That meant she had to take her hat with her and put it on at the last minute, being careful not to dislodge it when she got out of her car. Then there was the problem of carrying the boxes of papers and books she needed for research. There was no trunk and no backseat. She'd tried putting her things on the passenger seat, but they were heavy and the Mazda had a safety feature. The engine wouldn't start if there was weight on the passenger seat and the seat belt wasn't buckled. That meant her boxes had to go on the platform behind the bucket seats, and there they were difficult to put in and take out.

The seat belts were another feature that drove Katy crazy. Her Ford had been so old that it'd had lap belts. Her MX-5 was equipped with the newest in shoulder harnesses. While Katy realized that they were much safer than the lap belts, it meant she had to modify her wardrobe. She could no longer wear her favorite silk blouses without arriving at the office wrinkled diagonally.

Katy eased over two lanes to the right and drew a sigh of relief. She hoped she wouldn't have to speed up before she got to the freeway exit. She loved the concept of a high-performance engine, but she was a bit afraid of the surge of power that came when she stepped on the gas pedal. With the quick steering and the high horsepower, she sometimes felt as if the car were in control, not her. This was one of the days when she wished she'd ignored all the well-meaning advice of her new friends and kept her old car.

A few minutes later Katy turned in the driveway at the Wilshire Towers and parked in the empty space next to Sam's car. As she walked through the garage and approached the glass door that led to the lobby, she noticed that the ugly orange-and-green-striped carpet had been replaced with a lovely deep-pile royal blue. It looked much better, and she wished they'd done it earlier. She'd always hated the carpeting in the lobby.

Katy picked up the telephone by the door and dialed Sam's apartment. It felt strange to be dialing the number she'd answered so many times. When Sam picked up the phone, she had to swallow hard before she could talk.

"Sam? It's me, Katy."

Sam pressed the buzzer that unlocked the door, and Katy pulled it open. Again, a feeling of unreality struck her. She'd lived in the end unit on the sixth floor for most of her marriage, and it still felt like home. She reminded herself that she was only a visitor and pressed the button on the elevator for the sixth floor. While she rode up, she reviewed what she'd learned so far today. Cinescope Studios was doing a screenplay about the Video Killer. One of Alan Goldberg's secretaries had tipped her off. The writers of record were Tony Rocca and Erik Nielsen, and Katy had already started an investigation into their backgrounds. As far as the actual murder DVDs were concerned, several reliable sources at police headquarters had mentioned that they were in Sam's possession. They weren't in the evidence room, and they weren't in Sam's office. Katy had checked on that. And she had the advantage of knowing Sam's habits. She was positive that Sam had the murder DVDs here, in his apartment. And if the Video Killer ran true to form and struck tonight, she'd have plenty of time to copy them when Sam was called to the scene.

The moment Katy had figured it out, she'd called Sam. She was missing a few important facts for her article. Could she interview him tonight? At home?

Katy had expected resistance, but Sam had agreed almost too eagerly. That made her a little nervous, but she quickly squelched her suspicions. Sam wasn't the type to have an ulterior motive.

"Hello, Katy. Come in."

Sam pulled open the door before she had the chance to ring the bell, and Katy almost jumped out of her skin.

"Hi, Sam."

Katy gave him her very best innocent smile, but she trembled a little as he helped her out of her light summer coat. She noticed the eager look in his eyes, and now she was glad she'd rushed out at lunch to pick up this particular dress from the cleaners. It had always been Sam's favorite.

Katy watched Sam as he hung her coat in the hall closet. He looked sinfully handsome tonight in a wine-colored sweater and well-worn jeans. She'd forgotten how dark his eyes were when he wore that color.

"How about a drink, Katy?"

Katy was about to refuse; she never drank when she needed her wits about her, but she remembered her purpose for coming here and nodded. Sam had a low tolerance for alcohol, and if he had a drink, he might let something slip about the Video Killer.

"That's a wonderful idea, Sam, but only if you're having one, too."

"I'll have one to keep you company, but only one." Sam looked serious. "It's Sunday night."

"You're expecting something to break with

the Video Killer?"

"Maybe. Name your poison, Katy. I just stocked the liquor cabinet."

"Then let's have Manhattans."

While Sam mixed the drinks at the bar, Katy looked around the apartment with a calculating eye. There were no signs of another woman. She'd excuse herself and go to the bathroom later. Women always left makeup or perfume in the bathroom. Or a sexy negligee hanging up on the back of the door. Of course, it was really none of her business, but a man as handsome as Sam was bound to have a girlfriend by now.

Katy had barely started on her inventory of the apartment before Sam walked up with her drink. She took the glass and gave a pleased smile. There was a cherry in hers, and she knew Sam despised them.

"Oh, Sam. You bought maraschino cherries just for me!"

"Not really." Sam grinned. "They've been here since you left."

Katy felt her heart pound hard in her chest, and she cautioned herself not to assume anything. Sam's new girlfriend might hate maraschino cherries. Just because her cherries were still here didn't mean that Sam had been celibate.

"To us." Sam touched the rim of his glass

251

to hers. "And to the start of something new."

"I'll drink to that."

Katy looked deeply into his eyes and tried not to feel guilty as she took a sip of her drink. It *was* the start of something new, but Sam wouldn't be pleased if he knew that what they were toasting was her scoop on the Video Killer.

"Well, what do you think, Katy? Will we get to finish our drinks tonight?"

"I guess so, Sam." Katy took another sip to cover her embarrassment. It was their private joke. At bedtime Sam had mixed Manhattans. Most of the time they'd forgotten all about their drinks, and Katy'd dumped them out in the morning. Even though Katy tried not to speculate, she wondered whether Sam had kept the same bed she'd talked him into buying. They'd tried out every position they could think of on that bed, and it had been wonderful.

"Something wrong, Katy?"

Katy came back to the present with a jolt. A blush rose to her cheeks, and she quickly took out the list of questions she'd prepared. Why was she feeling nostalgic about that old bed now? Sam had probably replaced it the day she left.

"No, everything's just fine, Sam."

"Great. Then, let's talk about sex."

"Sex?" Katy's voice ended in a squeak, and she felt her hands start to tremble.

"That's right. Sex." Sam's voice was very calm. "You said you wanted to know my attitude toward women in the police force and whether their sex handicapped them in any way."

"Oh! Of course!" Katy pulled out her notebook and pen. "Go ahead, Sam. First of all, does a woman's gender influence her advancement in the field of law enforcement?"

Sam grinned, and Katy knew she was blushing. She took another sip of her drink and tried very hard to look professional as she jotted down Sam's answer.

14

Christie could barely contain her excitement as Mr. Brother set up his video camera. This date had turned out even better than her wildest expectations, and Christie felt like pinching herself to make sure she wasn't dreaming. Mr. Brother had promised that she could audition for the movie he was making. She was going to be an important movie star!

She paid close attention as Mr. Brother explained the camera and how he could operate it with a remote control. He would play Lars Thorwald, her husband, who killed her in front of the open window.

They were almost ready. Christie watched while Mr. Brother carried his tripod out onto the small master bedroom balcony that her parents had decorated with plastic ferns and flowers. He'd mentioned something about filming the scene from a different P.O.V., establishing a macrocosm leading to a microcosm in the critical scene. Or was it the other way around? She'd have to remember to ask her acting coach tomorrow if she could remember his exact words.

He looked so intense! Christie shivered a little even though the room was stifling. The balcony door was open, but there was no breeze to stir the muggy summer air. She was wearing her mother's high-necked flannel nightgown, a costume Mr. Brother had said was perfect for her scene. If any other man had told her to put on a nightgown and get into bed, Christie would have refused before the words were even out of his mouth, but it was different with Mr. Brother. He wasn't interested in her body, only in her talent as an actress.

Christie smiled slightly as she thought of what her parents would say if they saw her now. Naturally, they'd be upset that she'd invited Mr. Brother to the apartment when they weren't home. They'd ask all sorts of questions about his background. Now that she thought it, Christie didn't know much about him at all. They hadn't actually been introduced, something that was very important to her parents, but she'd seen him almost every Sunday at the Bijou. That should count for something.

As she took the deep, calming breaths that

her drama teacher had recommended before a performance, Christie glanced over at Mr. Brother. He was dressed in a black robe and heavy gloves that he must have brought with him in his camera case. Now he was pulling on a funny kind of black hood with holes for his eyes. Christie felt like giggling, but she managed to control herself. There was probably a very good reason for his silly-looking costume. She just didn't know enough about film techniques to recognize what it was.

One more check of the camera and Mr. Brother was ready. He raised his hand for her cue, and Christie went into the part of the nagging Mrs. Thorwald that she'd practiced so diligently. At first she was self-conscious and nervous about the camera, but after a few lines the magical moment that her acting coach had told her about actually happened. She ceased being Christie Jensen and became Mrs. Thorwald, berating her husband with the total force of her personality.

Mr. Brother took a step toward her, and Christie gave an involuntary gasp that she hadn't rehearsed. She knew she looked frightened, and it wasn't entirely due to her acting ability. He really did look menacing. As she went into her lines again, screaming and railing at him, Christie knew she was giving the best performance of her life.

As his black-gloved hands closed around her neck, Christie didn't have to act any longer. Now she truly was terrified. His hands were squeezing like a vise, and she couldn't get her breath. Her vision started to fade. She struck out at him with all the strength she had, but she couldn't dislodge his hands. Her scene was over. Why didn't he stop?!

Christie struggled, clawing at his hands with her fingernails, but her strength was gone. Still his hands squeezed tighter and tighter until her eyes bulged and her arms dropped limply to her sides. Then, as her tortured lungs screamed out for oxygen and she was rendered even more helpless than the invalid she had portrayed, she knew the awful truth. Mr. Brother was the Video Killer.

Allison sat in front of the large-screen television set, munching on blueberry-flavored popcorn and taking notes. In the past week she'd finished the first tier of the giant box, and now she was working her way through the other six flavors. Tony had been pathetically grateful when she'd agreed to help him with his research, but the whole thing had sounded more like fun than work to her.

Allison had been a dyed-in-the-wool Hitchcock fan ever since she'd taken a class on his films in college. It had been no trouble at all to watch several films each night, and she'd added quite a few names to the list of victims Tony had asked her to make. Allison was grateful for the diversion and the fact that the project was a lengthy one. Watching fifty-three films would keep her occupied for quite a while.

When Tony had called earlier to tell her he wouldn't be home until late, Allison had slipped into her most comfortable outfit and double-locked all the doors. Since it was Sunday, she was a bit nervous about being in the house alone. The Video Killer's three victims had all been murdered on Sunday nights. Of course, they had all been actresses, and she was no longer in the profession, but she'd taken precautions anyway. The gun that Tony kept in the bedroom was now sitting right next to her on the table by the couch.

Allison had started today's work by pulling out a DVD at random. It was *The Pleasure Garden,* Hitchcock's first complete film as a director. She'd never seen it before, and it kept her mind off the Video Killer.

The sun had been lowering in the sky when she'd completed her notes and selected her second film, *The Trouble with Harry,* which introduced Shirley MacLaine to the screen.

When that film ended, Allison took a break for dinner. Rather than preparing something herself, she dashed out for hot dogs from a stand a few blocks away. She ordered two of them, as well as a container of hot German potato salad and a side order of coleslaw, and went home to watch *Topaz.* She added Karin Dor to her list of Hitchcock's female victims and wrote a concise analysis of the film for Tony. The antique clock on the mantel was chiming nine in the evening when she slipped *Psycho* into the machine and pressed the play button.

The moment she heard the theme music, Allison rejected the DVD. Sharee Lyons had been murdered in the shower, and it would only make Allison more nervous to watch *Psycho* all alone at night. *The Birds* didn't seem like a good idea, either. Or *Notorious.* Or even *Suspicion.* She was all too aware of the Santa Ana winds blowing outside the window and the way the house creaked and groaned. The sound of the sprinkler system going on outside the family room window almost made her jump out of her chair.

Aware that she was being silly, Allison

managed to laugh at herself. She'd promised Tony that she'd watch four films for him every night, and she still had one left to go. There had to be some Hitchcock film that wouldn't frighten her out of her wits.

Allison looked through the titles carefully. *Under Capricorn* was simply too weighty, and she wasn't in the mood for the rambling and confusing plot of *The Paradine Case*. Finally she chose *Rear Window,* one of her favorites.

It was close to ten p.m. when Allison stopped the DVD to make a note. *Rear Window* had a female victim, Mrs. Thorwald played by Irene Winston. The murder itself hadn't been very scary, perhaps because Hitchcock had filmed it from James Stewart's perspective. Allison knew it would have been much more frightening if it had been shot from the victim's perspective, like in *Psycho.* Or even from the killer's. Had Hitchcock ever used that technique? Not that she could recall, but she'd know for a fact by the time she'd finished watching the complete collection.

Allison sat back and sighed. Suddenly she wished she'd taken time to finish her degree before she'd married Tony. A remake of Hitchcock's murder scenes from the killer's perspective would make an intriguing graduate project. She was surprised some enterprising filmmaker hadn't done it already.

Katy's list of questions went much more quickly than she'd expected, and they were finished in less than an hour. Sam had given her a great interview. Perhaps she could actually use it sometime. Katy closed her notebook with a snap and glanced at her watch. It was still early, and she had to think of some excuse for staying.

"Thank you, Sam. I really appreciate your help, and I know you probably missed dinner because of me, so maybe I could order a pizza or something to make up for . . ."

"I already thought of that, Katy. I ordered a large Sorrento's special for both of us. I hope you have time."

"I've got all night." The words were out of her mouth before she could stop them. Katy blushed furiously. Thank God Sam hadn't seemed to notice her blunder.

Katy hurried to the kitchen and collected plates, silverware, and plenty of paper napkins. Sorrento's pizzas were notoriously messy. She was about to bring everything back to the living room when she realized that Sam hadn't changed a thing in the kitchen since she'd left. The plates were still in the upper-right-hand cabinet, and the silverware was just where she'd placed it when they'd first moved in. Was that a sign that Sam hoped she'd come back? Or had he been simply too busy to change things around?

By the time Katy got back, the pizza had arrived. Her mouth watered in anticipation as Sam opened the box and put a piece on her plate.

"Are those anchovies, Sam?"

"Yup." Sam nodded. "I decided I liked them after all."

Katy frowned slightly as she took a bite. Sam had always claimed that the concept of fish on a pizza was bizarre. Why had he changed his mind now, after all these years? Had a new girlfriend managed to talk him into trying them?

They ate in silence until the last slices of pizza were on their plates. Then Katy's curiosity got the best of her. "How did you happen to try anchovies, Sam?"

"Oh, I don't know." Sam took the last bite and chewed thoughtfully. "I guess I just decided that if you liked them, they couldn't be all that bad. How about some coffee? I can make it."

"I'll do it." Katy pushed back her chair.

"You just sit here and relax, Sam. You look tired."

The moment Katy left for the kitchen, Sam glanced at his watch. It was almost eleven. The Video Killer could be out there right now, murdering his next victim. Even though a full complement of police officers was patrolling the streets, Sam had very few illusions. Los Angeles was a huge city, and their chances of catching the Video Killer in the act were very slim indeed. He was glad Katy was here to take his mind off the waiting. Of course she had an ulterior motive, but now that he knew what it was, he'd figured out a way to deal with it.

When Katy had first asked for help on her Sunday supplement article, Sam had known something was up. One telephone call to a buddy at the paper had confirmed his suspicions. There was no such article, and rumor had it Katy Brannigan had been assigned to something big. Sam knew it was the Video Killer story.

At first Sam had been furious at Katy's duplicity, but then he'd decided to turn the whole thing to his advantage. He needed help with the murder videos, and Katy had a fine mind. It was possible she'd spot some clue on the discs that he had missed. Sam was going to make sure Katy had access to the murder DVDs, although he wouldn't admit that to her. It would be interesting to find out just how far she'd go to get her story.

Sam knew he was taking a gamble. His job was on the line if there were any leaks to the press before the Video Killer was caught. But Sam was betting on the fact that Katy was too loyal to publish anything without coming to him first. Which would win out? Her loyalties or her ambition? Sam needed to find out.

"Is the coffee ready yet?" Sam called out to Katy in the kitchen.

"Just a couple minutes more, Sam. I'm waiting for it to finish perking." Katy leaned against the counter. Actually, the coffee wasn't perking at all. Sam had a drip pot, so she was waiting for the coffee to finish dripping. She arranged cups on a tray with plenty of Cremora and sugar cubes for Sam and wondered what excuse she could give for sticking around long enough to find the murder DVDs. So far it had been easy . . . almost too easy.

A tiny seed of suspicion began to grow in Katy's mind. Sam had agreed right away when she'd asked for the interview, and he'd been the one to arrange for the pizza. It was almost as if he was trying to keep her here.

Cherries in her Manhattan. Anchovies on the pizza. Sam was trying to butter her up for something. But what?

Katy picked up the tray and carried it back into the living room. She found Sam sitting on a floor pillow next to the fireplace with the stereo playing softly in the background.

"Bring it over here, Katy. We'll have our coffee by the fire, just like we used to do."

"Uh . . . fine." Katy set the tray down and joined him. There was no reason to be upset. She'd planned to stay the night. She'd even decided to go to bed with Sam if that was what he wanted. But suddenly the whole thing seemed so cold and calculated.

"I poured us a little cognac, Katy." Sam handed her a small snifter. "Let's toast your Sunday supplement article, the one about women cops."

"Oh, good idea!" Katy nodded solemnly. "To my article."

Katy tried to bring the glass to her lips, but suddenly she was so ashamed she couldn't do more than stare at Sam and blink back tears. She dropped her eyes and swallowed hard.

"No. That's silly. Let's drink to . . . to . . . Oh hell! I can't think of anything."

Katy looked at him with such distress that Sam couldn't help himself. He took the glass out of her hand and set it down on the rug. Then he pulled her into his arms and kissed her.

"Oh, Sam!" Katy uttered a sigh that turned into a sob as she melted into his arms. She hadn't realized how very much she'd missed him until now. They kissed for long moments, and she drew her breath in sharply as he slipped her dress from her shoulders. She reminded herself that this was completely familiar, that Sam had made love to her countless times before. Yet there was an element of renewed discovery. Had his arms always been this strong? His touch this exciting?

Katy wrapped her arms around his neck and pressed her body against his. And all the while he was carrying her into the bedroom, she told herself that she was in control, that she was using him to get what she wanted. But if she was only using him, why was she telling him over and over again that she loved him?

Erik sat up in bed, suddenly alert. It was almost eleven in the evening, and the pills Dr. Trumbull had given him had been aptly named. His headache was gone, and he had been zonked for over five hours.

There was a plaintive meow from the side of the bed, and Erik looked down to see Al staring at him hopefully. He patted the bed and Al jumped up, quickly claiming the warm spot on the pillow.

"Okay, Al. It's your turn. I've slept long enough."

Erik headed for the kitchen, where he warmed a cup of his breakfast coffee. Then he dialed the office, but the answer phone was on. Tony wasn't there. He must have finished his work and gone home. Even though it was late, Erik dialed Tony's home number. Allison answered on the first ring.

"Hello? Is this the gorgeous Mrs. Rocca?"

"You must have the wrong Rocca." Allison laughed. "Hi, Erik. What's up?"

"You are, obviously. What makes you so happy tonight?"

"I guess it's because I'm doing something worthwhile. Tony brought me a complete collection of Hitchcock films, and I'm watching all fifty-three, plus taking notes for him. It's fun being involved in an alumni research project again."

Erik frowned. He could understand why Tony might ask Allison to watch the three films they were using in the script, *Psycho, Strangers on a Train,* and *Frenzy.* But there was no possible reason to ask her to watch every film that Hitchcock had ever made. And what was this story he'd told her about an alumni research project?

"That sounds like a massive task, Allison."

"It is, but I really don't mind. Somebody from the UCLA alumni group is doing a study of the female victims in Hitchcock films, so I'm compiling a complete list for Tony."

"Oh, I see. Can I talk to Tony, Allison? I need to ask him a question."

Erik was careful to keep his voice neutral. He was willing to bet that there wasn't a UCLA study.

"He's not here, Erik, but you can probably catch him at the office. He said he'd be working all night. Something about blocking out the next scene so you could have it in the morning."

Erik's frown had turned to a scowl by the time he'd said good-bye to Allison. Tony could be at the office and not answering the phone, but Erik doubted it. And he was sure he wouldn't find the blocking for the second scene on his desk, as Tony had promised.

Erik grabbed his car keys and headed for the garage. A terrible suspicion was beginning to grow in the back of his mind. It was Sunday night, and the Video Killer had struck the past three Sundays. And no one knew where Tony was.

Tony needed money. Erik had taken enough calls from creditors at the office to know that. And their one chance of making big bucks was the *Video Kill* sale. It had been an impossible long shot until the Video Killer had appeared on the scene.

As Erik drove toward the office, he thought about the way that Tony had changed over the past few weeks. All those excuses he'd given that had turned out to be lies. The times he'd promised to show up at the office and hadn't. The way he seemed to know exactly how the Video Killer had murdered his victims, even though he swore he didn't have inside information. The fact that Diana Ellington had been murdered, right after they'd discussed casting her in the movie. And now the way Tony had conned Allison into watching a complete collection of Hitchcock films and making a list of the victims. There was no reason to watch all fifty-three of the films, unless Tony needed the information for something other than the script, something that Erik didn't even want to think about.

Erik told himself he was jumping to conclusions. It was insane to think that Tony was in so much financial trouble that he'd lost all touch with reality and become the Video Killer to sell the screenplay.

Traffic was light, and Erik pulled up in the parking lot at the office in record time. There was no car in Tony's space. He let himself in the back door of the building and headed for the elevator. His shoulders were slumped, and he felt the weariness of the world as he rode up to the office. He supposed the smart thing would be to call the police and tell them his suspicions, but there was no way they'd believe him when they found out he'd been locked up in the psych ward of the V.A. hospital for six months. They'd assume the whole story was a figment of his imagination, and maybe it was.

The lights were off in the office, and Erik frowned as he checked the coffeepot. Cold. Tony hadn't been here any time recently. And there was no second scene blocking on his desk and no sign of any work in progress.

Erik got out his video camera and took a few shots of the office. He wanted to show Jamie where he worked. Then he got a pillow and blanket from the closet and stretched out on the lumpy couch. He'd be right here to confront Tony, no matter what time he came in. As Erik stared out at the lighted dome of the Capitol Records building, he prayed that his suspicions were wrong, but as he dropped off to sleep, one hard fact remained. He needed some answers from Tony.

Katy was startled out of the deepest sleep she'd had in months by the shrill ringing of the telephone. She reached out to answer it, and her hand touched a very real, very warm arm. For a moment she was totally disoriented, and then she heard Sam's voice, as if it had come straight out of her dreams.

"Okay, Bob. I'm awake. Another one? Jesus! Give me that address again. I'm on my way."

Instantly alert, Katy rolled over and sneaked a look at her watch before she closed her eyes again. Past one in the morning. There was only one reason to call Sam at this hour. The Video Killer had struck again. All she had to do was play possum until Sam left, and then she could look for those murder DVDs.

"Katy?" Sam spoke her name gently.

"Hmmm?"

"I have to leave. Police business. I set the alarm for seven in case I'm not back by then."

"That's nice . . ."

Katy let her voice trial off and resumed

deep, even breathing so Sam would assume she'd gone back to sleep. She peeked out through her eyelashes as he switched on the light in the dressing room and pulled on his clothes. This was a perfect opportunity. She could hardly wait until he left to get a look at those DVDs!

Sam bent down to kiss her good-bye, and Katy started to react before she caught herself. Sleepy women didn't kiss that passionately. She let her body go limp and turned over to tunnel back down under the blankets. She didn't raise her head again until she heard the apartment door close behind him.

The moment she was sure he was really gone, Katy jumped from the bed and hurried to the kitchen for a cup of coffee. Her whole body was sated and lazy, the way only very good sex could make it. It had been a long time since she'd gotten out of bed with the urge to purr like a well-fed cat. She'd missed it. She'd known all along she'd missed it.

There was no time for dallying. Katy put the coffee on to reheat and opened the refrigerator. There was a quart of orange juice inside, and Katy poured herself a glass. Sam didn't drink orange juice. He must have bought it especially for her, in the hopes that she'd stay the night. Was that proof that he wanted her back? Katy's heart raced until she considered that he might have a girlfriend who liked orange juice for breakfast.

As Katy drank the juice, she cased the kitchen thoroughly, opening cupboards and drawers. She discovered that Sam had also stocked up on English muffins. She popped one in the toaster and jiggled it to make the element work. The same old toaster. She wondered if Sam had figured out how to work it. It wasn't until she had buttered the muffin and taken the first bite that she realized Sam had bought the kind she liked, with raisins. He hated raisins. Either he'd been sure that she'd be here in the morning or he'd found a woman with similar tastes to replace her. And what did that prove? Nothing. Absolutely nothing.

Suddenly Katy felt tears come to her eyes as she pictured another red-haired woman, probably twenty years younger and much prettier. The woman would wear Opium, Katy's favorite perfume, and she'd dress in long silk blouses, the kind Katy favored. She might even know all the lyrics to "The Wild Colonial Boy" like Katy did. Even worse, she might have discovered how to kiss that tiny sensitive spot on the side of Sam's neck that drove him to distraction. She could see them now, the beautiful younger woman with eyes even greener than hers, sleeping in Sam's arms on the very bed Katy had talked him into buying.

Katy stopped cold. Sam wasn't her husband any longer. She had no right to be jealous. She took a deep breath and switched off the kitchen light as she walked quickly to the living room. There was work to do, and she couldn't do it efficiently if she didn't concentrate on the problem at hand. She had filed for a divorce so she could be Katy Brannigan, woman reporter, and she'd better start acting the part.

A small stack of disks were sitting on top of the oak entertainment center they'd bought when they'd moved into this apartment. Katy got a chair from the dining room table and totally ignored the dirty dishes sitting there. She told herself she wasn't Sam's wife any longer, and she shouldn't feel she had to load them into the dishwasher, but she knew she probably would.

As Katy climbed up on the chair to grab the small stack of DVDs, she felt a rush of excitement. This could be it! But one glance told her it wasn't. This was a series she'd ordered from a catalogue and never watched on oil painting.

It wasn't until Katy had climbed down and was about to move the chair back to its place that she noticed a stack of disks in plain sight on top of the television.

Katy was so excited her hands trembled as she reached for them. Three disks and there had been three murders. The number was right. They were in black plastic cases with no labels. Sam always labeled his disks right after he recorded them, and he'd been furious with her when she'd forgotten to do the same.

Her hands trembled slightly as she slipped a blank DVD into the second slot of Sam's recorder and set it up to record Sam's disks. The murder videos were Sam's property, and she had taken advantage of his feelings for her to get them.

Should she do it? Of course she should. This was what she was here for, wasn't it? Katy pressed the button that would start the copying process. She knew she should be feeling excited and proud that she'd accomplished her goal. But all she felt was a terrible sense of guilt.

15

Monday, July 26

"Hey, Erik . . . it's daylight in the swamp."

Erik opened his eyes to see Tony standing over him, holding a steaming mug of coffee. He was wearing a pink T-shirt that said I'M THE ONLY GUY IN TOWN WHO DOESN'T WANT TO DIRECT. Erik reached out, blinking, and took the first scalding sip before he realized that he was sleeping on the couch in the office.

"What time is it?" Erik asked the first question that popped into his head.

"Just after seven in the morning. I figured you wouldn't want to sleep the day away when there's work to do. The Video Killer gave us another scene to write last night."

"That's nice." Erik took another gulp of coffee and struggled to sit up. "What was that about the Video Killer?"

"He did it again, last night."

"Another actress?"

276

"They didn't think so at first, but then they found out she was taking acting classes. Her parents didn't know about it, or they probably wouldn't have left her alone."

"She was young?"

Tony nodded. "Only nineteen. She worked part-time as a cashier at the Bijou Theater. I've got the whole news flash recorded."

"Let's see it." Erik got to his feet. It took him a minute to remember why he was sleeping on the office couch when he had a comfortable bed at home. "I've got to talk to you, Tony, about the Video Killer."

"Sure, Erik. The outline for the next scene is on your desk. It's good, even if I do say so myself. And the next time you decide to sack out on the couch, leave a note on the door to warn me, will you? I came in about midnight and worked for three hours before I even knew you were here. Then I heard snoring, and I just about jumped out of my skin."

"You came in to work at midnight?"

"Right around that time. I didn't look at my watch. You know me, Erik. I get my best work done in the middle of the night. No noise and no telephone calls. Now, come on. I'll show you that DVD."

Erik took another swig of his coffee and followed Tony to the reception area. Even though his head still felt fuzzy, he managed to catch the salient points of the news flash. The Video Killer had struck sometime between eleven and one. The victim, Christie Jensen, had been discovered by her parents shortly after one-twenty in the morning. She had been choked to death in the family apartment and then partially dismembered.

"Pretty gruesome, huh?" Tony flicked off the television set. "Did you catch that shot of that apartment building, Erik? Our guy couldn't have picked a better setting for the fourth scene. The minute I saw it, I thought of *Rear Window.* And guess what was playing at the Bijou yesterday?"

"*Rear Window?*"

"Right. And Christie Jensen looked a lot like Hitchcock's victim, Irene Winston. For all we know the killer watched the movie, picked up Christie from her ticket booth, and then acted it all out for real in her parents' apartment. How's that for sheer balls?"

Erik looked up to find Tony grinning. His partner's obvious pleasure made him feel ill.

"Balls isn't quite the word I'd use. We have to talk, Tony."

"Good idea." Tony nodded. "We'll have a

conference over breakfast. Come on, Erik. I'll treat you to three eggs and a full stack at Du-par's."

"You want to have breakfast after seeing *that*?"

"Why not? They didn't actually show anything. Come on, Erik. I can tell you're hungry. Your stomach's growling."

Erik hesitated a moment, but his appetite won out over his sensitivity. Dr. Trumbull's zonker had knocked him out over the dinner hour, and he hadn't eaten since yesterday's lunch.

"Okay. Just let me get cleaned up a little first."

"You'll have to use the bathroom at Du-par's." Tony grabbed his arm and steered him out the door. "The city shut off our water line for repairs, and it'll be off for most of the day."

Erik frowned. "But that's crazy, Tony. This whole block is office buildings. Why don't they do their repairs on Sunday or in the middle of the night, when no one's working?"

"Oh, they couldn't do that." Tony looked serious. "The city's on a tight budget, and they can't afford to pay overtime."

Twenty minutes later Erik came out of the bathroom at Du-par's to find a tall stack of pancakes, three eggs over easy, five strips of extra-crisp bacon, a side order of hash browns, and a cup of fresh coffee waiting for him. He slid into his side of the booth and took a forkful of hash browns before he said a word.

"Mmmm!"

"You bet." Tony took another forkful. He was having the special California omelet, and the waitress had said he was the only customer who hadn't asked what was in it. Allison had tipped him off, early in their marriage. Anything on the menu with the word *California* in it was mostly avocados.

As soon as Erik had eaten one pancake, he took the bull by the horns.

"I talked to Allison last night. Why did you give her all those Hitchcock films to watch?"

"Because she loves Hitchcock, and I needed her to do some research."

"But all we need are three scenes for our *Video Kill* script."

"Four scenes. You're forgetting *Rear Window.*"

"Okay, four scenes. But she told me you wanted her to watch all fifty-three films."

Tony took a sip of coffee to stall for time. He'd have to give Erik the same story he'd given Allison. "She's not watching them for the script, Erik. The UCLA alumni association conned me into researching a list of Hitchcock's female victims, and Allison's helping me out on it. As a matter of fact, that's what gave me the idea for the Video Killer's motivation."

"The alumni association asked you to do it?"

"Right." There was a moment of silence in which Tony refused to meet Erik's eyes. He picked up a piece of toast and smeared it with a package of jelly that was labeled MIXED FRUIT, but when he looked up, Erik was still staring at him. He had to lighten this up and divert Erik somehow.

"You ever wonder what's in this stuff, Erik? It says mixed fruit, but that could be anything. Even tomatoes. Tomatoes are a fruit, aren't they?"

"I'm not sure. My mother used to say that if you sprinkled sugar on them, they're fruit. And if you use salt, they're vegetables."

"A wise woman, your mother." Tony nodded solemnly. "But how about if you eat them plain?"

"Then they're a fregtible."

"Nice, Erik. Very nice. Please pass the peppalt."

Erik laughed as he handed over the salt and pepper. At the moment Tony seemed perfectly normal, smiling and cracking jokes. But hadn't the neighbors of that guy who'd murdered all those migrant workers claimed that he'd seemed like a perfectly normal, likeable guy? There were just too many unexplained facts to ignore, too many times when Tony had claimed he was going somewhere and then never showed up. Even last night was suspicious. Tony claimed he'd come in to work at midnight, but that was a lie. Erik had been alone in the office when he'd sacked out on the couch at twelve-thirty.

"More Swedish plasma?"

Erik nodded and Tony reached over to fill his cup. As the sleeve on Tony's T-shirt pulled up, Erik found himself looking for the scratches a young woman being strangled might leave on her attacker's arms. There was nothing there. Erik reminded himself that all his suspicions were circumstantial, and he might very well be a victim of his own overactive imagination. But his doubts still remained. Maybe Tony wasn't the Video Killer, but it was clear that he was hiding something. Erik had to find out what it was.

Tony leaned back and stretched. They were making great progress on the second scene, and it was possible they'd finish it by early afternoon if they kept on working.

"Why don't I call out for Deli and we'll eat lunch here? We're really on a roll. Get it, Erik? Deli? On a roll?"

"It's lunchtime already?" Erik looked up from the keyboard to glance at the clock on Tony's office wall. He had to meet Allison for lunch at Donny's. "What time is it, Tony? I can't read your damn clock."

"It's easy, Erik. The purpose triangle is the minute hand, the pink oblong thing is the hour hand, and the little turquoise circle counts off the seconds. Just remember that the hands don't move but the clock face does, and the twelve is marked by that little orange square. See? It's eleven purple rectangles and three green dots past the orange square."

"Fine, Tony. But what *time* is it?"

"Eleven fifty-seven give or take a few seconds. By the time I figure them out, they've changed anyway."

"I thought you were having lunch with Lon Michaels today. It's in your book."

"I was, but he canceled. So how about it? Do you want Deli?"

Tony turned to see Erik staring at the clock in dismay.

"Sorry, Tony. I've got something I have to

do. An important appointment. If I don't leave right now, I'm going to be late."

"It's really important?"

"Yes. I'm meeting with my tax man. Sorry, Tony. I'll try to be back early."

Tony was about to protest when he remembered that it was his fault that they hadn't worked on the screenplay yesterday.

"Okay, but hurry back. I'll keep on working, and maybe we can still finish this up today. I don't have to leave again until three."

"Three?" Erik frowned. "Do you really have to leave so early?"

"Sorry, old buddy." Tony thought fast. He'd arranged to see the new murder DVD with Sam at three-thirty. "I promised to meet Alan at the studio. I could always call and put it off until tomorrow but . . ."

"No, don't do that. Keeping up a good rapport with Alan is critical. I'm just getting nervous about meeting our deadline. He needs those scenes by August second."

"Don't sweat it, Erik. This is only the twenty-sixth and that gives us a full week. We'll be done long before then, especially if we put in a couple of marathon nights."

Erik sighed, resigned to missing his regular sleep. "Okay, Tony. You work up a schedule that's good for you, and I'll be here."

Five minutes later Erik was speeding through Hollywood, feeling guilty about lying to Tony. He didn't even have a tax man. But he hadn't wanted to admit that he was meeting Allison. Naturally, Tony would have joined them, and then they couldn't discuss Tony's problem. As Erik pulled into the parking lot at Donny's, he suddenly realized that he was doing the very same thing that Tony was doing. Telling outright lies to cover his actions. Of course, there was a good reason for Erik's lies. Were there also good reasons for Tony's?

Katy turned off her television with trembling hands and reviewed her notes. She'd just finished rewatching the murder scenes in the privacy of her own living room They were graphic, frightening, and amazingly well done. She felt ill.

Katy got up and went into her kitchenette to make a cup of herbal tea. The leader in her therapy group was death on coffee. She claimed that caffeine poisoned the body and caused negative personality changes. Katy had been scrupulous about restricting her coffee intake to one cup a day, and she'd already had her limit.

Katy took out the package of tea and read the ingredients on the box as she waited for the water to heat. Blackberry leaves, lemon-grass, and rose hips. It sounded like break-fast for a rabbit. She tossed the box of tea in the wastebasket and immediately felt bet-ter. She hated herbal tea. Maybe it was time she started thinking for herself instead of listening to her therapy leader. She'd been much happier before she'd started attend-ing the group. Using the microscope of introspection to examine the psychological motivation behind her every action was more bother than it was worth. If she spent hours thinking about why she wanted to do something before she did it, she never got around to doing it at all.

Suddenly Katy longed for the old days when she was lighthearted and impulsive. She grabbed a jar of instant coffee from the top shelf and spooned the freeze-dried crystals into a mug. If it was true that caf-feine caused personality changes, she might just be due for one.

Armed with a steaming cup of coffee, Katy returned to her spot in front of the television. She had noticed that Tammara Welles seemed half in a trance when she'd arrived at the murder scene. That was something she could dig into. Had the Video Killer used drugs to dull his victim's senses? She knew that Miss Welles had hosted a party for charity that night. Was it possible that the Video Killer had mingled with the guests to slip something in her drink?

Katy reached for the phone and put in a quick call to her boss. Billy Goat had told her to call if she needed anything from the newspaper morgue. The phone was answered on the third ring by his secretary, Margo.

"Bill Morgan's office. He's not in right now, but I can take a message."

"Hi, Margo. This is Katy Brannigan."

"Oh, Katy!" Margo sounded breathless. "Things are really popping down here with the new murder and all. Mr. Morgan's down at police headquarters. Your ex called a press conference. But he told me to beep him immediately if you called in with a story."

"No story yet, Margo. I just need some information from the files."

"I'll pull it for you. Mr. Morgan told me to give you anything you wanted."

"Thanks, Margo. I need a list of the guests who attended Tammara Welles's charity party on the eleventh."

"That's easy. I have a copy right here on my desk. Your ex requested one the day after Miss Welles was killed, and I haven't refiled it yet."

Katy sighed as she made arrangements to pick it up. Sam was ahead of her by two full weeks. What other information did he have? She simply had to find out.

A moment later Katy was back on the couch, watching the murder scenes again. There was something very familiar about the scenes the Video Killer had shot. They were a lot like Hitchcock films. That was it!

Katy fast-forwarded through them again. Yes, the first one was *Psycho,* the second was a remake of *Strangers on a Train,* and the third, with the necktie strangling of Diana Ellington, had all the elements of *Frenzy.* Had Sam noticed the pattern? Katy doubted it. Sam's movie collection consisted entirely of detective films. Naturally he'd heard of *Psycho,* but she doubted that he'd seen any other of Hitchcock's films. She knew she had to see the fourth disc, the one Sam must have in his possession right now, to find out whether her theory was correct.

VIDEO KILLER REMAKES HITCHCOCK MURDERS. Katy could see the headline now with her name below in twelve-point type. She'd be the first to break the story, scooping every veteran investigative reporter in the city. She'd be famous. Maybe she'd even win a Pulitzer. But first she had to find out if she was right.

There was only one way to get her hands on the fourth DVD, and Katy reached for the phone again. She took a deep, calming breath as she dialed Sam's private office number.

Sam answered on the second ring. He sounded tired and harassed, but the moment he realized who was calling, there was a special intimacy in his voice.

"I heard about the fourth murder, Sam. You must be exhausted. I just thought I'd offer to cook dinner for you tonight so you won't have to go out."

"That sounds great, Katy. Your place or mine?

"Yours. That way you won't have to drive. Is six all right?"

"It's fine. Do you want to stop by my office to pick up the key?"

"Uh . . . no." Katy could feel herself starting to blush even though she knew Sam couldn't see her. "I still have mine. Unless you've changed the locks."

"I haven't. I'll see you at six, then. And Katy? Last night was wonderful."

Katy smiled and hung up the phone. He hadn't changed the locks. She quickly stopped herself from looking for psychological motives and began to jot down a grocery list. She'd stick to Sam like glue this week.

It shouldn't be hard. He'd certainly been glad to see her last night. Naturally, she'd copy the fourth murder DVD, and if she got very lucky, Sam would slip and tell her even more. As Katy gathered up her things and headed for the door, she was surprised to find that she was trembling a little in anticipation of the evening ahead.

16

Lon flicked on the lights and glanced at his audience of one. Alan Goldberg was smiling. "Well, Alan? What's the verdict?"

"That shower scene is great, Lon. Just what we need. And it's subtle, too. All implied violence and no gross-out."

"The low light levels work?"

"Absolutely. Rocca and Nielsen'll be thrilled. Who did you use for the victim? She's good."

Lon winced. "That was Diana. She dropped by the night I was making the test."

"Diana Ellington? Jesus, Lon . . . that's one hell of a coincidence!"

"I know. We talked seriously about the possibility of casting her. Diana really wanted in on the project."

"Lon, I don't know what to say except that you've got my sympathies. You must feel like hell every time you run that test."

Lon nodded. "You could say that."

"What a colossal waste!" Alan took out a handkerchief and mopped his forehead. "That's the big trouble in this business, Lon. Guesswork. It's all guesswork."

"How's that?" Lon looked puzzled.

"Your test with Diana. If we'd only known, you could have shot the damn thing as a strangling instead of a stabbing."

The screen on the television in Sam Ladera's office went black, and Tony stretched to ease his tension.

"*Rear Window?*" Sam asked the question.

"That's right." Tony sighed. "Christie Jensen looks just like Irene Winston. Everything fits the pattern, Sam."

Sam nodded. "I really hate to push you, Tony. But do you think you can come up with a partial list of Hitchcock victims for me? I've got to start warning those look-alike actresses."

"Sure. I'll have something for you any day now."

"I appreciate this, Tony. I know how busy you are, and watching all these films is above and beyond. I really owe you one."

"No problem, Sam." Tony smiled, but his heart wasn't in it. Sam wouldn't be quite so appreciative if he knew that Allison was the one who was watching the DVDs. Now he'd have to think up another lie to urge her to hurry with that damn list. Tony remembered the phrase his mother had been fond of quoting. *Oh, what a tangled web we weave when first we practice to deceive.* It was true. With all these deceptions and half truths floating around, his life was getting very complicated. He just hoped he could keep them all straight until the Video Killer was caught.

Allison spooned up the last of her chili and smiled at Erik. Donny's was even better than she'd expected, but she could understand why Erik had thought it was a hangout for hookers. The blonde at the next table was wearing a red satin minidress that was so short she couldn't even sit on it, and her redheaded companion wore a silver peekaboo top that left absolutely nothing to the imagination.

"Well? What do you think of my discovery?" Erik finished his chili and wiped his mouth with his napkin.

"It's the best chili I've ever had, Erik, but I don't even want to think about what's in it. I'm surprised the bowls don't melt."

"True." Erik nodded. "Just look what it's done to the tabletops. They used to be white."

"You're joking!" Allison glanced down at the orange tabletop and then back up at Erik. "Aren't you?"

"You'll never know. How about dessert? They make a great lemon meringue pie, but I'd recommend their house sundae. The ice cream puts out the fire from the chili."

"Just coffee, Erik. I couldn't eat another bite."

Erik waved the owner over, a round-bellied man whose apron had seen better days, and ordered coffee. A moment later he was back, carrying two chipped white mugs filled to the brim and a sticky-looking sugar bowl.

As soon as the owner had left, Erik turned to Allison. "I forgot to ask you what happened on your anniversary."

"It was nice." Allison smiled. "Tony got home about three that afternoon, and he gave me a complete collection of Hitchcock movies and an assortment of gourmet pop-corn."

"Did you go out to dinner?"

"No. Tony only had an hour. Then he went back to the office to work."

Erik stared at her for a long moment, and then he shook his head. "He didn't come back to the office, Allison. I worked late that night, until almost eleven-thirty. I remember making a crack to the night guard at the complex about coming in just seconds before I turned into a pumpkin."

"If Tony wasn't home or at the office, where did he go?"

"I don't know, Allison." Erik turned to her seriously. "Have you noticed anything different about Tony lately?"

"Like what?"

"Oh, a change in personality. He still jokes around at the office, but I think something's worrying him. I just wondered if you knew what it was."

Allison shook her head. "I don't know, Erik. Tony doesn't talk to me anymore. I . . . I barely see him, and when he comes home he's too exhausted to do anything but fall into bed. I can tell he's under a lot of stress, but every time I bring it up, he says there's nothing wrong. He's got so much on his mind that sometimes he's positively insensitive."

"I noticed that, too. Think carefully, Allison . . . do you remember what Tony said when he told you about the first murder?"

"Of course. He called me at home and said, 'Great news, honey! I think we just sold *Video Kill.*'"

"And what was your reaction?"

"I asked him for details, and he told me

295

about the murder. He was very excited, but I felt a little sick about the whole thing."

"Tony acted the same way with me. He was almost euphoric. He kept telling me how lucky we were. He really didn't seem to care that a woman had been brutally murdered."

"But Tony's not like that, Erik! He cares about other people. At least, I think he does."

"That used to be true, Allison, but Tony's changed. You know how we work. Tony blocks out the scenes, and I write the dialogue. That means Tony's got to finish the blocking before I can do my part."

Allison nodded. She knew how the two men worked together.

"Well, I waited a full week for Tony's blocking, but when he kept putting me off, I finally went ahead and did the first scene without him."

"Tony didn't do any work at all?"

"Not then. After I was finished, I asked Tony to read it. He said it was well written but we couldn't use it because it wasn't the way the murder had actually happened. My whole point is, how did he know?"

Allison shrugged. "He probably got some inside information. Tony knows a lot of people."

"I asked him about that, and he swore he hadn't been able to find out a thing. Now, how could he be so positive about the full details of all those murders? Unless he was there when the murders were committed!"

"Erik! Are you saying that you think Tony is . . ." Allison stopped, unsure whether to laugh or get angry. "I can't believe you said that. It's ridiculous. Tony doesn't have any reason to . . ."

"How about money?" Erik interrupted her. "Think about it, Allison. What if Tony figured the only way to sell our *Video Killer* story was to make it into a reality?"

"That's absurd!" Allison began to get angry. "I don't know what's got into you, Erik. You know Tony would *never* do something like that! And if you even consider the possibility, then you're certainly no friend of Tony's and no friend of mine!"

Allison grabbed her purse and tried to stand up, but Erik grabbed her arm.

"Allison, wait. Maybe I'm way off base here. I hope to God I am. But something's wrong. You can't deny that. The only way to help Tony out of whatever trouble he's in is to figure out what it is."

Allison wavered a moment, but then she sat back down. It was true there was a problem, and denying it wouldn't make it go away. But Tony certainly wasn't the Video Killer!

"Look, Allison, forget all that Video Killer stuff for a minute and let's discuss this rationally. I've taken some calls from creditors at the office. I know Tony's hurting for money. Exactly how bad is his financial situation?"

"I don't know." Allison's voice broke, and she took another swallow of coffee. "Tony handles the money. I've asked him, but he says that everything's fine. And every time I bring it up, he gets mad."

"Check on it, Allison. You've got a joint account, don't you? Go to the bank and ask for a copy of your last statement. And if you find out that Tony's in financial trouble, maybe we can get a loan or something to help him out."

Allison thought about Erik's suggestion for a moment. "All right."

"And I think you should keep a log of the times Tony comes in. He's got to be going somewhere when he's not at home and not at the office. We have to find out where."

Allison shook her head. "I won't do that, Erik. I want to know where he goes more than you do, but I will not spy on him."

Erik looked down at the table for a moment and then he sighed. "Okay. Maybe that's carrying things a little too far. It's just that I'm worried about Tony, and I really want to help him."

"Me too." Allison opened her purse and took out a package of cigarettes. "Would you get me some matches, Erik? I forgot my lighter."

As Erik got up to go to the counter, he noticed that the redhead at the next table was lighting a cigarette. He asked if he could borrow her lighter for a second, and handed it to Allison.

"Thanks, Erik. This is just like the lighter I got Tony for our anniversary. See? You just hold the cigarette in here and it lights automatically."

Allison lit her cigarette and was about to hand back the lighter when she caught sight of the inscription. *YOU LIGHT UP MY LIFE.* This was Tony's lighter! She leaned close to Erik and spoke softly.

"Ask her where she got it, Erik. It's important!"

Allison watched as Erik engaged the redhead in conversation. Her knees felt weak, and she knew all the color had left her face. There couldn't be two lighters exactly alike with the same inscription. It was just too much of a coincidence. A moment later Erik was back.

"She said it was a present from a guy she knows. He gave it to her last week."

Allison stubbed her cigarette out in the ashtray with trembling fingers. How could Tony do such a thing? He'd given her anniversary present to another woman. You bet she'd keep that record of his comings and goings. And she'd use it when she filed for divorce!

"What is it, Allison?"

Allison glanced over at the redhead and shuddered visibly. She couldn't bear to stay here any longer, in the same room as Tony's mistress.

"Let's go, Erik. Tony's not the Video Killer. He's much worse than that!" Allison stood up and gave the redhead her iciest stare. "I've just discovered the source of Tony's problem. And if I stay here a second longer I'm going to tear her eyes out!"

17

Sunday, August 1

Brother was scowling as he climbed the stairs to his quarters. He had just come from brunch at the Crestview Hotel, and the experience had been most unpleasant. First there had been some confusion with the name on his reservation. It had taken a discreetly folded bill to the maître d' to secure a table. After he'd been seated, several people he hadn't recognized had stopped by his table to chat. It had obviously been a case of mistaken identity on their part, but the whole thing had been distressing. Even though the food had been excellent and the service exemplary, Brother knew he wouldn't brunch at the Crestview again. Now he needed to put the annoying experience behind him and concentrate on the work to be done.

Brother poured himself a glass of Perrier and settled down in front of the monitor in the screening room. As he searched tonight's movie for the scene he needed, Hitchcock himself appeared on the screen. He was walking down the street in this cameo appearance. Brother snorted slightly as he hit the fast-forward button. The conceit of the Englishman was appalling. He'd taken in everyone with that story of why he'd appeared in *The Lodger*. According to Hitchcock, he'd needed more extras, and he'd stepped into the scene himself rather than wait for them to arrive. From that day on, the audience had expected to see Hitchcock in every film he'd directed, and he had jumped at the prospect, making appearances in thirty-five of his features. His films had suffered because of it. Of course Hitchcock had staunchly maintained that he appeared early in his films so he wouldn't distract the viewers, but that was ridiculous, another case where Hitchcock's colossal vanity had overridden his integrity as a director.

As he continued to fast-forward, Brother thought about Hitchcock's cameo in *Psycho*. The rotund director had been standing outside the realty office, easily recognizable. In *Strangers on a Train* he'd boarded the express carrying a double bass, and in *Frenzy* he had played the part of a spectator at the opening rally. It was impossible to miss him in any of his cameos. There was always an excited murmuring from the audience when he appeared on the screen.

For one brief moment Brother wondered if he wasn't making the same mistake as the British director. It was true that he had appeared in every segment of his own film. But his own appearances were a necessary part of the story. Unlike Hitchcock, he was totally unrecognizable, therefore no one would be distracted by watching for him. It was the primary reason he'd worn the executioner's costume.

Tonight's film was a challenge. Brother considered it one of Hitchcock's best efforts. It had been remade in 1960 by director Ralph Thomas, but that had been wasted effort with the exception of the excellent color cross-country photography. At the time, several critics had spouted that no one could remake Hitchcock, and Brother intended to prove them wrong. Naturally, he admired Hitchcock's concept of sudden switches in the action, but the way he'd jumped from one scene to the next had been so overdone that the film became choppy. Brother intended to correct that error in his segment. He would keep Hitchcock's richness of detail and his undeniable sense of the macabre, but Brother's segment would flow smoothly to its inevitable conclusion.

The sky was beginning to darken when Brother had finished his preparations for the segment he was shooting tonight. He would treat himself to a leisurely dinner. Then it would be time to make personal contact with his star. Her career was fading because of a problem with alcohol, which he intended to use to his advantage. She wouldn't be able to refuse his offer of a drink.

As he switched on the light over his desk and examined the glossy publicity photo that had been distributed by the talent agency, Brother felt an overwhelming excitement. His newest actress fit all his requirements. If Daniele Renee knew how famous she'd be by tomorrow morning, she'd be overcome with gratitude.

Allison was in the middle of *Marnie* when she heard the front door open. She jotted down the time on the back page of her notebook, a quarter past five, and hit the pause button.

"Tony? Is that you?"

"It's me." Tony appeared in the doorway. "How are you coming with those Hitchcock movies?"

Allison swallowed hard before she answered. Tony looked so tired her heart went out to him, but she quickly steeled herself. He was tired because he'd been spending time with another woman.

"I have four to go."

"You're kidding!"

Tony rushed over to kiss her, and Allison had all she could do not to kiss him back. She knew she had to maintain her distance or she'd never get the answers to the questions she'd decided to ask.

"How could you finish so many, Allison? There aren't enough hours in the day."

"You forget I'm a Hitchcock fan. I know some of these films so well, all I had to do was glance at them to get the information you wanted."

Tony gave her an affectionate pat on the head and stepped back. He hadn't even noticed the lack of enthusiasm in her kiss.

"I'm beat, honey. Can you make me a sandwich? Then I'm going straight to bed to sleep for a couple of hours. I have to meet Erik at the office at eight. We'll be working all night."

Allison felt like refusing, but her old nurturing instincts were too strong. She got up and went to the kitchen to make Tony's sandwich as he followed along behind her.

"Aren't you going to ask how my mother is?"

"Sure, honey. I'm so tired I forgot to mention it. How's she doing?"

Allison bit back her angry retort. Tony didn't even care enough to ask.

"She's fine. They think they've got her medication stabilized. Did you send a check for her bill last month? The bookkeeper stopped me this morning and said they hadn't received it."

"I knew there was something I forgot." Tony groaned. "Tell them I'm sorry. I'll put it in the mail tomorrow."

Allison wavered slightly in her resolve. Tony looked genuinely contrite, but this was the perfect opportunity to ask about their finances. She cut a thick slice of roast beef, put it on a plate, and faced him again.

"There's enough money in the bank to cover the check, isn't there, Tony?"

"Sure, honey." Tony nibbled on a piece of cheese. "Remember when I told you I'd made some investments? Well, they worked out even better than I'd hoped. There's no problem with money. No problem at all."

Allison wasn't willing to let it go so easily, now that she had him talking. She had to know more about their finances. She put on her most helpful smile and looked up at him innocently.

"I know you're really busy, Tony. Why don't you leave me the checkbook, and I'll send out the payments."

"No! Thanks anyway, honey, but if I pay the bills myself, it's a lot easier for me at tax time. I'd rather have you concentrate on those Hitchcock films."

Tony realized his excuse was weak, but he sure as hell didn't want Allison to see the balance in their checkbook. He had to change the subject quick, before she noticed how her suggestion had upset him.

"Oh, that reminds me, honey." Tony cleared his throat. "I got a call last week about the Hitchcock research. They want me to give them what I've got so far. I'll take your notes with me tonight and print them out at the office."

"But my notes are a mess." Allison frowned. "Can't they wait until I'm finished?"

"I guess not. Their deadline's been pushed up, and they need to start compiling the data."

"Well, okay. Maybe I can finish it tonight, if I really work at it. Will tomorrow afternoon be soon enough?"

Tony winced. He really hated to put pressure on Allison, but Sam really needed that list.

"It'll be super, honey." Tony reached into his pocket and took out a cigarette. "I know it was wrong to dump all this on you at the last minute."

Allison turned just as Tony put a cigarette in his mouth. The timing couldn't be better for her next question. She was grateful for the years of acting lessons that enabled her to assume a guileless expression and hide her inner anger.

"Let me light your cigarette, Tony. I want to try your new lighter."

Tony fumbled in his pocket again and came up empty-handed. He'd been so busy, he'd forgotten to buy a new lighter to replace the one that Allison had given him. He had to think up something in a hurry.

"Sorry, honey. It's at the office. I used it all afternoon while I was working at the computer."

Allison slapped a slice of tomato on Tony's sandwich with more force than was necessary and handed the plate to him. She knew exactly where Tony had left his lighter, but this wasn't the time for ugly confrontations. She'd thought the whole situation through quite rationally this afternoon. She would give Tony enough rope to hang himself before she made any direct accusations.

Allison was so quiet, Tony began to get nervous. There was no possible way she could know that he'd given Ginger the lighter.

"I've been thinking, honey. I know I haven't been a good husband lately, but this rough time is almost over. Just as soon as we turn in the first part of the script to Alan, I can relax a little and spend more time with you. I've missed you."

Allison began to waver again, and when Tony held out his arms, she moved close and let him hold her. She wanted to believe him. She needed to believe him.

"Just hang on, honey. Things'll get back to normal soon, I promise. I know I've been a real louse the past couple of weeks, but you still love me anyway, don't you?"

"Yes, Tony. I still love you anyway."

Allison turned away and blinked back tears as she realized that it was the truth. She'd always love Tony, even if he had a mistress. And she'd still love him even if, as Erik so wrongly suspected, he was the Video Killer. She couldn't turn off her love the way she shut off the kitchen faucet. It just wasn't that easy. She could disapprove of Tony's actions, and even despise the new qualities that had surfaced in his personality, but she couldn't stop loving him.

"Eat your sandwich, Tony." Allison gave him a little hug before she stepped back. "And then you'd better go straight to bed if you want to get any sleep at all."

"I wish hugging you could take the place of eating and sleeping." Tony flashed his old grin at her. "Do you think it'd work?"

"I don't think so." Allison smiled back. "Go on, Tony. You don't have much time left."

As soon as Tony had gone into the bedroom and shut the door, Allison went back to her movie. She was about to start watching *Marnie* again when the doubts hit her. Tony's affection was sincere, she was sure of it. But she dialed the office anyway.

"Erik? I'm glad I caught you. Will you look on Tony's desk and see if his lighter is there? It's just like the one you borrowed from the girl at Donny's."

"Sure, Allison. Hold on a second and I'll go look."

As she waited, Allison could feel her heart pounding in her chest. If Tony's lighter was at the office, all her fears would be groundless.

"Allison?" Erik's voice came back on the line. "Sorry, but I couldn't find it. There's nothing on Tony's desk except a book of matches from the Traveler Motel on Fair-fax."

Allison was just struggling to find her voice to thank him when Erik spoke again.

"I'm afraid I've got bad news, Allison. I called UCLA about the Hitchcock project Tony has you working on. They referred me to about six different extensions, but nobody knows anything about it."

"You're sure?"

Erik's voice was full of sympathy when he answered her.

"Yes, Allison. I'm sure. I'm afraid it's another one of Tony's lies."

18

Daniele Renee studied her face in the wavy mirror over the sink and rummaged in the drawer for her lipstick brush. Her once-beautiful face was puffy from the drinking, but her makeup covered a multitude of sins. Her hands were shaking as she applied color to her lips. Another drink would help, but she'd already had three in the bar, and she didn't want to look like a lush. The man was waiting for her in the living room, so she had to hurry. She'd given him her scrapbook to look at, but she didn't have many screen credits, so there wasn't much in it.

When he'd first approached her in the bar and called her by name, she'd been puzzled. Had she met him before? He'd explained that he'd seen her on the screen, and since he'd been armed with her favorite drink, a Tequila Sunrise, she'd agreed that he could join her. By the second drink she'd been

312

impressed at how he'd followed her career. He'd praised the bit part she'd played two years ago in a low-budget film, and he was probably the one person in the world who'd recognized her in the elf costume she'd worn for a cookie commercial. After the third drink, when he'd asked if they could go somewhere quiet to talk about the movie that he was producing, she'd suggested dinner at the Bistro, just to check his reaction. Everyone knew it was expensive.

In the course of her acting career, Daniele had run into plenty of men who claimed they were producers. It was a standard line they used to pick up an actress. But this man was well dressed, and he appeared to have money. He might just be the exception.

The man had agreed immediately, even though he'd already eaten. There would be no problem getting reservations since he knew the maître d'. The Bistro was one of his favorite restaurants, and he tried to get there at least once a week. Had she tried their *Coquilles Saint-Jacques à la provençal?*

Daniele had been a bit nervous when she followed him out to his car. It was Sunday night, she was an actress, and there had been warnings on the news all week about the Video Killer. Then, when he'd unlocked the door to his expensive Mercedes, Daniele had thrown caution to the winds. She prided herself on being a good judge of character, and this man simply couldn't be the Video Killer. He was much too rich and much too nice. She'd suggested they skip dinner and go straight to her place. It was private, and she still had enough liquor in the bottle to mix him a drink. Kirstin, her roommate, had a job demonstrating all-purpose wonder knives at the annual boat show in the L.A. auditorium. The show didn't close until eleven, and since it was only a little after eight, Daniele knew she had at least three uninterrupted hours to convince him that she was the perfect actress for his movie. This could be her big chance, even bigger than the one she'd blown when she'd been married to Erik Nielsen.

A frown crossed Daniele's forehead as she remembered her other chance, the part in the comedy series that Erik had made her turn down. And she'd suffered through all the inconveniences of her pregnancy, watched her beautiful body change into something so bloated and ugly that she'd barely recognized herself in the mirror, all for a baby who had to be shipped off to some fancy sanitarium.

Daniele shuddered a little as she remembered the expression on Erik's face when she'd explained that she couldn't possibly take care of the baby. He'd looked at her like she was some kind of monster. But wasn't that better than ruining her career for a kid who'd never even know his own name?

There were tears in her eyes, and Daniele blinked them away quickly. Fourteen years had passed. Jamie was a teenager now, a child's mind trapped in an adult's body. Several times she'd almost called Erik to ask about Jamie, but she'd always hung up before his phone could ring. Sometimes it was better not to know.

A final pat to her hair, and Daniele was ready. The whole process of redoing her makeup had taken less than five minutes. Now she was glad that she'd brought the man here, to her apartment. The lamp she'd switched on in the living room had a rosy glow in which she knew she'd look beautiful. She put on her best smile, opened the door, and stepped out.

Where was he? Daniele's breath caught in her throat as she saw that the couch was empty. Had he grown tired of waiting and left? Then she heard a noise in the kitchen, and she began to breathe again. He was just freshening his drink.

"I hope I didn't take too long." Her voice was perfectly modulated, friendly, inviting. It was the voice of the innocent seductress she'd played in her first part.

Daniele stood in the center of the room with her best profile toward the kitchen doorway. As she heard his footsteps cross the floor, she turned, very slowly and very gracefully. Then everything seemed to speed up suddenly as her eyes focused on the camera, red light glowing. And the apparition that approached her. And the knife blade slashing down. And then the action stopped. Permanently. And her scream died stillborn on her perfectly drawn and colored lips.

It was past ten at night when Sam finished his third bowl of stew and pushed his chair back from the table. Katy had fixed his favorite meal, Irish stew with fresh vegetables and big man-sized hunks of meat. He'd eaten in hundreds of Los Angeles restaurants, but he'd never found one that served stew like Katy's. And the soda bread. She's told him her secret was ground cardamom seeds for flavoring.

She'd been here every night this week, cooking for him and sharing his bed. Sam

316

knew why, and he'd doled out just enough tidbits about the Video Killer to keep her coming back for more. He knew she had an ulterior motive, but so did he. He wanted his wife back for good.

Katy came out of the kitchen, carrying a steaming cup of fresh coffee and a whole pie. Some of the juice had bubbled up through the crust, and it looked like peach, his favorite.

"Coffee, Sam?"

"You bet. It's Sunday night, Katy. I have to stay alert."

"Do you think he'll do it again tonight?"

"There's no reason to think he'll break his pattern, but let's not talk about it now. I want to enjoy my dessert." Sam hooked his arm around her waist as she began to slice the pie. It was definitely peach. "I don't suppose there's any . . ."

"Ice cream to go on top? Of course there is. If you can hold off for a minute, I'll get it."

Sam stared down at his slice of pie as Katy dashed back to the kitchen. Then he reached out to lightly touch the crust. It was still warm and the aroma was tantalizing. He took his fork and cut off the very tip. The crust was light and flaky, the way only Katy could make it. An expression of rapture crossed Sam's face as he popped the forkful in his mouth. Delicious! He'd have just one more bite and then wait for the ice cream.

"Where's the ice cream scoop, Sam?"

Sam chewed quickly and swallowed. The pie looked a little ragged now, and Katy had always complained that he'd finished his dessert before she could dish out the ice cream, so he cut off a little more to even it up. She'd given him a big piece to start with and she'd never know the difference.

"Uh . . . I don't know, Katy. I haven't seen it since I hired the new cleaning woman. She must have put it somewhere."

The pie really looked lopsided now. Sam shaved a little more off the left side with his fork.

"Did you ask her where she put it?"

Sam frowned down at the pie. Perhaps a little more off the right would make it more wedgeshaped. "I can't ask her, Katy. I don't know the word for ice cream scoop in Vietnamese."

"Doesn't she speak English?"

Sam eyed his slice of pie critically and shaved off a bit more. It still looked lopsided. "Very little, but she's going to night school. I figure by Christmas she'll be able to understand me."

"It's okay, Sam. I'll use a big spoon and buy a new scoop tomorrow."

Sam heard Katy pull out the silverware drawer, and he made a last stab to even up the pie. Perfect.

"Here's the ice cream." Katy appeared at his elbow with a big spoonful. Then she looked down at his pie and started to laugh. "Oh, Sam! I knew I shouldn't have left you alone with that pie. You never could wait for the à la mode part."

Sam grabbed her and pulled her down in his lap. He kissed her, and neither one of them cared that the spoon was dripping on the tablecloth.

"I've got a great idea." Sam's voice was husky with passion. "Why don't you put the ice cream back in the freezer, Katy? Or better yet, just leave it here."

Katy set the ice cream down on the table. It was difficult to believe what she'd just heard. Ice cream was Sam's favorite thing. Or at least she'd always thought it was. She kissed him on the tip of the nose and cuddled even closer.

"But, Sam, don't you want a second piece?"

"Yes, honey." Sam got to his feet and carried her to the bedroom. "I definitely want a second piece."

Tony stashed his video camera in his carrying bag and slipped on his jacket, covering his orange T-shirt, which proclaimed BEING GOOD IS BETTER THAN BEING NICE in blue letters.

"That's it for tonight, gang. Do you girls have a ride? It's Sunday."

"We know." Ginger shivered a little. "Bobby's taking us home. Besides, Sunday's almost over, isn't it?"

Tony glanced at his watch and grinned.

"Nope. It's only ten-thirty. I thought we'd be here for another couple of hours, but your new scenes go a lot faster and they're easier to shoot."

"Oh, sure." Tina grumbled. "Easier for you guys maybe, but not for me. I just about died, bending over that chair. And look at my feet! Next time get roller skates that fit me, will you, Tony?"

Tony couldn't help it. He started to laugh. Ginger and Bobby joined in, and finally even Tina began to smile.

"Okay, okay. I guess I shouldn't complain. But if you decide to do another scene with wheels, put Bobby on 'em. My legs feel like rubber."

Ginger looked thoughtful as they started out the door. "Wheels, huh? Maybe one of those exercise bikes, the type that leans way back. We could open with Bobby pedaling away, and then we could —"

Tony grinned as the rest of Ginger's sentence was cut off by the closing door. She was bound to come up with something weird by tomorrow night. She had an active imagination, and she was a wizard at finding props they could use. Tonight they'd done a scene in a doctor's office, a bank, and a bakery. And they'd finished with Tina playing a topless pizza delivery girl on roller skates. Ginger's talents were being wasted, doing skin flicks like this, but at least she made enough money to support herself. That was more than he could claim.

Tony took a clean T-shirt from his camera bag and pulled it on. It was black with red letters that said WARNING: LIVING MAY BE DANGEROUS TO YOUR HEALTH. Then he made a final check of the room before letting himself out. The nap he'd taken at home had been worse than no sleep at all. It seemed he had barely closed his eyes when the alarm had sounded, and he'd crawled out of bed to shower and rush off. He'd found a pipe store that was open on Sundays, picked out a duplicate lighter, and paced the floor nervously while it was being inscribed. Then he'd rushed straight here and worked on the porn for five and a half hours.

As Tony walked quickly down the block to his car, he wondered what would happen if he just stopped, gave up, stretched out on a concrete bench at the bus stop, and took a little snooze like some deadbeat wino. Right now that prospect was immensely appealing. No responsibilities. No deadlines to meet. And plenty of good hot food from the Salvation Army soup kitchen.

Tony hesitated slightly as he walked past the bench, and then he laughed. If he actually did it, he'd probably end up getting busted by a couple of L.A.'s finest. Then, when Allison came down to bail him out, she'd find out there wasn't any money in their bank account. It would be one colossal mess. No. He couldn't give way to his exhaustion now. There simply wasn't time. At ten-thirty his evening was only beginning. First he had to get something to eat. His body wouldn't run without fuel. And then he had to drive to the office to work on the script. Maybe, if he really rushed and the traffic was light, he might catch a couple of minutes sleep on the office couch before Erik came in.

Tony unlocked his car door and got into the driver's seat. Before he started the engine, he gulped down two dexies with a swallow of cold coffee that was left in his dashboard cup. He had to keep going. There was no end in sight.

Katy and Sam were watching television. To be more accurate, Sam was watching television. Katy had stretched out on the couch, and she was currently sleeping through a rerun of a talk show. The topic tonight was the oldest profession, and a particularly succulent blonde had just come on to tell of her experiences in Vegas when Sam noticed that Katy was crying in her sleep.

"Katy? Honey, what's wrong?"

Drowsily, Katy said, "Uh . . . nothing. Just a bad dream."

"Tell me about it." Sam pulled her into his arms.

"I don't exactly remember it, Sam. I was doing something bad. Something terrible. And then you found out about it and . . ."

"And what?" Sam prompted her.

"And you didn't love me anymore!" Before Sam had time to reply, Katy found herself sobbing again.

"Don't cry, honey." Sam stroked her hair. "It was just a dream, and that's impossible anyway."

"What's impossible?"

"There's nothing you could do that would —"

The phone rang loudly, drowning out the rest of Sam's sentence, but Katy knew what he had almost said. *There's nothing you could do that would make me stop loving you.* His words were sincere. She knew that. But would he change his mind if he knew that she had taken advantage of his loving trust in her to copy the murder discs?

Sam reached for the phone and answered it before it could ring again. He listened for a moment, and then Katy saw his face harden into that of the professional cop as he barked out orders.

"Another one? Jesus! Get Jackson and the fingerprint team out right away, but tell them not to touch anything until I get there. I'm ten minutes away."

Sam hung up the receiver and jumped up. Then he turned to Katy, and his expression softened.

"It's another murder, honey. Do you want to come along? I hate to leave you here alone, and I could sure use your help. Bob said the victim's roommate is pretty shaken up, and you've always been good at calming people down."

324

Katy started to nod, and then she stared at Sam in disbelief. "But, Sam, you forgot. I might pick up some information at the scene and I'm a reporter!"

"I didn't forget." Sam smiled at her. "I just decided to bend procedure for the sake of humanity. I know I can trust you to check your story with me before you file it."

"Of course I will, Sam!"

As Katy climbed into the car and they raced toward the murder scene, she found herself thinking about what Sam had said. He trusted her to check her story with him before she filed it. And she'd promised she would. This time. If only she could do that with her feature on the Video Killer!

Allison shut off the television and returned the movie she had just watched to its case. It was past one in the morning, and she was exhausted. She wished she could go to bed, but she knew she couldn't sleep with work left to do. She had just watched the last Hitchcock movie for Tony's list, and now all that remained was to check the accuracy of her notes against the resource material she'd gathered.

Her eyes hurt from watching the screen so intently, and Allison took three aspirins before she opened the big cardboard box on the coffee table. She'd called Larry Edmunds Bookshop in Hollywood this afternoon and explained exactly what she'd needed. Within an hour a messenger had delivered seven books. Three were basic synopses of Hitchcock's plots, two contained stills from various features and a brief critique of his methods, another had a complete cast list with pictures of his stars, and the last was a biography of the man himself. These seven books, along with the notes she'd found from her college class, would prove that her list of Hitchcock's victims was valid and complete.

Allison yawned as she arranged the books in a pile. It would be a long night, and she wondered whether she ought to just throw the list in the wastebasket and quit. If what Erik had told her this afternoon was true and there was no UCLA research project, she had wasted her time. She was tempted to go straight to bed, but she couldn't let Tony down.

Without being consciously aware of what she was doing, Allison began to make excuses for Tony. She'd worked as a student assistant while she was in college, answering the telephones and taking messages. She remembered making several stupid mistakes. When Erik had called UCLA to ask about the project, he might have talked to a series of student helpers. Or even more likely, the person on the staff who knew about the Hitchcock study might be away on summer vacation.

Allison checked her first two references and then she sighed deeply. She could explain away the phone call Erik had made to the college, but there was the matter of Tony's lighter. He'd lied about that. Or had he? That might have been a simple mistake, a case of remembering something inaccurately. How many times had she been willing to swear that she'd left her purse on the ledge in the hallway and found it on the bed instead? Erik had looked for Tony's lighter on his desk, and it could have been anywhere in the office. She was jumping to conclusions, and that wasn't fair to Tony.

But was Tony at the office now? He'd told her he'd be working with Erik all night. If she called the office, and he wasn't there, she'd have definite proof that he'd lied.

Allison picked up the phone and dialed the number. Her hands were shaking. She gripped the phone so tightly her knuckles were white. One ring. Two rings. Then Erik's voice came on the line.

"Hello, Erik?" Allison had to work to control her breathing. "Is Tony there?"

"Hold on a second, Allison. I'll put him on. By the way, he found his lighter about ten minutes ago. He left it in the men's room. That silver's beautiful, but your inscription's something else. At first I thought it was a gift from Debby Boone."

"Oh, thank you, Erik!" Allison breathed a big sigh of relief. Tony was at the office. And he'd found his lighter. Erik had been very clever about telling her that it had the proper inscription.

"Honey? There's nothing wrong, is there?" Tony came on the line. "It's past two in the morning."

"Is it that late?" For a moment Allison didn't know what to say. She had to give him some reason for calling. "I just called with a progress report. I watched the last Hitchcock film, and I'm just finishing up my notes. I think I can have it ready for you by tomorrow afternoon."

"That's wonderful, honey!" Tony sounded tired but grateful. "I knew I could count on you."

Allison hung up the phone and smiled. Tony was at the office, just like he'd said. And he'd found his lighter. All the tension of the past few weeks began to disappear. She found herself so tired she could barely keep her eyes open. There was no need for her Valium tonight. She'd fall asleep the minute her head touched the pillow.

Five minutes later Allison was in bed. She'd set the alarm clock for six. It would be easier to finish checking the list when she was rested. It wasn't until she was dropping off to sleep, a contented smile on her face, that she remembered Erik's description of the lighter. Silver? The one she'd given Tony for their anniversary had been gold.

19

Monday, August 2

Erik finished proofing the *Frenzy* scene on the computer screen. "It works, Tony. As a matter of fact, I think it's the best thing we've done so far."

"Good." Tony nodded and rubbed his eyes. "Let's print the whole thing out and take it over to Alan's office."

"Now?" Erik glanced at Tony's clock. "I haven't figured out how to read your clock, but it's got to be early. It's still dark outside."

"You're right. It's only five in the morning. Remember what I told you about the pink oblong thing and the purple rectangles? The orange square is three green dots past . . ."

"Forget it, Tony." Erik interrupted what he knew would be another lesson on telling time. "I'm too tired to concentrate on something that complicated."

"Yeah. Me too."

Erik glanced at his partner closely. Tony looked as if he hadn't had any sleep in a week.

"Why don't you catch a nap on the couch, Tony? I'll wake you up after I print out and do the final proof."

"That'd be a lifesaver." Tony gave him a tired grin. Exhaustion was too tame a word for how he was feeling. "Are you sure you don't mind?"

"No. Go ahead. You can't walk into Alan's office looking like death warmed over."

Erik watched as Tony stumbled out into the reception area and stretched out on the couch. By the time he'd gone to his own office to bring back a blanket and pillow, Tony was already asleep. It was no wonder. They'd met at the office around midnight and worked on the scenes for Alan all night. They'd both been in rough shape in the service, but Tony looked even worse now. He'd lost weight and his face was pale and haggard. It was obvious that he was worn down physically from too many cigarettes, too much coffee, and not enough sleep.

A wave of pity washed over Erik as he stared down at Tony's sleeping face. When a person drove himself as hard as Tony was doing, the stress was bound to take a serious mental toll. It seemed impossible that Tony was the Video Killer, but Erik had done some research into serial murderers for their movie concept. They were usually tortured individuals under extreme stress. Most had no concept of the hideous crimes they had committed, and one man was quite honestly horrified when he was confronted with the evidence against him. If Tony really was the Video Killer, he might be totally unaware of his actions.

As he covered Tony with the blanket and slipped the pillow under his head, Erik began to feel guilty over the way his mind was working. Tony looked much more like a tired boy, worn out after a big day at the amusement park, than an insane killer. He had tried and convicted his partner in his mind without a shred of real evidence.

It wasn't until Erik had gone into the kitchen to pour himself a fresh cup of coffee that he realized what day it was. Tony had been at his desk when Erik had arrived, shortly after midnight, and they'd been together since then. The thought made Erik cringe, but he found himself hoping that another actress had been killed. If the Video Killer had struck after midnight, he'd have proof that Tony was innocent.

Erik ran the spelling program on the pages

they'd done and started the printout. The swishing sound of the paper emerging from the printer seemed suddenly deafening, so he switched on the radio to mask the noise. The classical music station he found was playing Beethoven's Fifth, and the booming crashes of the bass notes made his headache worse but at least he couldn't hear the printer.

As soon as the first scene was printed, Erik picked up and straightened the pages. When Alan's uncle coughed up with the *Video Kill* contracts and they finally got their money, it might be wise to invest in some updated office equipment.

About the time the Beethoven ended, Erik finished printing out the second scene. The classical station's next selection was German Lieder, sung by a lusty soprano. Erik got up to switch the station and caught the very end of a news flash. The Video Killer has struck again. And Tony had been here all night! Erik let out a whoop and ran to wake Tony.

"The Video Killer?" Tony sat up and blinked. "What was that, Erik?"

"He struck again last night. I just caught the tail end of the news flash on the radio. Turn on the television and I'll get up a cup of coffee."

Erik came back just in time. The words NEWS FLASH were blinking on and off with a recorded voice-over.

WE INTERRUPT OUR REGULAR PRO-GRAMMING FOR THIS ANNOUNCE-MENT. THE VIDEO KILLER STRUCK AGAIN IN HOLLYWOOD AT APPROXI-MATELY NINE O'CLOCK LAST NIGHT. THE FULL STORY IN A MOMENT.

As the announcement was repeated, Erik sighed. The Video Killer has struck at nine o'clock. He could account for Tony's where-abouts after midnight but not before. Tony was still a suspect.

The anchor's face appeared on the screen. He looked somber. "This just in. The latest in the Video Killer murders took place in Hollywood last night. Police arrived at the scene of the crime, the four hundred block of Irvine, at shortly after midnight this morning. L.A. Chief Detective Sam Ladera said that evidence found at the scene points to another in the series of murders that has been terrorizing the show business com-munity. The victim, Miss Daniele Renee, was an actress."

There was a crash as Erik's coffee cup fell to the table. Tony glanced over at his partner in alarm.

"Erik? Are you all right?"

"Huh? I'm . . . uh. . . ." Erik's face was bloodless, and his mouth opened and closed as he struggled to answer. "I'm fine."

"You had me scared there for a minute. What's the matter? You look like you've seen a ghost."

"I . . . uh . . . I just have a blinding headache, that's all. I get them sometimes. I . . . I think I'd better take a pill."

"Sure, Erik. I tell you what. Why don't you go on home and get some rest. I can finish printing out and deliver to Alan. There's no reason why you have to go along."

"Uh . . . well . . . maybe that's a good idea."

Tony watched as Erik fumbled in his pocket and took out a packet of pills. He tried to punch one out of its plastic bubble, but his hands were shaking too badly.

"Here. Let me."

Tony took the packet and got a pill out for Erik. Then he watched anxiously as his partner half staggered into the kitchenette for a glass of water. He'd never seen Erik like this before. It must be one hell of a bad headache.

The packet of pills was still in his hand,

and Tony glanced at it curiously. The name of the drug was printed on top. *Mezopropathalomine.* And the words *For Experimental Use Only* were written across the package in bright red letters. The doctor's name was stamped on the back, Dr. S. Trumbull, with a telephone number. He looked up just in time to see Erik headed for the door.

"Erik? You forgot your pills."

Tony got up and handed Erik the packet of pills. He noticed that Erik's hands were trembling as he took them.

"Thanks, Tony. I'd better get home right away. This stuff really zonks me out."

"Do you want me to drive you? I can shut off the printer and —"

"No!" Erik sounded panic-stricken. "That's not necessary, Tony. I'll be home long before it hits if I start right now."

"Are you sure those pills are safe? I mean, they say *experimental* all over them. There's nothing seriously wrong, is there, Erik?"

"Of course not." Erik tried to give him a reassuring smile. "I just get bad headaches, that's all. And those pills are nothing but a new kind of aspirin."

As soon as Erik was gone, Tony reached for a piece of paper to jot down the name of the doctor and his phone number. Erik was lying. Something as ordinary as aspirin couldn't zonk you out, and it certainly wouldn't have *experimental* written all over it in red letters. He'd call this Dr. Trumbull just as soon as his office opened to find the truth.

Allison was the first customer in line at the bank when it opened at ten in the morning. It had taken two coats of foundation to cover the dark circles under her eyes, but Tony's list was completed, and she'd decided to investigate their financial situation herself. The incident with the lighter had convinced her that if Tony could lie to her about one thing, he might be lying about others, too. She knew she couldn't relax until she knew that there was enough money to pay for her mother's medical expenses.

"May I help you, ma'am?" The young woman seated on a high stool behind the teller's cage gave Allison a brilliant smile. She was wearing a pin that said JOIN OUR CHRISTMAS CLUB NOW.

"I hope so." Allison smiled back. "I'm Mrs. Tony Rocca, and I need to know our account balance."

"Would that be passbook savings or checking, Mrs. Rocca?"

Allison thought quickly. She knew they had a checking account, and she vaguely remembered signing something Tony said was a signature card for a savings account.

"Both, please."

"And the accounts are under whose name?"

"Allison Greene Rocca and Tony D. Rocca."

"R . . . O . . . C . . . A?"

"No. R . . . O . . . C . . . C . . . A."

The woman jotted down the correct spelling on a piece of paper and looked up at Allison again.

"Do you have your passbook or your checkbook with you, Mrs. Rocca?"

Allison shook her head. Tony kept the checkbook, and now that she thought about it, she'd never even seen the savings passbook. Tony probably had it in his desk.

"That's all right." The woman smiled. "I can get it from the computer, but I need a little more information. Are these joint accounts?"

"I really don't know. My husband opened them. What other types of accounts are there?"

"We offer joint accounts, partnership accounts, and trustee accounts."

"Could you please tell me the difference?"

"Certainly, Mrs. Rocca." The woman smiled again, but Allison could tell it was wearing thin. "On joint accounts either person can sign to complete a transaction. Most husbands and wives have this type of account. Partnership accounts require both signatures. And on trustee accounts, the second party may sign only upon the death of the primary party."

"I believe we have joint accounts."

Allison glanced behind her and noticed that the line was growing longer. She had no idea this would be so complicated.

"Do you know if the accounts are business or personal?"

"Personal. Definitely personal."

"And what is your social security number, Mrs. Rocca?"

As Allison rattled off the nine-digit number, she heard people beginning to mutter in line behind her. She felt terribly guilty for taking up this much time, but there was no way around it. The bank wouldn't give out account balances over the phone.

"And now I need to see three pieces of identification, one with a photograph."

Allison fumbled in her purse and came up with her driver's license and two credit cards. The woman glanced at them and pushed the credit cards back.

"The driver's license is fine, Mrs. Rocca, but I can't accept these credit cards. They're in your husband's name. Do you have any other personal identification?"

"I . . . I don't think so."

The woman looked up, saw the size of the line behind Allison, and lost the last vestige of her smile.

"Then you'll have to fill out an exceptional cause application. Please follow me. I'll take you to see Mr. Thatcher."

Allison winced as the woman put out a NEXT WINDOW PLEASE sign. Several people groaned, and she gave them an apologetic look as she followed the teller to a desk in the rear of the building.

"Mr. Thatcher?" The teller approached a middle-aged man who wore a dour expression. Evidently, only tellers were required to smile. "This is Mrs. Allison Rocca. She wants to check her account balances, but she doesn't have the proper identification."

"Please sit down, Mrs. Rocca. Naturally we apologize for any delay that you may have encountered, but I'm sure you can understand why we must be scrupulous in the discharge of our duties. I am reasonably certain that you wouldn't want a stranger to walk into the lobby of this financial institution, request a copy of Allison Rocca's account balance, and receive it!"

"Of course not."

"And that, Mrs. Rocca, is precisely why we demand unquestionable proof of identity. You, our valued customer, have charged us with this obligation. It's for your own protection, you see. Now, do you carry anything with the name Allison Rocca on it?"

"Just a moment. I'll check again." Allison pulled out her card case and went through it. She felt so chastised that she wanted to get up and walk out, but she wasn't about to leave without learning their balance. Suddenly she remembered the discount card for a mail order jewelry store she'd received in the mail. She'd written her name on it herself and stuck it in her wallet. Surely a man who so scrupulously discharged his duties wouldn't accept it as proof of identification, would he?

"Will this do, Mr. Thatcher?" Allison handed him the discount card even though she was sure he'd reject it.

"That's acceptable. Now all you need is one more."

Allison checked the flap behind her driver's license and found an old library card from the time she and Tony had spent a summer in Connecticut. It had expired ten years ago, but she gave it to Mr. Thatcher and crossed her fingers.

"It's out of state." Mr. Thatcher frowned. "Don't you have anything else?"

"I'm afraid not."

"Well . . . I think we can make an exception this time. Now I need the answer to a few short questions. We'll start with the checking account."

Twenty minutes later Allison walked out of the bank, clutching a slip of paper with their account balances. She still couldn't believe what Mr. Thatcher had written on the paper. Their joint savings account contained four dollars and seventeen cents. And the checking account would show a negative balance once the monthly service charge was deducted. Tony had lied. They were broke. Flat broke.

For the first time in her life, Allison didn't listen to the traffic report before she got on the freeway. There was the usual jam at the top of the pass, but she barely noticed when she had to creep along at ten miles an hour. She was too busy rehearsing what she would say to her agent when she dropped in at the office to beg for work.

It was ten o'clock by the time Tony dropped off the script at Alan's office. He was only fifteen minutes from the house, and even though he still had what seemed like millions of things to do, he needed to talk to Allison. He wanted to tell her about Erik's medicine and ask her what she thought. When he'd told Dr. Trumbull's nurse that it was critical, she'd given him the earliest appointment possible. The doctor was away on vacation and wouldn't be back until next Sunday, but she could squeeze Tony in then, right after his morning rounds. She was sorry, but there was no way she could give him any information about a patient over the phone. Tony had tried all his usual tricks, but he'd run into a stone wall. Then he'd thought of Allison. It was a long shot, but perhaps Erik had confided in her about what Tony was sure was a serious illness.

Tony didn't make the connection until he was pulling up in front of the house. The Video Killer's latest victim. Daniele Renee. The name sounded very familiar when he'd heard it, but he'd figured that he'd probably met her at a party or something. Now he remembered. Daniele Renee was the actress Erik had married.

Tony's hands were shaking as he got out his key and unlocked the front door. No wonder Erik had been so upset! He'd tell Allison about it, and maybe she could run over to Erik's apartment to see if there was anything she could do. He'd go, but he had to meet Sam in less than an hour.

Allison didn't answer when Tony called out for her. He checked every room, but she was obviously gone. There was no note on the refrigerator. She was probably at the convalescent center visiting her mother. If he'd called first, he could have saved himself the trip.

Tony was ready to turn around and go back out to his car. He didn't have time to wait for her to come home. But now that he'd driven all the way here, he might as well check to see whether she'd finished her list.

A packet of paper was on the table, and Tony picked it up. Five copies of the Hitchcock list, collated and stapled. Allison had come through for him again. She always was a whiz at doing research. He'd get this right over to Sam, and they could start warning look-alike actresses.

Tony scrawled a hasty note and slipped it under a magnet that was shaped like a watermelon slice on the door of the refrigerator. It said, THANKS FOR THE LIST, BABY — AT OFFICE UNTIL LATE — WILL CALL. Then he rushed back out and tried not to speed as he drove to police headquarters.

Tony shuddered as the monitor in Sam's

office went blank. They had just finished watching the fifth murder DVD, the worst of the lot as far as Tony was concerned. It wasn't just the cold-blooded murder of Erik's ex-wife that was so horrifying. It was the list he held in his hand. Tony glanced at Allison's neat printout again.

THE 39 STEPS (1935) G.B.
Victim — Lucie Mannheim
Method of Murder — Stabbing

If they'd had that list yesterday, Sam might have been able to warn Daniele Renee in time to save her life.

"What's the matter?" Sam turned to Tony as he shuddered again.

Tony hesitated. He'd been about to tell Sam that the latest victim was his partner's ex-wife, but he'd quickly thought better of it. Sam would find out soon enough, and poor Erik didn't need some cop hammering on his door, asking him questions.

"I was just thinking that this one didn't have to die. We could have warned her if I'd had this damn list sooner. She's a Lucie Mannheim look-alike."

Sam put his hand on Tony's shoulder. "Sam Spade's first rule of good detective work. Don't get hung up on what might have been. You finished that list a lot faster than I expected, and now I'll start warning actresses personally. How many Hitchcock victims are left?"

"Too many." Tony sighed and referred to his copy. "We could narrow it down if we knew which movie he'd choose next, but I haven't been able to find a pattern. Hitchcock killed off a lot of actresses in his films, and for every victim, there are at least twenty or thirty look-alikes."

"That many?" Sam looked shocked as Tony nodded.

"I went to a costume party once, where everyone was supposed to come dressed like a famous character in a movie. There must have been twenty girls that came as Scarlett O'Hara in *Gone with the Wind,* and every one of them looked the part. All those Vivien Leigh's, Sam, at one random party. Those are the kinds of numbers you're up against."

"Okay, I'll just take those books of photos you gave me and start making calls. Why don't you run home and get some sleep? You look as if you've been up all night."

"Well, most of it." Tony got to his feet and yawned. "Call me if you need me, Sam. If I'm not at the office, the answering machine'll be on."

On his way out Tony noticed that Andy Mertens was at the desk again. He waved and started for the door, but before he could get outside, the older officer stopped him.

"Hey, Archer! Can I talk to you a minute?"

"Sure. What is it, Andy?"

"It took a couple of weeks, but I think I got it figured out." Andy lowered his voice. "If you're Archer, the chief's got to be Sam Spade! Am I right?"

20

Saturday, August 7

Alan Goldberg gave a weary sigh as he waited for the butler to call his uncle to the phone. He'd sent a copy of Rocca and Nielsen's sample scenes to Hawaii on Monday, and Uncle Meyer still hadn't called with his decision. Alan needed an answer today. Cinescope's option ran out at midnight tomorrow.

"Hi, Uncle Meyer." Alan made his voice deliberately cheerful. "I called to see what you thought of the *Video Kill* partial."

Static crackled from the receiver, and Alan held it away from his ear until it stopped. "What was that, Uncle Meyer? We have a bad connection."

Alan listened for a minute and then he winced. The old man was cranky this morning.

"Of course, Uncle Meyer. I'm very interested in the air pollution reading in Honolulu. I just forgot to ask, that's all."

Alan sipped his coffee and leaned back in his chair as Uncle Meyer went into a lengthy lecture on the levels of ozone and nitrogen dioxide and carbon monoxide. While he was listening, he flipped through the paper for a summary of the week's air quality ratings for the L.A. area.

"You're lucky you're not here, Uncle Meyer." Alan lit a cigarette and glanced down at the figures. "It was really bad yesterday. West L.A., downtown, and the airport had third-stage episodes. They kept broadcasting that the air was hazardous for everyone."

As his uncle reacted predictably and went into another of his tirades on pollution, Alan crumpled up the paper and tossed it in the wastebasket. Actually, the whole L.A. Basin had been in the safe zone, but Uncle Meyer didn't need to know that. He was looking out the window, watching a bird build its nest on the ledge below, when his uncle asked a question that made him sit up with a jolt.

"Yes, Uncle Meyer. I know our option on *Video Kill* runs out tomorrow. If we don't sew it up now, another studio could snatch it right out of our hands."

There was another burst of static, and

Alan caught the tail end of his uncle's question.

"Other offers? Yes, Uncle Meyer. I know for a fact that they have. Sony is very hot on the project, and Rocca and Nielsen have already taken one meeting with someone at Paramount."

Alan put down the phone very gently and got up to pour himself another cup of coffee as his uncle hemmed and hawed. Mentioning other offers had been a brilliant tactic on his part. It might even be true, for all he knew. As soon as there was silence from the other end of the line, Alan picked up the phone again.

"So, what's your final decision, Uncle Meyer? Shall I have the contracts drawn?"

Thirty seconds later, Alan said good-bye to his uncle and hung up the phone. Then he opened the manila folder on his desk and scanned the contracts for *Video Kill* he'd ordered from Cinescope's legal department a month ago.

"Good morning. It's Saturday, August seventh, at ten forty-five a.m. Time to get up. Good morning. It's Saturday, August seventh, at ten forty-five. Time to get up. Good mor—"

Erik sat up in bed and pushed the button

350

on his new alarm clock, cutting off its disgustingly cheerful synthesized voice. He'd finally replaced Daniele's clock with this new digital model. He didn't want anything to remind him of Daniele and the awful way she had died.

As he got out of bed, Erik realized what the clock had said. August seventh. Tomorrow was the day their option with Cinescope ran out, and Alan had promised that they'd know one way or the other today. Tony had called several times during the past week, but Erik had put off any meetings between them. He knew Tony wanted to talk about Daniele's murder, and he needed some time before he could discuss it. Naturally, they had to include the scene in their script. It was part of the Video Killer story. But Erik wasn't ready to face that prospect quite yet.

The day after Daniele's murder, Erik had left town. He'd driven up the coast and spent three full days with Jamie at Pine Ridge. Jamie had been glad to see him, and the reports on his progress had been very encouraging. It would have been a wonderful respite if he hadn't been plagued by the headaches. They were worse now, one a night, every night since he'd heard about Daniele. And Dr. Trumbull was out of town on vacation. Erik just hoped his supply of zonkers would last until his next appointment.

Now that last night's headache was completely gone, Erik realized that he was hungry as a hibernating bear. Evidently Al was hungry too. He could hear the big white cat pacing back and forth in the kitchen, meowing and rolling his empty food bowl across the tile floor.

"Hold on, Al. I'm coming."

Erik pulled on a pair of jeans and an old Minnesota Vikings sweatshirt. As he walked into the kitchen, he could swear that Al smiled. A few minutes later Al was chowing down on his microwave-heated food and Erik was standing at the refrigerator door, trying to find something to eat.

The egg carton was empty and the milk that was left in the carton didn't smell right. The bread had some green stuff on the edges that had to be mold, and there wasn't a thing in the apartment to eat. He'd get some take-out Chinese from the place across the street, eat his lunch, and then call Tony to see if he'd heard from Alan.

Tony let out a whoop of joy as he hung up the phone, and several people passing on the street turned to look at him. He'd just finished talking to Alan and the news was fantastic. Cinescope had finally made an offer on *Video Kill,* and the terms were better than either Tony or Erik has expected. They would be going into production as soon as the script was ready. The only hitch was Lon Michaels. Alan's uncle had insisted that he be a part of the deal, and Lon was still dragging his feet. Tony had lied through his teeth when he'd told Alan that Lon was ready to sign. Now he had twenty-four hours to turn that lie into a truth.

With hands that were shaking slightly from the excitement, Tony took out the card with Lon's home number. He dialed, and the phone was answered on the third ring.

"Lon? This is Tony Rocca. Erik and I finished the first three scenes. I know it's your day off but, well, if I bring this partial over to you, do you think you'd have time to read it today? I know I'm asking a lot, but quite frankly we're stuck and we need your advice on which direction to go."

There was a long silence, and Tony gripped the phone so tightly, his knuckles turned white. He wanted to grovel, plead, even cry if that would convince Lon to sign on to the project, but he knew that he had be perfectly silent and wait for Lon's response.

At last Lon broke the silence. "I'm flattered you want my advice, but wouldn't you be better off discussing this with Alan?"

"Come on, Lon." Tony forced a laugh that he hoped would sound lighthearted. "Alan's a money man. I'm not putting that down, but he's not exactly known for his sensitivity."

"That's true." Lon gave a bitter laugh. "Did I tell you what he said about Diana when I ran that test for him?"

"Yes, you did. Alan can be pretty crass at times. And that's precisely the reason we can't use him for a sounding board. We need advice from someone who's in sync with the concept we're trying to present."

"Yes, I can see that." Lon sounded pleased. "All right, Tony. I'll read what you got so far. Can we meet at my house at four?"

"You bet!" Tony wrote down the address and hung up with a grin. As long as he could keep up the bullshit to con Lon into thinking he was indispensable to the project, he'd sign on with no trouble.

The liquor store across the street had a banner advertising a sale on California champagne. Tony dashed in to buy a chilled bottle of Korbel Brut. Then he ran back out again. He had to call Allison right away.

"Damn!" Tony swore as he got the answering machine. He didn't want to leave a message. News this good should be delivered in person. He was just starting to punch out Erik's number to share their good fortune when he noticed the time. He'd have to call Erik later. He was due at the Traveler Motel in twenty minutes and he couldn't be late. He had the only key to the room, and the management might start to get suspicious if they saw Ginger and Tina standing around outside.

Allison let herself in the door and dropped her purse and her tote bag on a chair. She'd just come from a session with the photographer her agent had recommended, and it had gone well. His studio had been a reconverted garage with a shower curtain strung in one corner for a dressing room, but since he was just breaking into the business, he worked cheap.

Once she had seen the state of their bank balance, or rather, the absence of their bank balance, Allison had decided to take matters into her own hands. Rather than phone her agent, she'd dropped by the office and gone into her rehearsed speech. She needed work badly. She'd take anything. She was available day or night. Her agent hadn't promised anything, but agents never did.

She'd just given Allison the photographer's name so she could update her portfolio and promised to call if anything came up.

The red light was blinking on the answering machine. Allison grabbed a Diet Coke and drank it while she listened to the messages. The first two were hang-ups, but the third was the call she had been anticipating with dread for the past twelve months. It was from Doris Stanley at the convalescent center. Could Allison call her as soon as she got in? Helen Greene had experienced a reaction to her medication, and they had moved her to the hospital.

Erik sat at the kitchen table, struggling with his chopsticks. He had finished an order of Szechuan Beef, and one stubborn peanut was left in the carton. After chasing it around for what seemed like an eternity, he had just managed to pick it up when the telephone rang. Startled, Erik's grip on the chopsticks faltered and the peanut dropped to the kitchen floor in Al's territory. By the time Erik had said hello, Al had the peanut cornered between the dishwasher and the stove.

"Erik? This is Allison. Thank God you're home! Do you know where Tony is?"

"I'm not sure, Allison. Did you try the office?"

"I called there but the answering machine's on. I've got to find him right away!"

Allison sounded rattled, and Erik kept his voice deliberately calm.

"He didn't tell me his schedule, Allison. What's wrong?"

"It's Mom." Allison's voice broke in a sob. "She had an allergic reaction to her medication. They've taken her to the hospital."

"Which hospital?" Erik reached for a pen.

"West Community on Fairfax, room three forty-two. I'm there now."

"I'm so sorry, Allison. Did you leave a message for Tony?"

"Yes, I did. But I'm not sure what I said. I've got to go, Erik. They're paging me."

"Keep calm, Allison." Erik grabbed his car keys. "I'm on my way."

Erik had no sooner hung up the phone when it rang again. It was Tony.

"I've been trying to reach you for twenty minutes, Erik. Where have you been?"

"I just ran across the street for some food. Listen, Tony . . ."

"No, you listen." Tony interrupted him. "Alan's finally offered us a contract! He got the okay from his uncle this morning, provided Lon Michaels signs on. I called

357

Lon and I'm heading over there in a couple of minutes. From the way he sounded on the phone, I'm eighty percent, no, make that ninety percent sure he'll sign."

"That's great, Tony. But is there any way you can reschedule that talk with Lon?" Erik took a deep breath. He didn't like to be the bearer of bad news. "Allison just called. They've moved her mother to West Community Hospital, room three forty-two. She wants you to meet her there right away."

"Oh no. Not again!" Tony sounded exasperated. "Listen, Erik, I know I sound hard-hearted, but it's not like this hasn't happened before. Allison didn't say it was life-threatening did she?"

"Not exactly. She said her mother had an allergic reaction to her medication."

"That's what I thought." Tony sighed. "Look, Erik, if I really thought this was something serious, I'd drop everything. But Allison's mother has been in and out of the hospital four or five times for the same thing. Will you just go and keep Allison company until I can get there?"

"Sure. I'll go. I was going anyway. But what should I tell Allison?"

"Tell her, oh, hell, Erik! Tell her you couldn't reach me."

"I can't lie to her, Tony."

"Then tell her the truth. Say I've got to sign the cinematographer for *Video Kill* or the deal won't go through. I'll have her paged when I'm through, and if she's still there, I'll come right over."

"Okay. I'll tell her."

There was a click, and Tony hung up. Erik followed suit, but he was frowning as he hurried out to his car. He just hoped that Tony's meeting with Lon was actually taking place, that it wasn't just another of Tony's lies.

Katy shuddered as she read the last page of Rocca and Nielsen's partial script. Her friend at Cinescope had come through, and the result was staggering. Rocca and Nielsen's first three scenes paralleled the murder DVDs exactly.

This script was too accurate to be a coincidence. Rocca and Nielsen had known exactly what to write. Katy knew that Sam had been very careful about his press releases and the details contained in this script were highly confidential. Had either Rocca or Nielsen seen the murder DVDs?

Katy disregarded that possibility immediately. Sam was sitting on those DVDs like a mother hen. No one had seen them except Sam . . . and her, of course. There was no one else who could possibly know their content with the exception of the person who had actually shot them. And that meant either Tony Rocca or Erik Nielsen was the Video Killer!

Her hands were trembling, and Katy forced herself to calm down. She was making a snap judgment, and a good reporter didn't jump to conclusions without plenty of evidence.

There was a determined expression on Katy's face as she found her car keys and went out the door. It was time to gather some evidence. As far as she knew, no other reporter had ever interviewed a murderer *before* the police arrested him.

Erik found Allison in the waiting room on the third floor of the hospital, huddled on a green plastic sofa.

"Allison, I'm here."

Allison looked up, startled. "Erik! I've never been so glad to see anyone in my life! Did you find Tony?"

Erik sat down on the sofa next to her and put his arms around her. She was shaking.

"Yes. I talked to him on the phone. Cinescope's made an offer on *Video Kill,* and he's trying to sign the cinematographer. It's important. Without that, the whole deal falls through. He said to tell you that he'll call the hospital as soon as he's finished, and if you're still here, he'll drive right over."

Allison tried to smile. It made her look even more vulnerable.

"Congratulations on *Video Kill,* Erik. But do you think Tony's telling us the truth?"

Erik sighed. "I don't know, Allison. He sounded sincere, but I just can't tell anymore."

"Neither can I. Not even when we're face-to-face. I love Tony, but I just can't trust him. My husband's turned into a stranger."

Tears began to well up in Allison's eyes, and Erik brushed them away.

"I know, Allison. Don't try to deal with it now. How's your mother?"

"Much better. The doctor says she's stable now. They just moved her out of intensive care and into a regular room."

Erik sighed audibly. "Thank God for that! I wasn't sure what to think when I saw you crying."

"I was crying because I was so relieved." Allison gave him a shaky smile. "I always cry after a crisis. I bet I look awful."

"No, you look beautiful. Even with swollen eyes and a red nose."

"Oh, Erik!" Allison started to laugh, but it came out more like a sob. "I think that was a compliment, and if it was, it's the nicest thing anyone's said to me in weeks. You've got to be the sweetest guy I know."

Erik felt his cheeks turning warm, a reaction that would have been more appropriate for a schoolboy. To cover his embarrassment he got up and pretended great interest in the scene outside the window. He didn't turn around until he heard someone calling Allison's name.

"Allison?" A doctor stood in the doorway. "You can see your mother now, but limit your visit to a moment or two. She's resting comfortably. I've given her something to make her sleep through the night. Your husband can come along, of course."

"He's not my husband." Allison smiled at Erik. "Dr. Naiman? I'd like you to meet Erik Nielsen, my husband's partner. And my best friend."

Dr. Naiman shook Erik's hand. Then he turned to Allison.

"Go ahead, Allison. I'll stay here with Mr. Nielsen."

As soon as Allison had left, the doctor turned to Erik. "Can I be frank with you, Mr. Nielsen?"

"Of course."

"I'm very concerned about Allison. She's been under a severe strain the past few weeks. I've refilled her tranquilizer prescription." Dr. Naiman handed Erik a bottle of pills. "There's really no need for her to stay here, so drive her home, give her a Valium, and make sure she goes straight to bed. She can't be a comfort to her mother if she falls ill herself."

Erik sighed as Dr. Naiman hurried off to answer a page. Of course he was happy to help Allison in any way that he could, but this was really Tony's responsibility. If he found out that Tony had been lying about his meeting with Lon Michaels, he'd personally knock his block off.

No more than a minute passed before Allison was back. She was smiling and the tension lines had disappeared from her face.

"Oh, Erik! She looks so much better. It's a miracle!"

"That's wonderful, Allison." Erik hugged her. "Now Dr. Naiman said I should drive you home. Then I've got strict orders to put you to bed."

"Put me to bed?"

"That's what the doctor ordered."

Allison laughed. She felt so relieved about her mother, she almost made a joke about what he didn't have to do to stand in for Tony, but Erik was so clearly embarrassed, she decided not to add to his discomfort.

Instead, she took his arm, rode down the elevator with him, and let him lead her out to the parking lot.

"Leave your car right here, Allison. You can pick it up tomorrow. Dr. Naiman didn't think you should drive."

"That's ridiculous!" Allison fumbled in her purse for her car keys and promptly dropped them on the ground. Her hands were still shaking, and she did feel a little weak-kneed.

"See?" Erik reached down and scooped up her car keys, dropping them in his pocket. "That settles it, Allison. You're riding with me."

Allison didn't resist as Erik led her to his car. Perhaps Dr. Naiman was right. She was still too nervous to drive.

The moment Erik started the car and pulled out of the lot, Allison's eyes closed. She half dozed as Erik negotiated the afternoon traffic and headed toward the freeway entrance. It was nice to have someone take care of her. She wished Tony would be as considerate as Erik. She was almost asleep when she heard Erik swear softly under his breath. She opened her eyes just in time to see a man who looked a lot like Tony coming out of a room at the Traveler Motel.

The man turned slightly, and one quick glance told Allison everything. It was definitely Tony. And he had his arm around the redhead in Donny's who'd loaned her the lighter.

21

Tony was grinning as he walked down the street with Ginger. Everything was rolling along just fine today. They'd finished another two scenes in the porn movie, and if they really hustled, they could wrap it up in a week.

"Are you sure you have time to drop me off at my place?" Ginger hesitated as Tony opened the car door for her. "I can always take the bus."

"It's no problem, Ginger. Thanks to you, I'm running ahead of schedule today. Do you want me to pick you up tomorrow?"

"No. My car should be out of the shop by then. If it isn't, I'll catch a ride with Bobby or Tina."

Tony drove along in silence until he pulled up in front of Ginger's apartment building. He'd been thinking about offering her a job ever since she'd started acting as his unofficial production assistant. She was a hard worker, and no one had to know how they'd met.

"Wait a second, Ginger." Tony reached out to take her arm as she made a move to open the door. "Would you be interested in a job on a real movie? One that isn't X-rated?"

"Sure. Why wouldn't I? But I'm not good enough to be an actress, Tony. I've not had any training."

"I wasn't thinking of acting, Ginger. What I'm talking about would be a production assistant job. You'd work on the set of a movie as a sort of glorified schlepper. Do you know what that is?"

"Sure. Somebody asks for something, and I run to get it. Right?"

"That's part of it. You'd also take notes, answer phones, and deliver messages. The pay's not much and the hours are miserable."

"It sounds like heaven compared to some of the jobs I've had." Ginger laughed. "Who do I have to screw to get on the payroll?"

"No one. If you want it, you've got it. The only stipulation is that you never mention the porn movies we made. What do you say?"

"I say yes. And don't worry, Tony. I'll never open my mouth," Ginger gave him an impish grin, "unless I'm in another one of your movies of course."

Katy walked down the hallway again and stared out the window at the parking lot. The place marked ROCCA was still empty, but the message on the answering machine had said that he'd be in before two-thirty. She'd been waiting outside the office door for close to forty-five minutes, and she was about to give up and come back later when a dark green Volvo pulled into the lot and backed into the space.

It seemed to take forever for the elevator to rise to the top floor. When the doors slid open, Katy ducked into an alcove and watched while Rocca unlocked his office door. She didn't want him to know that she'd camped out on his doorstep. If she appeared too eager, he might be suspicious.

Katy waited five minutes, long enough she thought. Then she knocked at the door and put on her most innocent expression as he opened it.

"Mr. Rocca? Or is it Mr. Nielsen?"

"Tony Rocca."

"I'm glad to meet you, Mr. Rocca." Katy reached out and shook his hand. "I'm Karen Daniels from the Equitable Management Company, but don't worry. I'm not here to sell you anything. Equitable had just taken management of this building, and I'm here to find out what improvements are needed. Do you mind if I come in and ask you a few questions?"

"I'm in a rush. Will it take long?"

"Not at all, Mr. Rocca. It's just a quick walk-through and inspection."

"Well, all right. Follow me, Miss . . ."

"Karen Daniels. Now, do you have a kitchenette with this suite?"

Tony nodded and led her to the kitchenette. Katy tried to look professional as she peered under the sink and inside cupboards. All the while she kept up on a lively chatter, asking questions that had nothing to do with building management. By the time they'd left the kitchenette and gone into Erik Nielsen's office, he'd told her that they'd been partners for five years, that they'd written the script for *Free Fire,* and that they were currently in the process of writing a script for Cinescope about the Video Killer.

"That must be fascinating, Mr. Rocca!" Katy crawled under the desk to check the outlets and pocketed several scraps of paper on the floor. "Will it be fiction or based on fact?"

"It's factual." Tony stopped suddenly, realizing his error, but Katy gave him such a guileless smile that he continued. "We're writing a parallel of the actual murders."

Katy nodded and ran her fingers up and down the window casing, supposedly checking for termite damage. "I read all about the latest murder in the paper. That poor woman! She was strangled, wasn't she?"

"No, she was stabbed. Eight times."

"Terrible!" Katy checked the edge of the rug by the door and shivered a bit. There was no way Tony Rocca could have known the victim was stabbed precisely eight times. Sam hadn't released that information to anyone.

"This rug will have to be retacked, Mr. Rocca. I'll send someone in just as soon as I can. And now, if I could have a peek at your office?"

Katy's eyes went straight to Tony's desk. There were some papers on top that she wanted to examine, but that was impossible while he was in the room with her.

"Oh, Mr. Rocca? I know this is an imposition, but do you suppose I could trouble you for a glass of water? I'll just check your cold air return while you get it."

"Of course. I'll be right back."

The moment he was out of the room, Katy made a beeline for the desk. There were several copies of what looked like a list, and she grabbed the one on top. She'd barely had time to stuff it in her pocket before he was back.

"Oh, thank you, Mr. Rocca!" Katy drank the water in one long gulp. "Well, that just about does it. Unless you have any specific complaints?"

Five minutes later Katy was in the parking lot of a strip mall, three blocks away. She'd run down all twelve flights of stairs, afraid that he'd notice the missing papers and come after her while she waited for the elevator. Even now, she didn't feel completely safe. Her hands were trembling as she drew the papers out of her pocket to examine them.

It took a moment for the list to make sense. When it did, Katy gasped aloud. It contained the names of Hitchcock's female victims, along with the movie titles, the methods of murder, and a synopsis of each plot. It was suspicious, but what made it into incriminating evidence was the way that Tony Rocca had marked it. Five movies were crossed off in red ink, the ones the Video Killer had duplicated on the murder DVDs. There was no doubt in Katy's mind that Tony Rocca was the Video Killer. And she'd just stolen his worksheet to prove it!

■ ■ ■ ■

"Tony." Lon reached out to shake Tony's hand. "Come up, and we'll talk in my work-room."

"Jesus, Lon! Do you think you have enough equipment?"

"Now you know my deep dark secret, Tony." Lon laughed self-consciously. "I'm a pack rat. I can't stand to throw away anything that still works. Just shove that garnelite voltage booster out of the way and have a seat."

Tony handed Lon his copy of the first three scenes, moved the heavy black box with switches and knobs off the couch, and sat down. Then he leaned back and waited impatiently. Most people would have flipped through the pages quickly, but Lon seemed to be reading every word. Tony wasn't sure if that was a good or a bad sign.

Twenty-five minutes passed with no sound except that turning of pages. Lon asked no questions, and Tony was wise enough not to offer any comments. It was the hardest thing he'd ever done, keeping his natural tendency to talk under control. Finally Lon closed the binder and looked up at Tony.

"What you've done is very good, Tony. But

you told me you were planning to explore the character and motivation of the Video Killer. There's nothing here that touches on his personality."

"That's true, Lon. We'll have to put in those scenes later, when we know his identity. If we wrote anything about his personality now, it would be pure guesswork."

"That's a good point." Lon nodded. "But why did you choose Hitchcock segments for all of the murder scenes?"

Tony decided to use the same excuse he'd used with Erik. He still couldn't admit he's seen the murder videos.

"That's an excellent question, Lon. Let me tell you my reasoning on this whole thing. The first girl was killed in the shower. Naturally, that suggested *Psycho* to me. And, maybe, you haven't noticed the connection, but the victims have all resembled Hitchcock's stars. To tell you the truth, I was thinking of you when I wrote those scenes. I kept thinking, how would the best guy in the business shoot this? And I came up with the parallel."

"Then you're under the impression that the Video Killer is trying to copy Hitchcock?"

"Not exactly. My theory would be that he's trying to *improve* on Hitchcock."

"That's fascinating, Tony. But you said on the phone that you were stuck. How can I help?"

"If we carry our Hitchcock theme all the way through, I have to decide which segments should be included. That's where I'm running into trouble. I figured we'd do *Rear Window* next. It lends itself to the Christie Jensen killing."

Lon nodded. What Tony said made sense. He still felt a curious reluctance to commit to the project, but perhaps he was being too cautious. He really wanted to film it. It would be gratifying to try to improve on Hitchcock.

"That's a good idea, Tony." Lon paused for a moment. "And then what do you think about *The 39 Steps*?"

Tony beamed. "That's exactly what I had in mind. How did you happen to pick that one, Lon?"

"It's a natural progression dramatically. Where do you think we should go from there?"

Tony shrugged. He couldn't very well tell Lon he'd have to wait to see the next murder scene. "That's where I'm stuck, Lon. What do you recommend?"

Lon laughed, and the voice in the back of his mind that told him to wait was suddenly silenced. There was no reason to wait. He wanted to do *Video Kill,* and he would!

"I think we better get our jobs straight, Tony. You're the writer. I'm only the cinematographer."

Tony couldn't help it. A grin spread across his face. "Then you've decided to sign on with us?"

Lon nodded. "It's just too exciting to pass up. I'm definitely in. Do you have time to listen to a couple of ideas?"

"Of course." Tony sneaked a glance at his watch. He knew he had to sit here and listen to every one of Lon's suggestions, and that could take hours. And then he had to block out the next scene for Erik. The way it was stacking up, it might be morning before he got home. Naturally, Allison was bound to be upset, and he really wanted to be with her. But Erik was there, and she'd just have to understand.

Erik opened the bedroom door noiselessly and peeked in on Allison. She was sleeping soundly, curled up in a ball in the center of the bed. The tranquilizers Dr. Naiman had given her had worked like magic. Her hair was spread out over the pillow, and she looked so peaceful that Erik felt his own eyelids growing heavy. He tiptoed up and

375

covered her with the quilt that had been folded at the foot of the bed. It was a warm, muggy night in the valley, and the air-conditioning was turned up full blast.

Allison smiled as he covered her, but she didn't open her eyes. She mumbled something that sounded vaguely like "thanks" and immediately went back to sleep. Erik shook his head as he left the room. How could Tony treat her this way? Allison had needed Tony this afternoon, and that excuse about a negotiation meeting with Lon Michaels had been an outright lie. Erik just hoped that Allison hadn't seen Tony coming out of the motel room with that redhead.

Erik's hands were clenched into fists as he walked back down the hall to the telephone. He'd given himself over an hour to calm down, but he was still furious over Tony's duplicity. He just didn't know what to believe anymore. Had Cinescope really made an offer on *Video Kill*? If he found out that Tony had lied about that, he was going to dissolve their partnership. There was no way he could work with a man he couldn't trust.

It didn't take long for Erik to get his answer. Alan was delighted to hear from Erik. Had he heard the good news? Tony had managed to sign Lon Michaels. Lon had called Alan to confirm not more than ten minutes ago. Erik was lucky to have such a partner. Tony was a dynamo.

Erik was having second thoughts when he hung up the phone. Tony had obviously gone to his meeting with Lon, and he'd done a bang-up job. And Cinescope was committed to making *Video Kill*. Alan had said the contracts were ready, and they could sign them in the morning. That meant Tony hadn't lied at all, and maybe there might be a reasonable explanation for his appearance at the Traveler Motel.

After debating the question in his mind for a moment, Erik picked up the phone and dialed the office. Tony wasn't in, but the answering machine was on.

"Tony? This is Erik. You were right about your mother-in-law. She pulled through just fine. I'm at your house with Allison, and I'll stay with her until you get home. The doctor gave her some tranquilizers, and he said she'll sleep through the night. And Tony? Congratulations on signing Lon. I just talked to Alan, and both of us are really impressed."

Erik hung up, feeling much better. He went into the family room and switched on the television, but the commercial channels didn't have much to offer. The Hitchcock

377

movies Allison had reviewed for Tony were in a box by the couch. *The 39 Steps* was on top, and Erik shivered as he realized that Daniele had looked enough like Lucie Mannheim to be her twin. Thoughts of Daniele brought on a dull, throbbing sensation near his right temple. He pulled out his packet of pills and took one before it could develop into a full-fledged headache. The zonker would knock him out for a couple of hours, but Allison was sleeping soundly and there was no reason why he had to stay awake. Tony was bound to be home by the time he woke up, and then he could offer his congratulations in person.

22

There was no way that Katy could relax. She paced the floor of her apartment, listening to the recording she'd made of her conversation with Tony. There was no doubt that he'd incriminated himself, but what should she do about it? A responsible citizen would notify the police immediately, but she was a reporter first and a responsible citizen second. At least she'd always thought of herself that way.

She'd already sketched out her story, and she knew she'd win every award in the book. But how would Sam feel, reading her words in the morning edition? He'd be furious at the way she duped him, and it was doubtful he'd ever speak to her again. Everything boiled down to a question of priorities. Which was more important? Her career? Or Sam?

Suddenly Katy was struck with a sense of déjà vu. She'd faced this same decision right before she'd left Sam. Back then she'd chosen her career. Could she honestly say she was happy with her choice?

Katy looked around her small, cramped apartment and sighed. She'd have the money for a bigger place when her promotion came through, but that wouldn't change the way she felt when she came home and there was no one to greet her. Living alone wasn't all it was cracked up to be, and she was willing to bet that the other divorced women in her therapy group felt exactly the same way about it. Oh, they all talked about how nice it was not to have to fix dinner and pick up their husbands' clothes, but Katy didn't believe a word of it. After ten solid months of coming home to an empty apartment, she knew she would have welcomed the chance to pick up Sam's clothes and put the toilet seat down before she used it.

Why was she so lonely? Katy blinked hard as tears came to her eyes. She had plenty of friends, other single career-minded women, and they went out to dinner at least once a week. Of course they split the tab six ways and drove home by themselves, but they all claimed that they were perfectly content without men. Katy knew better. She still missed Sam's jokes over dinner, the way he knew which wine to order and just how much to tip the valet parker and the waiter. Going out with the girls wasn't at all like going out with Sam. Especially afterward.

Katy glanced at the calendar and frowned. Tonight was her therapy group, but she'd already decided to miss it again. She was tired of the soul-searching they did and all the problems they couldn't solve. Sex and sexism was all they seemed to discuss. They didn't get enough of the first and too much of the second. It was a waste of time searching for answers with other women who were as screwed up as she was. The blind couldn't lead the blind, and that was precisely what they were trying to do.

Her head hurt, and Katy reached for the aspirin bottle before she remembered that she'd taken three less than an hour ago. This was a tension headache, and the sooner she solved her dilemma, the sooner her headache would leave. So which was more important? Her career? Or Sam? It was time for an honest decision.

Katy tried to remember all the things that had bugged her about her marriage. Sam's habit of falling asleep while she was trying to talk to him in bed. The mess he left in the kitchen when he made a snack. The way he left the little twist tie off the bread wrapper so the bread dried out. The wet towels he left on the bathroom floor. The way he always got specks of toothpaste on the mirror when he brushed his teeth. Suddenly all that didn't seem as serious as it had before.

To be fair, Katy considered the positive side. Sam's surprise gifts, things he picked up on a whim because he knew she'd like them. The way he hugged her sometimes, for no reason at all. The umbrella he stored in the trunk of the car so she wouldn't get wet if it rained. The decorative nail he hung by the front door for the car keys she was always losing. And the warm comfort of cuddling next to him in the dark of the night.

Katy jumped to her feet and gathered up her notes. She'd let all those bitter women in her therapy group talk her into values that weren't hers, like the red convertible and the herbal tea. And leaving Sam. Her career was important, she'd never deny that. But no career, no matter how prestigious it might be, was worth the loss of her husband. Katy knew she'd be the biggest fool in the world if she didn't set things straight while there was still time.

She found her car keys under the sofa and grabbed her purse. She'd reached a decision, and this time she knew she was right.

As she got into her car and started the engine, suddenly she realized that her headache was completely gone.

Sam put down the phone and checked another name off his list. He'd spent the whole afternoon calling actresses, warning them to take precautions. Tony had been right. There were a surprising number of actresses who could double for the remaining Hitchcock victims, and he still had hundreds of calls to make. He was about to go into the kitchen to rummage for something to eat when the telephone he'd just put back in the cradle started to ring. It was Katy.

"Oh, Sam! I've been trying to reach you for fifteen minutes. I've got to see you right away!"

"Okay, Katy. Come on over."

There was a second's pause, and then Katy spoke again.

"No, Sam. You don't understand at all. I'm here already, at the outside door. Is it all right if I come up?"

"Of course it is." Sam looked puzzled. "Why didn't you just use your key?"

"Well." Katy hesitated. "It just didn't seem right, that's all. I mean, you might have had company or something."

Sam chuckled a little. "You were afraid you'd unlock the door and run into six or seven gorgeous women in various stages of undress?"

"Something like that. I'll be up in a flash, Sam. This is really important."

No more than two minutes later Sam's doorbell rang. He opened it, and Katy rushed in. She looked as if she'd been crying.

"It took a lot of nerve for me to come here and say what I'm going to say."

"Katy. What's wrong?" Sam moved to take her into his arms, but she pulled back.

"Don't interrupt me, Sam. And don't touch me, either. If you kiss me or hug me or anything like that, I'll lose my nerve."

"Okay." Sam shrugged. "Go ahead, Katy."

Katy took a deep breath and faced him squarely. Then she rattled off the speech she'd thought out in the car.

"I'm a louse, Sam. I'm working on the Video Killer story, just like you suspected at first. But I'm not going to file my story, ever. I decided my self-respect is more important than my career, but that doesn't change what I've done. I came back into your life under false pretenses. And I lied to you. And I copied your murder discs. You trusted me and I, I let you down. It's that simple. And

384

I came to say I'm really sorry, Sam."

"Oh, Katy —"

"Not now!" Katy interrupted him. "I'm not finished yet. And I also want you to know that I've decided I made the biggest mistake of my life when I left you and I'd like to come back, but you probably won't want me after what I just —"

"Shut up, Katy. Of course I want you back."

Sam pulled her into his arms and kissed her so thoroughly she didn't have time to finish her prepared speech. By the time he let her go, she'd forgotten most of it.

"But, Sam, I bootlegged your murder discs."

"I know. I was hoping you would. I figured you might spot a clue I missed. That's why I left them out in the open where you'd be sure to see them."

"Sam." Katy's eyes began to glisten. "You're as big a louse as I am!"

"True. I guess we deserve each other. Did you find any clues on the murder discs, Katy?"

"Not on the discs themselves, but did you know that a Hollywood writing team is doing a screenplay about the Video Killer? And their script exactly parallels the murders! Now, how could they know about the mur-

385

ders in such detail unless . . ."

". . . one of them was the murderer." Sam finished the sentence for her.

"Yes! That's exactly what I figured. So I went to their office this afternoon, and one of the guys had a list of Hitchcock victims on his desk!" Katy took out the list and placed it on the coffee table. "And he definitely incriminated himself while we were talking." She plunked her mini-recorder on top of the list. "See this, Sam? I recorded the entire conversation! I'm almost positive that the Video Killer is . . ."

". . . Tony Rocca, right?" Sam picked up the recorder and grinned at her.

"How did you know?"

"Because he made the list for me. And because I showed him the murder discs. Tony Rocca's an old friend who's been working on the investigation with me. I gave him permission to use the material on the murder discs as long as he didn't tell anyone where he got it."

"Damn!" Katy shook her head. "All that work and I wound up with nothing."

"Maybe, maybe not. Let's go over your notes together. I'll get us a glass of wine."

Katy sighed as Sam went into the kitchen to pour the wine. Naturally she was disappointed that she hadn't identified the Video

Killer, but somehow it didn't matter quite so much as she'd thought it would. She imagined her Pulitzer flying out the window, and she found she really didn't give a damn as long as Sam wanted her back.

Tony saved his file on the computer and glanced at the clock on his office wall. It was either eleven-twenty at night or five minutes to four in the morning. He checked his watch to be sure. Eleven-twenty. He could finish up *The 39 Steps* segment tonight, if he could just remember whether Daniele Renee had been faceup or facedown on the bed. Sam was probably awake. He'd call just to make sure.

Sam answered on the second ring. He sounded in surprisingly good spirits. "Can you drop by on your way home, Archer? There's someone here I'd like you to meet."

"This late?"

"I'll be up for a couple more hours. Of course, if you're too tired . . ."

"No, I'm fine. I've got another couple minutes of work here, and then I'll come right over."

It was a few minutes past midnight as Tony drove through Hollywood. The streets were practically deserted. Since this was a Saturday night and the nightclubs and bars didn't close until late, this area was usually jammed with people.

The Video Killer. The moment Tony thought of it, he knew he was right. Technically, it was Sunday, and everyone was staying in, behind locked doors. Tony couldn't blame them. Most of the girls in this area were struggling young actresses, and they knew they were targets for the Video Killer. Still it was eerier to drive past the clubs and the comedy houses and see no lines of people outside, waiting in line to get in.

Because of the nonexistent traffic, Tony arrived at Sam's high-rise much sooner than he'd expected. Sam buzzed him right up.

"Nice place, Sam." Tony nodded when Sam answered the door. "Westwood. Very plush. Do you think I'm dressed for it?"

Sam glanced at Tony's T-shirt and grinned. Tony was wearing a bright pink one with Day-Glo green letters that said MY OTHER SHIRT HAS A DESIGNER LABEL.

"You'll do. Come in, Tony."

Tony stepped into the living room and stopped in his tracks as he caught sight of the woman on the couch.

"Karen Daniels?"

"Not exactly. This is my wife, Katy Brannigan."

Tony started at Katy. "But, I thought,

didn't you say you worked for Equitable Management?"

"I lied." Katy shrugged. "I'm a reporter, and it was the only way I could get an interview with you."

It took a while to explain. Tony sat on the couch, sipping the wine that Sam had brought him, and just shook his head in disbelief that Katy told him all about her suspicions, the copy of the partial screenplay she'd received from her friend at Cinescope, the Hitchcock victim list she'd snatched while Tony was getting her a glass of water, and how she'd thought Tony had incriminated himself on her concealed voice tape recorder.

"Wait a minute." Tony frowned. "You actually thought *I* was the Video Killer!?"

"I was sure of it. It made a lot of sense at the time."

Sam stepped in. Tony looked really confused.

"When she came here tonight with what she thought was a closed case, I explained why you knew about the murder discs. You can understand why Katy thought you were guilty, can't you? She had a whole pile of circumstantial evidence and everything pointed directly to you."

"Jesus, Sam! I'm glad *somebody* knows

the truth!"

Tony shook his head. "Now, I've only got one question for Katy."

"Yes?" Katy leaned closer. "What is it, Tony?"

"Now that you're not Karen Daniels anymore, does that mean you won't fix the loose carpeting in my office doorway?"

23

Sunday, August 9

Erik swam up from the layers of his disjointed dream to see Allison's face. For a moment he didn't know where he was, and then he recognized the interior of the room. He was at Tony's house. On the family room couch.

"Good morning, Erik. How about some breakfast?"

"Uh, that'd be nice, Allison, but you don't have to put yourself out. Did Tony get home?"

"Yes. He's upstairs, sleeping. It was already getting light when he came in, so it must have been about five in the morning. He mumbled something about a new scene on your desk and passed out like a rock."

Allison's voice shook a little, and Erik sensed trouble. Perhaps she had seen Tony yesterday at the motel. He wasn't about to open that can of worms first thing in the morning. Tony and Allison would have to work it out themselves.

"So, how about pancakes, Erik? I've already mixed up some batter."

"That sounds great!" Erik smiled at her. "But, really, Allison, are you sure you feel up to it?"

"I'm fine. I already called the hospital, and they're going to move Mother back to the convalescent center this afternoon. She's much better. And I like to make pancakes, especially when there's someone here to eat them."

A bitter expression crossed Allison's face, but it was gone in a flash.

"You'll find fresh towels and everything you need in the guest bathroom." Allison smiled again. "Breakfast's in twenty minutes."

As soon as Allison had left, Erik got up and headed for the guest bathroom. He could use a shower and a shave. Then he'd have breakfast with Allison, stop off at the condo to feed Al, and go straight to the office.

An hour later, pleasantly stuffed with Allison's blueberry pancakes and plenty of coffee, Erik arrived at his condo. Breakfast with Allison had been a real treat. She'd served his food and poured his coffee, and they'd laughed when the kids from next door had chased their soapy dog, an obvious escapee from an early morning bath, through Allison's backyard. It certainly beat out the breakfasts at the coffee shops he'd been frequenting for the past sixteen years. How could Tony jeopardize it all for a cheap-looking redhead in a sleazy motel room? If Tony didn't realize just how lucky he was, maybe it was up to Erik to set him straight.

"Play it again, Sam!"

Sam hit the freeze-frame button, and the third murder disc stopped in its tracks. "I don't believe you said that, Katy."

"I don't, either." Katy groaned. "Just rewind a little and run it again. And no jokes about Bogey."

"It's important?"

"It could be. I didn't notice it before, but there's a shot of a telephoto lens in Diana Ellington's house."

"You mean here?" Sam stopped the video as a black cylindrical object appeared in the frame.

"Yes. That's definitely a telephoto lens. What's it doing in Diana Ellington's bedroom? She was an actress, not a photographer."

"Maybe she's an amateur shutterbug."

"No, Sam. That's an expensive lens, and it's strictly professional. There's absolutely no reason for her to have it propped up so prominently right there by her bed."

"So?"

"So it's out of character, Sam. And completely out of context. I think the Video Killer brought it with him. Check to see if it's still there in the pictures your men took at the scene."

Sam unsnapped his briefcase and drew out a bulky file. He flipped through several photographs and looked up at Katy with amazement. "You're right. There's no lens."

"I knew it. Sam. Now why did he put it right there by the bed?"

Sam got up and paced the floor. "A telephoto lens, I just saw one in . . . hold it, Katy! What's the next disc in the sequence?"

"Christie Jensen's murder. *Rear Window.*"

"That's it!" Sam snapped his fingers. "We've got it now, Katy, as long as he's consistent. That shot of the lens is a segue to the next murder! Remember James Stewart looking out the window with his telephoto lens?"

"Oh, Sam, I hope you're right. Let's start from the beginning and go through them. Once we catch on to the kinds of segues he uses, maybe we can predict —"

Sam clamped a hand over her mouth. "Don't say it, Katy, just in case it jinxes us."

Allison was quiet as she stacked the dishes in the dishwasher. She didn't want to wake Tony. She wasn't sure she could face him today. After the scare with her mother and the way he'd refused to come to the hospital, she wasn't feeling very friendly toward him. Of course, her mother had rallied and it hadn't turned out to be the emergency she'd thought it was, but Tony'd had no way of knowing that. And there was no possible excuse for what she'd seen at the Traveler Motel. Not only had he been coming out of the room with that redhead, he'd given her his anniversary lighter. That certainly showed what he thought of their marriage.

A tear slid down Allison's check as she stacked the last plate in the rack. She'd leave Tony this second if she had a way of paying for her mother's medical bills. She still loved him. It was useless to deny it. But she just couldn't live with him any longer.

The container of dishwasher soap felt empty. Allison rattled it just to make sure, and tossed it into the trash. Everything was going wrong today. There was a convenience store only three blocks away, and she decided to walk there. The fresh air might clear her head.

Allison had just come out of the tiny little market when she spotted a familiar car rounding the corner. Tony's dark green Volvo. He was obviously in a hurry, and she was glad he was gone. At least she wouldn't have to talk to him now.

There was a note fastened to the refrigerator door when she got home. It said GOTTA RUN — CALL LATER — LOVE YA. Allison pulled it down, crumpled it in her fist, and was about to throw it in the wastebasket when the phone rang. "Hello?" Allison's voice was trembling a little. She prayed it wasn't bad news about her mother.

"Allison! I'm so glad I caught you! This is Nina."

"Hi, Nina." Allison drew a big breath of relief. It was her agent. "Did you find me a starring role in a major motion picture?"

"Not quite, but I do have a line on something quite interesting. Hold on just a second, Allison."

As Allison held on she heard papers rattle. Nina's desk was always a disaster area. It was a wonder she was able to do any business at all.

"Here it is. A very, very dear friend of mine called this morning. He's doing a project, and I convinced him that you're just what he needs. He saw that commercial you did eons ago, and he thinks you look like Joan Fontaine. Mind you, his film's experimental. One of these auteur-type things that probably won't ever be shown anywhere, but he's paying scale if you want the job."

Allison laughed. "I wasn't kidding when I told you I'd take anything. What do I have to do?"

"To tell you the truth, I'm not sure. He wants to set up a meeting tonight to discuss it."

"Fine with me. Where?"

"I'll try to get him to come to you. That way you'll have more leverage. How about your house, eight o'clock?"

"That'll be fine."

"Good. I'll call him back right now and tell him you agree. Good luck tonight, kid."

There was a click and then a dial tone. Nina had hung up. Allison was smiling as she dialed Nina's number again. Nina had been so excited she hadn't even mentioned the name of the filmmaker.

After ten minutes of busy signals, Allison gave up. She really didn't care who the film-maker was as long as he was willing to pay scale.

■ ■ ■ ■

Erik had just picked up the papers on his desk when there was a knock at the door. It was a messenger from the studio with their contracts. Alan wanted them signed today, if possible, and that meant he had to call Tony at home.

When Allison answered the phone, she sounded cheerful. Perhaps she'd patched things up with Tony.

"Hi, Allison. The contracts came in from Alan, and we're supposed to sign them today. Is Tony up yet?"

"Sorry, Erik. He left about a half hour ago, but I'll tell him if he comes back. Guess what?"

"You guys kiss and make up?"

There was a long pause, and he could hear Allison sigh. "Not a chance, Erik. But I just had a great telephone call from my agent."

"Your agent?"

"That's right. I was an actress before I married Tony. I guess I never mentioned it. Well, there's a part in some kind of experimental film, and it looks like I've got it. The producer thinks I look just like Joan Fontaine. He's coming over to the house to discuss it with me at eight tonight."

"Congratulations, Allison. That sounds like fun. Have you told Tony?"

"Not yet. I'm going to leave him, Erik. Just as soon as I can. I can't live with a man who lies to me and keeps a mistress on the side in a sleazy motel room."

Erik swallowed hard. Allison had seen Tony with the redhead.

"Are you sure you're not making a mistake, Allison? Maybe Tony has some sort of reasonable explanation."

"Forget it, Erik. If I ask him, he'll just lie to me again."

There was a pause where Erik tried to think of something to say, something that would make everything all right again. For a man who could put great dialogue into other people's mouths, he was as total failure in real life.

"I don't know what to say, Allison, except that I'm here if you need me."

"Thanks, Erik. That means a lot to me. Wish me luck tonight?"

"Of course. I'm sure you'll do just . . ." Erik stopped in midsentence as the full implications of what Allison had told him sunk in. "Uh . . . Allison? Will you do me a favor and not mention to Tony that you're up for a part in that movie?"

"Why?"

"Well, all the Video Killer's victims have been actresses and —"

Allison sounded exasperated as she interrupted him. "Oh, Erik, not *that* again! Tony's not going to hurt me, even if he *is* the Video Killer. I'd stake my life on it."

"That's exactly what you'll be doing if you tell him."

There was a long silence, which Allison broke. "I can't talk about that now, Erik. I have to run out to see Mother. I'll call you later."

Erik was frowning when he hung up. Allison hadn't promised not to tell Tony, and she probably would if the opportunity presented itself. She refused to believe that she was in danger. He had to protect her, and there was only one way to do it. Tony would come in to sign his contract sometime today, and Erik would be waiting. And he'd stick to Tony like a Siamese twin until the night was over.

Tony glanced at his watch and frowned. He'd been waiting for over an hour. The nurse behind the desk looked bored, and Tony gave her his most endearing smile, the one Allison said could charm the birds down out of the trees.

"Do you think it'll be much longer,

Miss . . . uh . . ." Tony glanced at her plastic nametag, "Miss Woods?"

"It shouldn't be long now. Dr. Trumbull's almost never late for his Sunday rounds. There must have been a problem in surgery this morning."

"Why don't we save Dr. Trumbull some time when he comes in? I'm here to discuss a patient with him. Erik Nielsen. Could you possibly pull his file so it's ready?"

"It's already pulled, Mr. Rocca." The nurse indicated a stack of files on her desk.

Tony eyed the stack of files and nodded. If he could just get his hands on Erik's file, he wouldn't have to wait around for Dr. Trumbull.

The telephone on the desk rang before Tony could come up with a plan. Miss Woods answered immediately.

"Yes, Dr. Trumbull. Of course. I'll tell Mr. Rocca and reschedule."

"There's a problem?" Tony stood up. He was sitting no more than three feet away, and he'd heard her end of the conversation.

"I'm afraid so. That was Dr. Trumbull. He'll be tied up for at least another hour, and he asked if you'd reschedule your appointment."

"Of course." Tony flashed his smile again. He waited until she had checked the doctor's schedule and given him an appointment for next Wednesday at nine. Then he started coughing.

"Are you all right, Mr. Rocca?" The nurse looked concerned.

"Fine. Just fine." Tony coughed again, a whole series this time, as he sat back down in the chair. "Could I . . . Please . . . ? Water . . . ?"

"I'll get it. Just sit right there, and I'll be right back."

Tony coughed while the nurse left the room. He coughed all the way to the desk and continued to cough while he slipped Erik's file into his briefcase. He was still coughing when Miss Woods came back with a paper cup of water. He drank it and let his coughing taper off to a stop.

"Thank you!" Tony cleared his throat noisily and stood up. "I'm fine now. It must be the pollen count today. I understand the ragweed is blooming."

"That was a moderate to severe reaction, Mr. Rocca." Miss Woods looked concerned. "Are you seeing an allergist?"

"Oh, yes. I've got everything under control. Thank you so much, Miss Woods. You have no idea how much you've helped me."

Miss Woods was smiling as Tony left the reception area. What a nice man. He'd been so gracious about thanking her for her help, and all she'd done was bring him a glass of water.

24

Brother checked his equipment carefully and packed it in its carrying case. He was ready to shoot tonight's scene, and he knew his interpretation would be nothing short of brilliant. Even Tony Rocca, that college acquaintance of Lon's, would be impressed when he saw it.

There was a frown on Brother's face as he thought about Lon's meeting with Tony Rocca. Some might say it was ironic that Lon had signed a contract to film the murders that Brother had already perfected, but Brother found that type of humor impossible to appreciate.

There had been a painful confrontation after Tony Rocca had left. For the first time since their mother had died, Brother had been unable to affect Lon's behavior. It had taken all of his strength to bend Lon's will to his, but at last he triumphed.

Today Lon was subdued, just the way

Brother wanted him. He was silent as Brother stepped forward to put a movie in the machine. This was *Suspicion,* the segment they were shooting tonight. When this film had been completed, an RKO executive who believed that it was a mistake to portray Cary Grant as a killer had removed every indication that Grant was the villain. The resulting edit, done on Hitchcock's final cut, had reduced the running time of the film to less than an hour. At that point the head of the studio had realized the absurdity and had allowed Hitchcock to reinstate many of his scenes. The ending had been revised, however, so that Grant was innocent.

Before they could start their work, the phone rang and Brother permitted Lon to take the call. Lon was smoother and he'd learned more social skills. He always dealt with the phone calls and interviews. Brother stepped back and merely advised as Lon made all the arrangements with the star's agent. It was no longer necessary to be quite so cautious. The final segment would be finished tonight, and his masterpiece would at last be complete.

Katy got up and stretched. She'd been sitting on the floor, reading synopses of Hitchcock's plots, but she had gotten nowhere. And Sam was in the kitchen, trying to find someone who could help them. They'd found the segue to the next murder, at least Katy thought they had, but neither one of them could figure out which film it represented. The fifth murder disc had ended with a shot of the mailbox outside Daniele Renee's window.

The moment they spotted it, Sam had called Tony's office. He hadn't been in, and there was nothing on his list about mailboxes. They had to find out which film was next, and they didn't have much time. Katy walked to the kitchen and found Sam sitting at the table with the phone to his ear. "Any luck?"

"No, I'm on hold. It seems the only man at UCLA who teaches a class about Hitchcock is on vacation somewhere in the Baltic."

"No one else knows?"

"I called the film institute, and they referred me to a Professor Nash. He's not home, but his housekeeper's trying to locate him now."

"Did you find out anything?"

"Oh, sure. Lots of things. I've already spoken to six film buffs and three critics, but they couldn't answer our question."

"Don't worry, Sam." Katy gave him a hug. She knew he was frustrated. It was already midafternoon, and they had no idea which actresses to warn. "Maybe this Professor Nash will . . ."

She stopped speaking immediately as Sam held up his hand. Someone had to pick up the phone.

"Yes. I understand. No, that's quite all right. Will you please leave a message for him to call me at home the minute he gets back? It's very important."

"She couldn't find Professor Nash?"

"No. He's not at any of the places she called. That was my last hope, Katy. We'll never figure it out in time."

"Yes, we will." Katy put on a smile for his benefit. Sam looked haggard and his hands were shaking from too much coffee. Suddenly Katy realized that they hadn't eaten since dinner last night. All that coffee on an empty stomach wasn't good. Sam might feel better if he had a hot meal.

"Why don't you run out and get us some food from that deli across the street? The fresh air will do you good. And I'll go through the plot book again. Maybe I'll come up with something while you're gone."

Sam hesitated, but Katy was right. He was going crazy cooped up like this. "Okay. But if Professor Nash calls . . ."

"I'll ask him exactly the right questions. Stop worrying, Sam. I can handle it."

After Sam left, Katy went through her notes again. The first murder was *Psycho,* and the segue was a shot of two pairs of shoes, one pair gaudy brown and white, the other ultraconservative. That clearly pointed the way to the *Strangers on a Train* segment. The segue in the second murder disc was early, long before Tammara Welles's murder, when the camera had panned some businesses on a street. Among them was a dating service, a clue to the next film, *Frenzy,* where the victim had owned a matrimonial agency. Then there was the telephoto lens in the corner of Diana Ellington's bedroom. They'd already identified that as a segue to *Rear Window.* And the shot of the train tracks near Christie Jensen's apartment building was a clue to the next segment, *The 39 Steps.* And last Sunday's murder video had concluded with a shot of the mailbox outside Daniele Renee's window.

Katy held her head and groaned. There was no use going through the plot book again. She'd already skimmed it three times. There had to be someone who knew the significance of the mailbox. Someone who was a real Hitchcock fan, like Tony's wife.

Katy raced to the phone. Tony had mentioned that Allison helped him research the list. Of course he hadn't told her why he needed the list because of his promise to Sam. Katy knew she'd have to be very careful how she phrased her questions to Allison. Sam still wanted things under wraps.

"Hello?"

The phone was answered on the first ring.

"Hi." Katy smiled. Someone had told her you could hear a smile over the phone. "Is this Mrs. Tony Rocca?"

"Yes."

"This is Katy Brannigan. From the *Times*."

"Oh, yes. You write for the health section." Tony's wife sounded friendlier now. "What can I do for you, Miss Brannigan?"

"We're having a subscriber contest this month at the paper, and your name was drawn. It's a movie trivia quiz."

"Oh, dear. I haven't seen a movie in . . . I don't know how long."

"Just try it. You may be lucky. In which film did Alfred Hitchcock use a mailbox as an integral part of the plot?"

"An *integral* part of the plot?"

"That's right."

There was a long pause, and Katy began to despair. Then Allison spoke again.

"I thought I knew my Hitchcock, but that's a tough question. The only film I can think of is *Suspicion*. With the original ending, I mean."

"Could you tell me a bit more, Mrs. Rocca?"

"Well, it was made in 1941, and it starred Joan Fontaine and Cary Grant. In the original ending Cary Grant poisons his wife, but he mails the letter she gives him before she dies, not knowing that it contains her suspicions about him. RKO made Hitchcock revise his ending because they didn't want Cary Grant cast as a villain."

"You're right, Mrs. Rocca!" Katy had all she could do to keep from shouting.

Allison laughed. "I can't believe it! I've never won anything before in my life! What did I win?"

Katy thought fast. "You just won dinner for two at . . . Spago! We'll mail your gift certificate today. Thank you, Mrs. Rocca and, uh . . . congratulations."

Allison hung up the phone with a smile on her face. Imagine, a Hitchcock trivia question right after she'd watched all those movies! Then her face fell as she realized that, by the time her gift certificate for the free dinners arrived, she'd no longer be here.

She was leaving Tony just as soon as she could.

An hour later Allison was seated in front of the television, switching through the channels. There was nothing on but baseball. Pittsburgh was slugging it out against the Braves, but they were down by six runs. The Minnesota Twins were at Boston, losing quite predictably. The L.A. Dodgers were stomping the Cubs in the bottom of the seventh, eleven to three. Allison wasn't a sports fan, but there was nothing else to watch except reruns of programs she'd already seen. She finally settled for her home team, the Dodgers, even though it wasn't an exciting game.

When the game ended in a Dodger victory, the announcer came on to do an update on the baseball scores around the country. Allison remembered the joke Tony had told her at their Fourth of July party about the nervous rookie sports announcer: *These scores just in . . . five-three, eight-one, three-zip, seven-two, and ten-nine.* Everyone had cracked up when Tony had told it. He was a natural-born stand-up comedian.

Allison blinked back tears. She had to stop thinking about Tony. As she switched through the channels to find something, anything to watch, she had an unsettling thought. They didn't subscribe to the *Times*. Tony bought it at the newsstand on the way to work, and he brought it home for her to read at night. Since they weren't subscribers, how had Katy Brannigan happened to pick her name?

Tony put his video camera in the case and gave Ginger a big hug. They were finished. Wrapped up. No more porn and no more sneaking around to cheap motels. His debt was paid off, and now that *Video Kill* had sold, he sure as hell wouldn't have to do this again.

"That was just great, gang." Tony grinned at them all. "And just to show how much I appreciate you . . ."

"Champagne?" Tina actually squealed as Tony brought out the chilled bottle and popped the cork. "That stuff's expensive, Tony!"

"Yeah, but you guys are worth it. There's a bottle for each of you, and the room's yours until eleven o'clock checkout time tomorrow morning. Have a blast."

"Aren't you staying to celebrate with us?"

Ginger looked upset, and Tony pulled her over to the side while Bobby and Tina filled their glasses.

"I can't stay, Ginger. I've got tons of

things to do on that movie."

Ginger glanced over her shoulder, but Tina and Bobby were too busy enjoying the champagne to pay attention to what they were saying.

"You mean you were really serious about that job you offered me?"

"I was serious. As a matter of fact, I spoke to the head man on the phone this morning, and he promised to use you. You're supposed to report to the business office at Cinescope Studios tomorrow morning at ten. But remember what I said, Ginger. Not a word about how you met me."

"You've got it, Tony." Ginger hugged him, hard. "I just can't believe it. It's the first job I ever got where I don't have to take off my clothes."

By the time Tony gathered up his things and left the motel room, the party was in full swing. Tina had called her boyfriend to join them, and Bobby was trying to contact a couple of girls he knew. Ginger had finished one glass of champagne, and then asked Tony for a ride to the Beverly Center. Some of the boutiques were open late, and she wanted to pick out a conservative dress for her interview at Cinescope tomorrow.

Tony dropped Ginger off at Anestelle's, a dress shop on the ground floor, and headed for the office. His stomach growled loudly, and he realized he hadn't eaten all day. There was a Beefy-Burger ahead of him on the right, and Tony parked the Volvo and went inside. He ordered two triple chili burgers, coffee, and a disgusting-looking chocolate chip sandwich with what looked like fudge between the cookies. Then he paid, took his numbered receipt, and went to sit at a blue plastic table with an attached blue plastic chair under a blue plastic framed picture of a giant chili burger. Beefy-Burger might not have much in the way of ambience, but their food was edible. And while he sat and waited for the counter girl to call his number, he'd have time to read Erik's medical file.

Allison dressed in a green hostess gown and applied careful makeup. She wanted to look her best tonight. When she was finished, she went back to the family room and stared at the silent phone. Where was Tony? Probably at that room in the Traveler Motel again with his redheaded mistress. If she knew for sure, she'd leave him tonight without a backward glance.

This wasn't good. She was getting nervous, and that was no way to be when she had a meeting with an important producer.

Allison reached for the phone and dialed directory assistance. She still remembered the room number at the Traveler Motel. She'd simply call and ask for Tony. And if Tony answered, she'd know the truth.

Allison gripped the receiver tightly as the motel switchboard rang the room. One ring. Two rings. Then a woman answered. There was the sound of a party in the background.

"Hi. Is Tony there? He left his number."

"Tony? Oh . . . he left about a half hour ago. Ginger went with him."

"Ginger? Oh . . . she must be the red-head."

"Right. Ginger Watson." The woman giggled. "Except she's not really a redhead and Tony knows for sure."

"Thank you. Thank you very much."

Allison hung up the phone and went back to the bedroom. The truth didn't hurt as much as she thought it would. As a matter of fact, she was almost relieved to have it all out in the open.

Her leather suitcase was in the back of her closet, and Allison's hands shook slightly as she pulled it out. How strange. She was completely calm, but her hands were trembling. She packed carefully, with every item she'd need for a few days. She could come back later to get the rest of her things. Then she carried the suitcase out to her car and put it in the trunk. Her mind was curiously cold, and she felt nothing as she came back inside to sit by the window and count the minutes until the producer arrived.

Tony opened his briefcase and took out the file he'd liberated from Dr. Trumbull's office this morning. He was rather proud of himself for using Katy Brannigan's trick about the glass of water, and his performance had been convincing enough to make Miss Woods leave the room. Not bad for an amateur. He'd have to thank Sam's wife for teaching it to him.

The file was thick, and Tony opened it to the first page. It was a list of vital statistics. Height, weight, sex, age, blood type, and so forth. Tony glanced at it and turned the page. Erik's service record was next.

Tony scanned the information quickly and nodded. That was old hat to him. He'd served with Erik and their service records were practically identical. But the fourth page was more detailed, and Tony began to read with interest. That was more like it.

Erik had come to the V.A. hospital with severe headaches. Various medications had been tried, but none of them had been successful. Erik still had severe pain and blackouts during what the doctor called his "episodes." Tony flipped the page and found a psychiatrist's report. It was hard to believe that Erik had consulted a psychiatrist. He'd always claimed he didn't believe in head-shrinkers.

There was a section about Erik's disastrous marriage to Daniele Renee. Tony'd known about that, but he hadn't realized the whole thing was so traumatic for Erik. And this was the first he'd heard about Erik's son, Jamie. According to the file, Jamie lived at Pine Ridge, a full-time care facility for severely disturbed children. That explained why Erik had been so uptight about the sale of *Video Kill*. Places like Pine Ridge don't come cheap, and he probably needed every penny to pay for his son's care.

Tony began to feel like he was sorting through someone's personal laundry as he read on. The psychiatrist claimed that after Erik's divorce, he'd avoided all intimate contact with women. Such an extreme avoidance reaction, the psychiatrist insisted, indicated Erik's probable tendency toward violence, especially toward women who reminded him of his ex-wife.

Dimly Tony heard someone at his elbow. He looked up to see the counter girl with his order.

"Is there something wrong, sir?" She looked concerned. "I called your number six times, but you didn't answer me."

"Sorry, I guess I didn't hear you."

"Two triple chili burgers, coffee, and a fudgey-chipwich. Is that right?"

"Right. Thank you."

Tony slipped her a dollar, and she looked pleasantly surprised.

"Thank *you,* sir. If you need anything else, just holler at me."

The moment she had gone back to the counter, Tony turned to the file again. He still couldn't believe what he'd read. He was Erik's best friend. Why hadn't Erik confided in him?

Tony shuddered as he mentally ticked off the salient points. Erik had told his doctor that he'd felt like killing Daniele Renee when he'd come home and found their infant son unattended. By his own admission, he'd barely managed to control his rage. And after Daniele had left for good, Erik had put Jamie in Pine Ridge, filed for divorce, and then suffered a major breakdown. He'd been hospitalized in the locked ward of the V.A. for almost six months. Since then he avoided women entirely, and the psychiatrist thought he was violent. And, as if that weren't enough, Erik had admitting experiencing episodes in which he blacked out for hours and couldn't recall where he'd been or what he'd done.

"Oh, my God!" Tony stared down at his triple chili burgers. The orange grease was beginning to congeal on the plate, and suddenly he wasn't hungry at all. Everything fit, even something that wasn't in this file. Erik had a new video camera, and he'd been carrying it around with him lately.

"Sir? Was there something wrong with the food?"

The counter girl called out as he rushed for the door, his food left behind untouched. Tony didn't even hear her. He was in too much of a hurry to get to the office and find out if what he feared was true.

25

Erik was asleep on the couch near the office door. His neck was in an extremely awkward position that was sure to result in stiffness when he awoke, but he felt no discomfort now. Late in the afternoon the stress of waiting to confront Tony had taken its toll in the form of the worst headache yet, a blinding, screaming, excruciating migraine that had driven Erik to pacing the floor with his jaws clenched tightly together before he'd finally give in and taken one of Dr. Trumbull's zonkers. Now, two hours later, the telltale lines of pain had disappeared from his face, but he was still out cold.

There was the sound of footsteps in the hallway and a key rattled in the lock. Erik didn't wake. The door opened and a hand reached out to switch on the lights.

"Erik! What the . . . oh, no!"

Tony shook his head as he stared down at his partner. Erik was lying there like a corpse. For one heart-stopping moment Tony imagined Erik deliberately committing suicide rather than face the consequences of his crimes. Then he realized that Erik's chest was moving regularly up and down. He was sleeping. And there was a packet of pills on the table near the couch.

Tony swore and headed for the kitchenette to make coffee. Just as soon as it was done, he carried out a steaming cup and set in on the table next to Erik's head. Erik had to wake up. They had some serious talking to do.

Erik began to stir slightly. His arm moved, and he slid further on the couch to a more comfortable position. Tony held the cup directly under his nose and waited.

"Na yet. . . ." Erik mumbled.

"Erik?" Tony waved his hand over the cup of coffee so the aroma would go directly up Erik's nostrils.

"Wake up, Erik. Hot coffee. Come and get it."

Erik's eyelids began to twitch.

"Sit up. Come on, Erik. Just sit up, and you can have coffee."

It took a minute, but Erik struggled to a sitting position. His eyes opened, and he started up at Tony with a dazed expression on his face.

"Tony. I have to talk to you. But I can't remember . . ."

"I have to talk to you, too. Just drink this, Erik. And try to wake up. It's important!"

"Yeah. Yeah. Sure." Erik reached out for the cup and took a sip. He winced as the steaming liquid burned his tongue.

"Okay, Tony. I'm waking up."

Erik's eyes were threatening to close again, and Tony went to open the window. It was stuffy in the office, but the air outside was so muggy, it wasn't much better.

"More coffee." Erik held out his cup with an unsteady hand. He'd managed to finish it with his eyes closed. Tony brought a fresh cup, as Erik obediently drank it down.

"Sorry, Tony. I'm trying. The pills, you know. One more?"

"You got it."

Tony refilled Erik's cup and poured one for himself while there was still some left in the pot. He blinked hard as he started a fresh pot. He'd burst into the office angry, ready to confront Erik and haul him off to the police, but he hadn't found the cold-blooded killer he'd expected. If Erik committed those murders, he'd done it unconsciously, without even knowing he was hurting anyone. Erik deserved his pity, not his anger.

When he got back to the reception area with the coffee, Tony found Erik struggling to his feet.

"Hey. Sit down, Erik. You're still zonked out."

"Can't. The Video Killer! Tony?"

"Yes, Erik."

Tony winced. From his alarmed expression, he was sure Erik was about to confess. Somehow, he must have discovered what he'd been doing in those blackout episodes.

"Tony, I know!"

Erik looked so tortured that Tony reached out to grip his shoulder. As he did, Erik pulled back. For a moment Tony was confused. It was almost as if Erik was fearful of his reaction to the confession.

"Look, Erik. This sounds really corny, but I want you to know that I'm here for you. I'm your buddy, and I'd never hurt you."

Erik looked confused, but he nodded. "Tony, I know you're the Video Killer."

Tony was so startled, he was sure he'd heard Erik wrong. It took him a minute to find his voice.

"Would you repeat that, Erik?"

"I said I know you're the Video Killer. But you're still my friend, Tony. I'm no stranger to what stress can do to a man's mind. I also know that there's help for you if you'll only —"

"You think *I'm* the Video Killer?" It took a supreme effort of will to calm down enough to speak in a reasonable tone of voice, and Tony didn't quite make it. "How did you ever come up with a hare-brained idea like that? No. Don't answer that. It doesn't matter. The important thing is that I know what you've been doing during your blackout periods. You may not realize it, Erik, but *you're* the Video Killer. And the fact that you're accusing me is a symptom of your disease. Psychiatrists call it projection. I read your medical file, Erik. I know all about Daniele and Jamie and your violent feelings toward actresses."

Erik was awake now, and he looked totally astounded. "Now, *wait* a minute! It's true about Daniele and Jamie. Maybe I should have told you, but that part of my life is over. I'd rather not talk about it. But if you honestly think that I killed my ex-wife, you're the one who's crazy!"

"Okay." Tony sighed. "I can see this isn't going to be easy. Let's start again. Where were you the night that your ex-wife was killed?"

"I was here, with you. We worked all night to meet Alan's deadline. Don't you remember?"

424

Tony stopped cold for a second. Then he remembered what time the murder had taken place. "That's no alibi, Erik. She was killed at nine, and you didn't get here until after midnight. Where were you before that?"

"I was home. In my condo. Why don't you check it out with the security guard? You'll find out that I didn't leave the complex until a quarter to twelve."

"Fine. Get the guard on the phone."

Erik dialed the number while Tony watched. Suddenly Tony wasn't as sure as he'd been a moment before. Erik seemed sincere in his denials, but it was always possible that his conscious mind didn't know what his unconscious was doing.

"Hi, Norma." Erik spoke into the receiver. "What are you doing there so late?"

There was a pause, and Erik spoke again.

"The flu, huh? I understand there's a lot of it going around. Listen, Norma. I want you to talk to my partner, Tony Rocca. We're having an argument over what time I left the complex last Sunday night."

Erik handed the phone to Tony. He listened for a moment, and then he hung up with a chagrined expression on his face.

"You're right, Erik. You left at eleven forty-three. Look, I'm really sorry about this whole thing."

"Not so fast." Erik looked grim. "Now it's my turn. Where were *you* that night?"

"You still think *I'm* the Video Killer?"

"You haven't provided otherwise. I have."

"Okay, okay." Tony winced. "I was hoping this wouldn't come out. Hand me the phone. I'll call someone who can vouch for me."

In less than five minutes Tony had his alibi. Bobby and Tina were still at the motel room, and they vouched for him to Erik.

"A porn flick?" Erik hung up the phone and shook his head.

"Well, at least it was steady work. And I had to do it to pay off a loan."

Erik stared at Tony for a moment, and then he started to laugh. "If *you're* not the Video Killer, and *I'm* not the Video Killer, then we just spouted some of the worst dialogue I've ever heard in my life. I'm really sorry I didn't trust you, Tony."

"And I'm sorry I didn't trust you. I should have known better than to believe a medical chart. Why, when Allison's mother —"

"Oh, my God!" Erik's eyes widened. "We've got to call Allison right away. I tried to convince her that you were the Video Killer."

Tony grabbed the phone and dialed, but

426

the answering machine was on at the house. He left a message for Allison to call right away and hung up.

"She's not home."

"That's strange." Erik frowned. "What time is it?"

"A quarter after eight."

"That explains it. She told me she had a meeting with a producer at the house tonight, and probably switched on the answer phone when he got there."

"Which producer?"

"She didn't tell me. All I know is that she was really excited this morning about some producer who's making a movie. He wanted someone who looked just like Joan Fontaine."

"Joan Fontaine?" Tony looked amused. "Yeah, I guess she does look a little like . . . Oh, my God!"

Tony's face turned white, and Erik reached out to steady him.

"What's the matter, Tony?"

"*Suspicion*! The original ending. Move out, Erik! I'll explain in the car. I think the Video Killer's after Allison."

"My agent's very impressed with your project." Allison turned to smile at him. "Would you care for a drink while we discuss it?"

Brother stepped back and let Lon take over. He could afford to wait a few minutes. He'd give Lon time to get the lighting and the angle perfect before he moved in to start his work. Lon was the expert when it came to the camera, but Brother was the creative genius behind the project.

"Thank you, yes." Lon smiled. "But only if you join me. And only if you let me mix you my favorite cream drink."

"Oh, well, of course."

Brother silently congratulated Lon as he went behind the bar. It would be simple to slip the poison in a cream drink. Lon was a master at social graces, while he had never been any good at them at all. Lon had been the one to attend his mother's tedious teas in the rose garden after Brother had refused to appear.

Lon smiled at her as he mixed the drinks. "As your agent probably told you, I'm very impressed with your resemblance to Joan Fontaine. You're practically her twin, Miss Greene."

Allison almost looked over her shoulder to see if anyone else was in the room. Miss Greene. That was her. She'd been Mrs. Rocca for so long, it was difficult to respond to her old maiden name.

"Yes, she mentioned that. Are you doing a remake of a Joan Fontaine film?"

"Not precisely. I like to think of it as an improvement rather than a remake."

Allison smiled, even though she knew that most remakes were doomed to failure. "Which film are you doing?"

"Her best. Or perhaps I should say, it could have been her best. *Suspicion.*"

"That's very interesting." Warning bells went off in Allison's mind. *Suspicion.* The Hitchcock film Katy Brannigan had asked her about. And in the original ending Joan Fontaine was the victim. Allison's mouth was dry, and she almost screamed as she realized that she was alone with the Video Killer!

"Is something wrong, Miss Greene?"

He was looking at her now, and Allison drew on every acting skill she possessed to maintain her pleasant smile. "No, nothing's wrong. I'm just trying to recall the film. That was Alfred Hitchcock, wasn't it?"

"Yes. Unfortunately."

Allison's mind spun in several directions. She had to keep him talking about the movie, and there had been an expression of distaste on his face when she'd mentioned Hitchcock's name. She had to capitalize on that.

"I probably shouldn't say this, but *Suspicion*'s never been one of my favorite films. Are you planning on basically changing the plot?"

"Yes. How perceptive you are! Tell me your impression of Hitchcock as a director."

He was leaning on the bar now, watching her intently, and Allison gathered all the poise she could muster. She had to keep him diverted until she could figure out how to get away.

"Well, I'm certainly no expert. But I can't help but feel that Hitchcock's technique is often overly self-indulgent."

"In what way?"

He looked interested, and Allison plunged in. Thank God she knew her Hitchcock!

"Take *Rope* for instance. It's amazing that it was filmed without actual cuts, but I do wish Hitchcock had paid less attention to his gimmick and more attention to basics. James Stewart was terribly miscast as Professor Rupert Cadell."

"Yes. Quite right. You're very observant, Miss Greene. What did you think of *Vertigo*?"

"Well, I thought the camera work was superb, but he did tend to repeat that one shot. I'm sorry, I don't know exactly how to

430

describe it."

"Do you mean the shot where he tracked backward and zoomed forward?"

"Yes. That's the one." Allison beamed at him. "And I did think the plot line was quite unbelievable, although I'm not sure how it could have been improved."

"But *I* know!"

He smiled at her, and Allison almost cried in relief as he started to lecture on the film. He certainly wouldn't kill her while he was in the middle of an explanation. She had to stock up enough questions to keep him occupied until . . . until what? Tony wouldn't be home until late, if he came home at all. And the police had no way of knowing that the Video Killer was stalking her. There was no one who would come in to save her. She was alone, all alone, and she had to make her move soon or he'd grow bored and tired of talking to his next victim.

". . . and so naturally, I would have turned Kim Novak's suicide attempt into an actual drowning."

"Brilliant!" Allison got to her feet as gracefully as she could and inched carefully toward the door. "I'd love to hear your analysis of *Notorious* right after I slip into my best Joan Fontaine costume. It just happens to be a copy of something she wore in

Suspicion. Would you excuse me for just a moment?"

"But, Miss Greene, you haven't even tasted the drink I made for you."

"It looks delicious." Allison gave him her most innocent smile. She knew what was in that drink. Joan Fontaine had been poisoned. "Could you put it right there on the table by the couch? I promise to enjoy every drop, the moment I come back."

Allison's legs were shaking as she fled to the bedroom and locked the door behind her. Then she raced to the phone to call the police. No dial tone. She pressed the buttons frantically, but there was only the distant crackling of an open line. And then . . . the sound of someone breathing?

"Hello? Hello? Who's there?" Her voice was a terrified whisper.

"This is Brother, Miss Greene. You tricked Lon, but I know how to deal with reluctant actresses. Now, be a good girl and come out. Or I'll be forced to come in and get you."

The phone fell from Allison's nerveless fingers and landed with a clatter on the night table. She was trapped! She ran into the bathroom and threw the lock on that door, too. It would take him a while to get through two locked doors. And then . . . Allison's mind went absolutely blank as she

432

huddled in a corner and let terror wash over in waves.

Katy and Sam were pouring over pictures of actresses when Sam looked up.

"Do you know an Allison Greene? The name's familiar."

"Allison Greene?" Katy grabbed the pile of background material she'd gathered on Tony and paged through it quickly. "Oh, my God, Sam! Allison Greene is Tony's wife!"

Tony screeched around the corner and pulled up with one wheel resting on the curb.

"Let's go, Erik!" Tony reached under the seat and pulled out the little twenty-five automatic he'd been carrying ever since he started working at sleazy motels for the porn job. "Take this, I've got the tire iron."

"You take that pop gun. I'll handle the tire iron and go in from the front."

"Okay. We'll cover the house fast and meet in the master bedroom."

Tony crouched as he ran around the corner of the house and crossed the back patio. He unlocked the kitchen door noiselessly and eased it open. The breakfast nook was deserted. No sign of struggle in the living room, but there was a carton of cream on the bar. Allison hated drinks with cream, and she'd never make one for herself.

Suddenly a scene from *Suspicion* came back to Tony in horrifying detail. He could see Cary Grant walking up the staircase with a glass of milk for Joan Fontaine. It had been poisoned milk in the original ending.

Tony raced through the deserted hallway and met Erik in front of the bedroom door. He started to push the door open, but Erik held him back with a gesture. Faint voices carried through the heavy oak door. Allison's voice, desperate. She was still alive! And the deeper, ominous tones of a man.

Erik pushed Tony to the side with one well-placed shove and barreled into the room in a frontal assault. Tony caught a glimpse of a man in a black executioner's hood. He was bending over Allison, holding a glass to her lips.

Erik yelled and the man whirled, dropping the glass to the rug. A knife appeared in his hand, and he slashed out as Erik tackled him, drawing blood.

"Take cover, Allison!"

Allison scrambled from the bed and rolled under it as Tony leveled the gun. Erik and the Video Killer were grappling in a deadly contest, and he couldn't get a clear shot.

The knife flashed again, and Tony heard Erik grunt in pain. Then the Video Killer moved into his sights, and Tony squeezed the trigger. Once. Twice.

The sound of his little automatic echoed off the walls of the room and the Video Killer dropped to the rug, still clutching Erik. In the sudden silence Tony rushed to his friend and freed him.

Sirens sounded faintly in the distance, then louder as Tony grabbed a towel and tried to staunch the flow of Erik's blood. A moment later police cars screeched up in front.

"Erik. Hang on, buddy. Help's coming."

"Allison?" Erik's voice was so weak that Tony could barely hear him.

"She's all right. You saved her life, Erik."

"Jamie . . . ?" Erik said weakly. "Promise, Tony!"

"Sure, Erik. I'll take care of Jamie for you. I promise."

Tony didn't even feel the tears that were streaking down his face. Erik looked bad. Very bad. His face was pasty and his skin was cold to the touch. And his blood was soaking through the towel, even though Tony kept up a steady pressure on the wound.

At that instant Sam Ladera rushed in, followed by a full complement of his men. Tony stood by helplessly while the paramedics loaded Erik onto a stretcher and carried him out to a waiting ambulance. He turned just in time to see Katy with her arms around Allison, leading her from the room.

"Allison?" Tony rushed up to her, but Allison stared right through him with wide, unfocused eyes. She seemed not to recognize him at all. "Allison, honey, you're not hurt, are you?"

"It's the shock, Tony." Katy squeezed her arm.

"I'm taking her to the hospital for a thorough check, but it wouldn't be good for her to come back here tonight."

"No. Of course not. Thanks, Katy."

"Tony?" Sam was standing next to two paramedics who were removing the Video Killer's body. "Bad news, Tony. He's going to make it. Both of your chest shots were deflected by ribs. If I'd known, I would have given you my forty-five."

Tony knelt to stare down at the Video Killer's exposed face. He gasped as he recognized him.

"Lon? Lon Michaels!"

Lon looked up, and then he tried to smile.

"Tony. I'm sorry. I wanted to work on your project, but Brother had to finish his first. Maybe you can . . ."

Lon's voice trailed off and his face changed into a fierce mask of hatred. Tony stepped back involuntarily as a raspy voice spoke from Lon's lips.

"Lon's gone away. Forever. I'm Brother."

EPILOGUE

One Year Later

Allison's high heels sank into the grass as she walked across the rolling green lawn toward the entrance to Pine Ridge. One year had passed since she had narrowly escaped becoming the Video Killer's sixth victim.

It had been a year filled with grief and pain. Erik had been flown to a veteran's hospital in the East, a place that specialized in the care he needed. He was recovering, but it would be months before he was on his feet again. The Video Killer's knife had caused massive damage, and he'd undergone several bouts of reconstructive surgery.

From the very first, Katy Brannigan had taken charge, letting Allison stay in her old apartment until she felt well enough to face the world again. Allison had gone back to the expensive house in Studio City only once, to pack her belongings. She'd known that she needed time away from Tony.

Allison had visited her mother every morning, managing somehow to hold down the job that Katy had gotten her. She was just beginning to get back to normal, to feel the nightmare receding, when her mother had died. Then there were more months of grief and work, work and grief, refusing to answer the calls she received from Tony and hiding from the world in the cramped little apartment she'd rented.

She hadn't asked, but Katy had told her that Tony had finished the movie and sold the house. He was living in Northern California now, somewhere in the foothills above Sacramento on a ranch he'd bought with his share of the movie money. No one seemed to know his exact whereabouts, not even Ginger Watson.

Ginger had arrived on Allison's doorstep yesterday, and Allison had recognized the redhead from Donny's immediately, even though she hadn't seen her in almost a year, as the woman who'd been with Tony that afternoon at the Traveler Motel, Tony's mistress. Allison's first impulse had been to shut the door in her face, but something had stopped her.

Ginger had told her everything. That was the reason she had driven to Pine Ridge today. She had to visit Jamie, to see if she could help. Then she had to find Tony to tell him that she'd made a dreadful mistake.

As Allison reached the front entrance, she straightened her shoulders and pulled open the door. The reception area had a homey touch with braided rugs and a fireplace. A gray-haired, motherly woman sat behind a desk by the window.

"I'd like to see Jamie Nielsen. My name is Allison Greene."

"Jamie?" The older woman smiled. "He's lucky today. Two visitors."

"Shall I wait until his other visitor has left?"

"Oh, no. I'm sure Jamie will be delighted to see you. They're out by the pool, enjoying the sun. I'll call for an aide to show you the way."

A moment later Allison was back outside again, following a smiling man down a flagstone path to the pool area.

"Are you a member of Jamie's family?"

"No." Allison couldn't help but respond to the man's friendly smile. "I'm a friend of his father's."

"A terrible tragedy." The man's face grew sober. "Jamie had a rough few months, but having his father's cat helped a lot and he's making wonderful progress now. He's done so well, we hope to release him in six months or so."

"Where will he go? Erik's still in the hospital."

"It seems Mr. Nielsen has some very generous friends. There's a man who's been paying all the bills for Jamie's care, and he's going to look after him until his father comes home. There they are, over there, under the blue awning."

Allison's breath caught in her throat as she saw a smiling blond boy sitting at a table. He looked so much like Erik. He was talking to a man whose back was turned toward Allison, and their body postures indicated that they were fast friends.

"But Jamie looks almost . . ." Allison stopped, suddenly ashamed of her expectations.

"Normal? Yes, he's come a long way, and most of it's due to the man you see with him. He's been here every weekend. Last year, at this time, Jamie was just beginning to speak. Now he's up to grade level on all his subjects except math. We think he'll be ready for a regular public school very soon."

"The math part may run in the family. Erik always claimed he'd flunked algebra three times. That man, is he the one who's going to take care of Jamie?"

"Yes. I'll have Jamie introduce you.

They've just come back from a fishing trip. Two weeks in a cabin by a stream in Oregon."

The aide crossed the last few yards and tapped Jamie on the shoulder.

"Jamie? You have another visitor. This is Miss Greene. She's a friend of your father's."

"Hi, Jamie." Allison smiled as the boy stood up to shake her hand. His eyes were the same shade of blue as Erik's.

"I'm glad to meet you, Miss Greene. And this is my best friend. He's going to be my stand-in dad."

"That's wonderful, Jamie." Allison turned with a smile on her face. Then she froze and time seemed to stop. It was Tony.

"Allison?"

Tony stood up, and Allison saw her uncertainty mirrored on his face. Although the actual distance was only inches, there was a wide gulf that separated them. It was filled with grief and guilt and misunderstanding. Could she cross it?

Allison swayed slightly on her feet. She still loved Tony. She had never stopped loving him. And she could see very plainly that he loved her, too.

Tony moved then. It was just a simple gesture, but it broke her awful inertia. He held out his hand.

And Allison took one step forward to find that she'd hurtled over the immense gulf. She was safe at last, in Tony's arms.

Dimly she heard Jamie's voice. "Hey, Tony, is that Allison?"

And Tony's answer.

"Yes, Jamie. And I think you just got yourself a stand-in mom."

ABOUT THE AUTHOR

New York Times bestselling author **Joanne Fluke** was born and raised in a small town in rural Minnesota, but now lives in sunny Southern California. She is also the author of the Hannah Swensen mystery series, which began with *Chocolate Chip Cookie Murder,* and is currently working on her next book in the series. Readers are welcome to contact her at the following email address, Gr8Clues@aol.com, or by visiting her website at www.MurderSheBaked.com.

The employees of Thorndike Press hope you have enjoyed this Large Print book. All our Thorndike, Wheeler, and Kennebec Large Print titles are designed for easy reading, and all our books are made to last. Other Thorndike Press Large Print books are available at your library, through selected bookstores, or directly from us.

For information about titles, please call:
  (800) 223-1244

or visit our Web site at:
  http://gale.cengage.com/thorndike

To share your comments, please write:
  Publisher
  Thorndike Press
  10 Water St., Suite 310
  Waterville, ME 04901

CPSIA information can be obtained
at www.ICGtesting.com
Printed in the USA
FFOW03n0816220814
7030FF